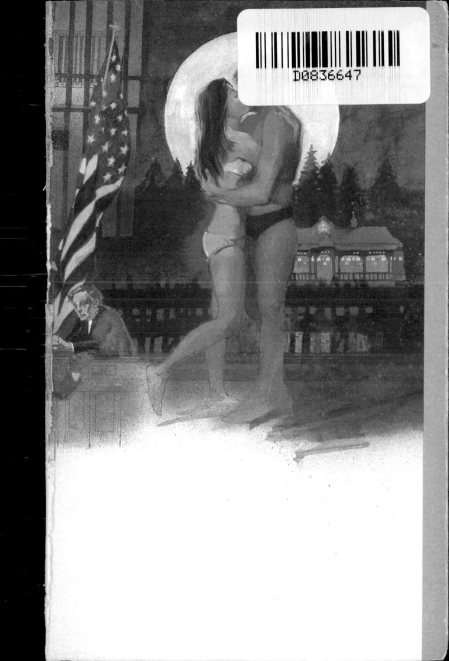

BERNARD F. CONNERS
DANCEHALL

A BERNARD GEIS ASSOCIATES BOOK.

BERKLEY BOOKS, NEW YORK

For C.C.C.

This Berkley book contains the complete
text of the original hardcover edition.

DANCEHALL

A Berkley Book / published by arrangement with
The Bobbs-Merrill Company, Inc.

PRINTING HISTORY
Bobbs-Merrill edition published 1983
Berkley edition / May 1984

ISBN: 0-425-07062-X

A BERKLEY BOOK ® TM 757,375
Berkley Books are published by The Berkley Publishing Group.
200 Madison Avenue, New York, New York 10016.
The name "BERKLEY" and the stylized "B" with design
are trademarks belonging to Berkley Publishing Corporation.

PRINTED IN THE UNITED STATES OF AMERICA

The author wishes to thank the following persons who furnished technical assistance with portions of this novel:

The Reverend Carl L. Cooper
Albany, New York

Francis J. Daley
Deputy Commissioner
New York State Department of Correctional Services

John T. DeGraff, Jr., Esq.
Albany, New York

Anthony J. DeTommasi, M.D.
Clinical Associate Professor of Psychiatry
Albany Medical College

Joseph L. Glenn, Ph.D.
Professor of Biochemistry
Albany Medical College

David Harris
Warden, Green Haven Prison
Stormville, New York

Livingston Hatch, Esq.
Elizabethtown, New York

William A. Petersen, M.D.
Albany, New York

Arthur A. Stein, M.D.
Professor of Pathology
Albany Medical College

On June 4, 1982, the body of a young woman surfaced from some three hundred feet of water off Pulpit Rock in Lake Placid, New York. Because of the depth and intense cold of the water, the body, which was determined by medical examiners to have been submerged for twenty years, was remarkably well preserved. At the time, the authorities were unable to establish the identity of the woman but concluded that her death had been violent.

PROLOGUE

Green Haven Prison
Stormville, New York
September 1984

It was the end of a day, the end of a life. Death floated in with the autumn night and settled on the grim umber buildings, muting sounds of living things. The inmates, the guards on the towers, the demonstrators grouped in candlelight prayer beneath the long gray wall, all sensed its presence as an uneasy stillness enveloped the Green Haven Maximum Security Prison.

With darkness, lights blinked on and formed strings of neat yellow lines that delineated areas within the compound. Between the wall and buildings was no man's land—a narrow corridor where the slightest sound or movement would alert guards on the towers overhead.

Off to one side were the prison laundry, the gymnasium, the machine shop, the power plant. Usually all were dark. But this night the lights in the power plant were on.

Just beyond were tiers of illuminated windows in Building No. 1. These were the galleries that housed Green Haven's nineteen hundred inmates. As eleven o'clock approached, the lights in the galleries were extinguished. So, too, the lights in Building No. 2, where the prison hospital was located—with the exception, that is, of a small superstructure on the roof. This was the Special Housing Unit at Green Haven. Ordinarily, like the prison power plant, it would be dark. But on this particular night, the lights blazed.

Inside the Special Housing Unit were two rooms. One was a small cell few in the prison had seen but of which everyone had heard. It was the "last cell," the holding area next to the execution chamber housing New York State's seventy-year-old electric chair, the same chair that had been used to execute such notorious persons as Julius and Ethel Rosenberg, and the alluring Ruth Snyder. Here a condemned prisoner was taken for his final day, to spend his last torturous hours before execution.

It was now seven minutes before eleven. The occupant of the cell, wearing a plain gray prison uniform and dark felt slippers, was sitting on a metal bunk smoking a cigarette. The top of the uniform had been slit and then lightly basted together so that it could be opened easily to provide access for a stethoscope. A small patch on the prisoner's head had been shaved to permit direct contact with an electrode affixed to the electric chair. Outside the cell, in view of the inmate, sat a uniformed guard. The guard seemed nervous; the prisoner, remarkably calm.

In precisely five minutes two men would appear. They would open the door of the cell, support the prisoner by the arms, and march at a brisk pace around a turn in the corridor into the execution chamber. Here, in a carefully prescribed ritual before a score of witnesses, the prisoner would be strapped into the chair. Electrodes would be attached to the head and right leg, and then a long black switch would be thrown on the executioner's control panel. The whining cry of the current would break the stillness as an initial charge of two thousand volts of electricity was sent coursing through the prisoner's body. After three seconds, the voltage would be reduced to five hundred volts for fifty-seven seconds (to avoid unnecessary burning of the body) and then accelerated rapidly once again to two thousand volts. The procedure would be performed three times. With the initial shock, the brain would be charred as it reached a temperature exceeding two hundred degrees Fahrenheit. The body would lunge against the straps. A loud gurgling sound would come as air was driven from the lungs. A crackling, almost a sizzling, would emanate from the chair. Sparks would fly from the electrodes. Although unseen by the witnesses because of the death mask and clothing, the body would turn a vivid red. The index finger of the right hand would rise ever so slowly, and from the death cap would come a puff of blue-gray smoke that would float up and collect against the ceiling.

After the application of electricity, a whirring exhaust fan in the ceiling directly above the chair would remove the odor of death as an examination was conducted by a prison doctor.

The examination would reveal no life. Death would have come quickly . . . as it had twenty-two years earlier on a dark midsummer night on Lake Placid.

◊ ◊ ◊

PART
I

Lake Placid, New York
July 1962

"Police!" The man looked up abruptly from his desk. "Did you say police?" His expression turned from stern to sour. "Why should I ask the police for your address?"

"No, no," said the girl sitting in front of him. She shifted uncomfortably, a touch of panic in her brown eyes. "I said As-tor *Place*—'place,' not 'police.' *Place!*" She repeated it slowly, but with her New York City accent, it did sound like "ask the police."

"That's my address. You know, Lower East Side."

"It's that accent," said the man, shaking his head disapprovingly. "You mean lower, not low*a*. *Lower*."

His admonition helped little. It was Ann Conway's first job interview, and it was not going well. She was out of her element. Until that morning she had been north of Yonkers only once before—when her father, who was separated from her mother, had died in Poughkeepsie. Now here she was in Lake Placid—somewhere, she thought, near Canada.

"How did you know we were hiring waitresses?" the man asked.

"I saw the sign in town when the bus stopped to let some people off. I was on my way to Saranac Lake." As soon as she mentioned her destination she was sorry.

"Why were you going to Saranac?"

She swallowed hard and shifted her eyes. She could see no advantage in saying she was on her way to visit her mother. He would then ask where her mother was, and she would have to say she had just been admitted to Raybrook, the tuberculosis sanatorium. Then he would probably ask her if she had had a physical lately. People were unpredictable when it came to TB.

"I was going to look for a job." It was the truth. She needed to find something near her mother.

The man leaned back in his chair and folded his arms, lightly drumming his fingers on his biceps. Middle-aged, with gray hair, he had cold gray eyes and a thin mouth. A knitted brow suggested his predominant mood was one of annoyance. His appraising stare from behind rimless glasses increased Ann's uneasiness.

"You ever work in Saranac before?" he asked.

"No, sir."

"How old are you?"

"Nineteen."

"Where have you worked?"

"That's a good question." She gave a quick, nervous laugh. "Actually, my only job was with my mother. She had a gift shop on Second Avenue. I worked there until a few weeks ago."

"You really don't have any waitress experience is what you're saying."

"If I work real hard I'm sure I can learn quickly." She followed the comment with a bright smile. "And I could really use the job."

Her eagerness seemed to soften him. "We don't ordinarily hire someone on the spot like this. I suppose we can give you something temporary. They're short-handed in the dining room—an advertising convention." Picking up the form on which he had written her name and address, he scribbled his initials and handed it to her. "Take this down to Miss Hallenbeck. She's in the office where you came in." He glanced at his watch. "You'd better hurry, they're closing. You can come back in the morning to fill out the application forms."

"Gee, I really appreciate—"

"I understand." The man rose, indicating matters of more importance awaited him elsewhere.

Ann left the office, her heart pounding. God, how she needed the job. She had only forty-seven dollars left, and her future was bleak. Actually, the interview had been easier than she had expected. It could be more difficult in the morning. She still had to fill out the application forms. But that was tomorrow. For now, she was employed. She gave a little skip. She felt light as a feather.

It was easy to understand why Ann Conway had been elected the most popular girl in her class two years earlier. Her friendly, easygoing manner and an almost perpetual glad-to-see-you expression had endeared her to the girls at St. Catherine's high school. Nor was her popularity confined to the girls. She was average looking, with dark brown hair, a tiny nose, and teeth that were slightly crooked. But when her face crinkled into a smile, she was an instant success with the boys. The smile radiated a sense that she was happy with herself and more than ready to share her happiness with others.

If her pleasant face and winning way did not attract men, then her figure certainly did. At five seven, she had long, shapely legs, slender hips, and a twenty-inch waist. If there were any deficiency in her bearing, it was a slight drooping of her shoulders that came from a tendency to fold her arms across her chest—a holdover from earlier years when she had tried to shield expanding breasts from the nuns at St. Catherine's.

Perhaps it was some of these qualities that influenced the employment manager of the prestigious Adirondack Club to delay the more formal application procedures and hire her. But such relaxation of club standards did not prevail down the hall in Eleanor Hallenbeck's bailiwick. She ran a dining room staffed by some sixty waitresses and busboys and brooked no inefficiency. Under her, job motivation consisted of an explicit warning for any failure, with the promise of instant dismissal for any subsequent transgression. The casualty rate among employees could be high, depending on the mood of the guests and the state of Eleanor Hallenbeck's peptic ulcer. At this moment she was still smarting from a guest's recent criticism that a member of her staff had been observed eating while on duty.

Grim eyes greeted Ann as she stepped into the office.

"Hello, my name—" She had no time to finish.

"The form, please." The woman held out her hand, barely looking up. "What experience have you had as a waitress?"

Ann Conway's hopes for the job plummeted. "Ah . . . only at home, ma'am."

"Where did you work before?"

"With my mother. She ran a gift shop on—"

"There's absolutely *no* eating in the dining room! Is that clear?"

Surprised, Ann hesitated, then nodded.

"Pick up your uniforms from Frances at the dormitory. Report to the kitchen at five o'clock this evening."

Ann was barely through the door before it was shut behind her.

Outside, she felt both relief and exhilaration. For now, she had a job *and* a place to stay. If they liked her maybe they'd keep her on. It would be a wonderful surprise for her mother. Ann had not told her of her plans to find a job near Raybrook. She would go to see her in the morning.

A uniformed workman carrying tools came toward her. "Hi!" she greeted him. "Could you please tell me how to get to the dormitory?"

After receiving directions, she stood for a moment to look about her. Glistening in the distance, ringed by extraordinary mountain peaks, stretched beautiful Lake Placid. She was awed by the sight; for a girl accustomed to the frenzy of Manhattan, it seemed deathly still. Even the puffy white clouds looked as if they had been painted above the mountains. There was something odd about it, she thought. Almost forbidding.

◊ ◊ ◊

CHAPTER 2

Eleanor Hallenbeck was easygoing compared to her counterpart in the kitchen. Alex Gunder, the head chef, was a gargantuan creature whose iron-fisted supervision terrorized the help. Having recently completed seven tough hitches as a chief petty officer in the submarine corps, he was slow in adjusting to civilian life. Lumbering amid the kitchen hardware, perspiring, swearing, booming instructions into a microphone, he was commanding a U-boat under attack, and every decision, every mistake, was a crisis of epic proportion that sent a waitress crying or an assistant chef packing.

Ann Conway's assignment was to carry a heated bin the size of a large breadbox and dispense hot rolls to diners. Once familiar with the routine, she moved easily among the tables under the watchful eye of Miss Hallenbeck, raising the lid of the bin for guests to make their selections. In a crisp tan uniform with a dark brown trim that matched the color of her hair, she was a pretty addition to the dining room staff.

She had been on the job for about an hour when she noticed a tall, handsome blond busboy standing with an older waitress in a corner of the kitchen. When he looked in her direction, she had the impression that he was talking about her.

Suddenly a torrent of expletives erupted from the far side of the kitchen where Alex had uncovered some employee's mistake. Shaken, Ann headed back for the dining room.

The small band that provided music was playing as she emerged from the kitchen. She paused, gazing across the broad expanse of tables and glittering candles to the dance floor, where several guests twirled to the strains of a waltz.

"Why are you standing here?" She was startled by Miss Hallenbeck's voice. "Don't you see Mr. Billings?"

Ann then noticed a heavy-set, middle-aged man waving at her from across the room. With an apology to Miss Hallenbeck, she hurried to the table where the guest sat with two elderly women.

"Well, here you are." Mr. Billings forced a smile as Ann raised the lid on the bin. "I thought maybe you'd forgotten us. I don't see any of those caramel ones. You know, the ones with the raisins?" He glanced up inquiringly. "We had them last night."

"Oh, yes," Ann said. "I know the kind. We may be out of those. Excuse me, I'll find out."

Back in the kitchen, Ann discussed the matter with an older waitress named Lucy who had helped her earlier.

"If it was me, I'd just say we were all out," Lucy said. "You can take a look in the pantry, though."

"Looking for the pantry?" asked a voice from behind.

Ann turned to see the busboy she had noticed earlier, carrying a tray of condiments.

"Follow me," he said, smiling.

Ann hesitated.

"Cute, isn't he?" said Lucy. "If I was twenty years younger—"

"Lucy, table twelve near the door wants something." It was a younger waitress who joined them from the dining room. "How you doing?" she said to Ann.

"I was just talking to her about Dave," said Lucy.

"Oh, he's a doll," the girl said. "Trouble is, he spends all his time in the woods. We tried to get him to come to a party last week, but he had to take care of a family of owls. He said the mother had abandoned them and he had to go home to feed them. Oh, oh, Alex!" Ann turned to see the chef glowering at them from the other end of the kitchen.

Lucy and the younger waitress left abruptly. Ann picked up the bin and followed the busboy through a pair of swinging doors into a hallway at the rear of the kitchen.

"In here," called the busboy.

Ann walked into a large storeroom lined with shelves containing reserve supplies for the kitchen. She rested the bin on a table and straightened her uniform self-consciously.

"Just start?" the busboy asked.

"Yes, this afternoon."

It was her first opportunity to see him closely. He was even more handsome than she had thought. In his early twenties, he had high cheekbones that accentuated deep-set blue eyes. Unruly blond hair, bleached white from the sun, hung down on his forehead. His features were smooth, even delicate, but his face was a trifle thin, giving him an adolescent look.

"I'm Dave Powell." He smiled, revealing teeth that were astonishingly white and marred only slightly by a chipped incisor.

"Hi. I'm Ann Conway." There was an awkward pause. She glanced around the room, looking for the rolls.

"Are you from around here?" He began stacking the condiments from the tray onto a shelf.

"New York. I just came up today—"

Suddenly, the clunking of the swinging doors in the kitchen signaled someone's coming. It was Lucy, who arrived in the pantry carrying a tall hot-fudge sundae topped with whipped cream.

"Here you are, Mandrake." She put the sundae on Dave's tray. "Make this disappear fast."

"Thanks, Lucy," Dave said. "I appreciate it."

"Forget it." The waitress brushed off his thanks as she

moved toward the door. "If some of those other young guys helped out like you, this would be a decent place to work."

Dave picked up the sundae as the waitress departed. "Want some?"

"No. No, thank you." Ann eyed the stenciled sign on the wall behind him: NO EATING—VIOLATORS DISCHARGED.

"There don't seem to be any rolls here," she said, replacing the strap over her shoulder and picking up the bin. She hesitated and then nodded toward the sign. "Won't they fire you if they catch you eating?"

He smiled and raised his eyebrows. They were very blond against his tan. "I wish you wouldn't make me nervous while I'm eating."

Ann was about to leave when he said, "You going to be here all summer?" He looked directly at her, fixing her with his blue eyes. She felt a pleasant tingle.

"I'm temporary, but I hope—"

Sounds of the swinging doors and talking interrupted from the hallway. "Don't tell me you can't find it!" roared a heavy voice. "I know goddamn well it's in here!"

"Oh, boy!" Dave swallowed a mouthful of ice cream. "It's Alex!" Holding the towering sundae away as if it might explode, he looked frantically for a place to hide it. Desperate, he opened the bin Ann was holding and dropped the sundae in among the rolls. He flipped the lid down just as Alex and one of his assistants burst into the room.

"What the hell are you two doing in here? Why aren't you out on the floor?" Furious at having been drawn from the kitchen at a crucial time, Alex was in no mood for explanations. "Get your asses in the dining room!"

Ann moved quickly, but her trouble was just beginning. At the kitchen door she was greeted by the crusty features of Miss Hallenbeck.

"Where have you been, girl? Mr. Billings has been waiting. Come with me."

On the verge of panic, she trailed her employer into the dining room. The bin was now a ticking bomb. This can't be happening, she thought as they crossed the dining room.

"Well, at last," said Mr. Billings, watching them approach.

"We're *so* sorry." Eleanor Hallenbeck shifted smoothly into her dining-room manner. "There was a delay in the kitchen." The way she said it left little doubt where the blame lay.

Desperate, Ann hoped Miss Hallenbeck, having absolved herself, would move on. Instead, she planted herself directly behind Ann.

Ann hesitated. It had to be a hundred degrees inside the bin. The sundae would have melted all over the rolls by this time. Maybe she should faint. From the corner of her eye she saw Dave Powell. He had maneuvered near the table and was watching aghast. She glanced at him helplessly.

"Ah—young lady. Ah—would you mind?" Mr. Billings, with a bemused expression, looked from the girl to the viselike grip she had on the lid. There was nothing else to do. Ann flipped up the top.

Mr. Billings's mouth opened, but no sound came as he stared into the bin. Baffled, he raised his eyes to Miss Hallenbeck. "Rolls à la mode?" His reaction was enough for Eleanor Hallenbeck to take a look.

For Ann Conway, it had been a long day. Not knowing what else to do, she started to cry.

◊ ◊ ◊

CHAPTER 3

When she came out of the dormitory, he was waiting for her, head down, hands in pockets, his expression remorseful. Any resentment she felt was dispelled by his look of dejection.

"I really feel bad," he began, as though uncertain what her reaction would be.

"Well, it's probably all for the best," Ann said. "I was on my way to Saranac Lake to get a job, anyway."

"I'm glad you're not angry." He relaxed noticeably. "I guess I panicked when I heard Alex coming. I wish there were something I could do."

Ann felt herself begin to melt; the sun was setting and in the twilight he looked even more handsome. She wondered about her own appearance. She had left hurriedly after Miss Hallenbeck dismissed her. The dormitory matron had been sympathetic, telling her she could probably get permission to remain the night. But Ann had declined, not wanting to share the embarrassment of her discharge with the other waitresses.

Transferring her suitcase to her left hand, she smoothed her hair. "I hope you won't be nervous when you're eating in the pantry from now on." She gave a wan smile.

"I won't be eating in the pantry. I got fired too."

"Oh, no!"

"I tried to tell them it wasn't your fault, but Alex wouldn't listen." He shrugged his shoulders. "I did what I could."

"You told them. Oh, you shouldn't have."

There was an awkward pause, and she was about to leave when he said, "Can I give you a lift somewhere? My car's right over there." He motioned toward a shiny black Ford convertible. The top was down, revealing a red-leather interior. The car was old but immaculate.

Ann hesitated. "Well . . . maybe you could drop me off in town."

"You bet." Taking her bag, he headed for the car.

Within minutes they were rolling along the lakeside road. It was a warm evening, and the wind rushing past the open car provided relief from the heat.

"Where are you going?" he asked.

"I have to get a room somewhere." She felt uneasy. "I don't know whether to try here or Saranac Lake. I'm not sure there's a bus that goes there tonight."

"There's no problem getting to Saranac. I can take you. It's only a few miles. The only difficulty may be finding a room." He glanced at his watch. "It's getting late and everything gets pretty well booked during a holiday week."

Ann felt helpless. Her mother would be worried. She hadn't talked with her for two days.

As though sensing her concern, Dave adopted a more cheerful manner. "Look, there's a rooming house over in town. Maybe we can find something there. Don't worry, we'll get you settled." He looked at her confidently and smiled. "It's the least I can do after getting you fired, right?"

The rooming house was a large gray structure sandwiched between two stores on the main street. As they stopped, they saw the sign in the window. "No vacancies."

"I was afraid of this." Dave shut off the ignition and turned toward her. "Look, Ann, if you want to, you can stay where I do. It's over on Lake Placid—on an island. It belongs to a family I know. They let me stay there while they're away."

Two young men strolled past the car. One paused briefly. "Hi, Dave. All set for tomorrow night?"

"I'll be there."

"They'll be tough," the boy said. With an oblique, appraising look at Ann, he went on his way.

"I hope tomorrow won't be any tougher on you than tonight," Ann said wryly.

"What? Oh, he's talking about the Lake Placid Majestics. It's a local baseball team I play with."

"What position do you play?" She really was not that interested. It was getting dark and her options were dwindling.

"Pitcher. Listen, do you want to stay at this place I mentioned?"

"I don't know." She was hesitant. "An island? Will anyone else be there? Maybe I should go to Saranac Lake."

"Whatever you say. I don't think you're going to be too lucky, though." He regarded her thoughtfully. "Why don't you at least look at this place?" He started the engine. "Then, if you want to, you can stay. How does that sound?"

"Would I have my own place?" She knitted her brow. "That is, would there be separate . . . ?"

"Oh, sure. There's a little apartment over the boathouse. I sleep in the main house." He looked behind for traffic and pulled away from the curb. Smiling, he patted her arm gently. "Don't worry."

They drove through the main part of the village toward the lake. Within a few minutes they arrived at a harbor and parked in a lot next to a large red wooden building that rambled along the edge of the lake. Extending from the structure out over the water was a long pier with outdoor dining facilities. Although old, the building was freshly painted.

As they left the car and started across the parking lot, Ann heard music; a low pulsating sound that reverberated beneath her feet.

"Where's the music coming from?" she asked. "It's not on the wharf."

"The Dancehall." Dave nodded toward the building. "It's downstairs, around back. Come on, we'll have a drink. You'll feel better."

With her suitcase in one hand, he guided her around the corner of the building and down several steps to an entrance. Above the door in white letters appeared the words:

DANCEHALL
You Must Be of Legal Age to Enter

"How old are you?" Dave asked as they approached the door.

"Twenty-one," she said quickly.

He glanced at her dubiously. "You only have to be eighteen, you know."

Inside, an enormous hall was jammed with young men and women. On one side was a long bar where customers stood three deep, jockeying for position. On the other, separated by a room divider, was a large dance floor teeming with gyrating forms. At the far end of the hall on a stage were five musicians.

Dave tucked the suitcase into a corner. "What would you like?" he asked, guiding her toward the bar.

"I don't care. Whatever you have."

"How about a gin and tonic?"

"Sounds okay."

As Dave was ordering, two people left the bar. Ann eased into one of the chairs. "Some spot. Spend lots of time here, do you?"

"Quite a bit," said Dave, taking the other chair. "Most everyone ends up here at night." The drinks came and he reached for his wallet.

"Here, I'll get mine." Ann produced a small change purse.

"No, don't be silly." He withdrew several bills from the

wallet. Keeping a few dollars, he handed the rest to Ann. "Here's twenty-five dollars. I wish I had more. It'll help you out till you land another job."

"Oh," said Ann, surprised. "No, I could never take it. Thanks, but I couldn't."

"Please, Ann." He tried to press the money into her hand. "I'd feel better. Honestly."

"No, no." Touched by his generosity, she patted his hand lightly. "Thanks anyway."

With a slight shrug, he returned the money to his wallet. He seemed embarrassed. Picking up her glass, she began to sip. The drink was cold and tasted good. She stirred it as she looked around the room. "Where do all these people come from?"

"Most of them are college kids. They come here to work in the summer. You know, like you."

The comment made her uncomfortable. She wondered if he thought she were a college girl. She hoped he wouldn't ask. "Where are you from?" she asked.

"Rochester."

"What brought you up here?"

"I went to Cornell. It's not too far from here—Ithaca. Lots of kids come up to work during the summer. How about you?"

"I'm from New York City. Manhattan."

"That's pretty obvious. You know, the way you talk. New Yawk," he said, imitating her accent.

She shrugged. "You all sound funny to me, too."

They turned to watch the musicians. Ann stole a glance at him. He was so darn good-looking and nice. And he seemed to like her.

"Do you go to school up this way?" he asked.

"No . . . No, I don't."

"Where do you go?"

She knew it was coming. "Down in the city."

"Whereabouts in the—"

"I once knew a Mike Powell," she said, determined to

change the subject. "I suppose Powell is a pretty common name. What kind of name is it?"

"What's that?" he said, surprised. "Oh, you mean what nationality? I'm Polish."

"Polish? No kidding." She paused reflectively. "It doesn't sound Polish."

"Well, actually our name originally was Polanski, but my father changed it. He was in the newspaper business. He figured he saved the paper some money over the years by shortening it."

There was another pause, then Dave said, "You go to school in the city? Whereabouts?"

"Hunter." She said it without batting an eye.

"Hunter?" he repeated vacantly.

She looked at him, surprised. "You never heard of Hunter College? It's on Lexington and Sixty-eighth Street. The Sixty-eighth Street stop on the IRT," she added confidently. "Ever ride the IRT?"

"I don't know that much about the subway."

Well, she did, and she sure hoped they could talk about that, rather than college. She should have told him the truth. She had never gone to college, and as far as she knew, no one even remotely connected with her family had.

"What's your major?" he asked.

"What?"

"What's your major in college?" He looked at her closely.

"Major?" Jeepers, she had to get off the subject fast. "What time is it, do you know? It must be getting late."

Dave glanced at his watch. "Ten after ten. You want to go?"

"Maybe we should. I've been up since five-thirty this morning."

"Sure, let's go." Dave downed his drink and led her through the crowd toward the entranceway where they had left her bag.

As they pushed toward the doorway one of the bartenders

called out to Dave. "Some girl was here looking for you earlier."

"Who was it? Do you know?"

"No, I think there were two of them. I've been too busy to even look up." He turned to wait on a customer.

Outside, Ann smiled up at Dave. "Two girls looking for you, huh? I guess baseball isn't the only thing you've been pitching."

He laughed. "It was probably a couple of the waitresses I've been ferrying to work. Now that I've been fired they're probably worrying about transportation."

On the boardwalk it was dark. They passed through an interlocking series of docks onto a wharf that jutted out onto the lake. A full moon, already high in the sky, appeared at intervals from behind patches of silver-edged clouds. A light breeze occasionally drifted from the lake, offering momentary relief from the oppressive heat and causing water to lap gently against the pilings. But for the most part it was still, and only the sounds of their heels against the dock broke the quiet.

From the moment she stepped onto the wharf, Ann was uneasy. The broad expanse of black lake was unnerving. She was glad when he took her hand as they came to a narrow part of the dock.

"The boat's right up here," he said. "Watch your step on that rope."

"You know, Dave, I've been thinking. This is a lot of trouble for you. Maybe I should try to find a room in Saranac."

Dave laughed. "I'm beginning to think you're chicken. Look, it's only a couple of miles up the lake." His hand tightened, drawing her along with him. "Here's the boat."

She could see the outline of a thirty-foot launch with a substantial cabin. She drew some confidence from its size. Dave put her suitcase in the cockpit and stepped aboard. He held out his hand to help her.

"Sit here while I cast off," he said, guiding her toward a

wicker chair in the stern. He then moved forward and disappeared into the cabin. Soon the engine started with a thunderous roar. Dave's head reappeared in the cabin entranceway. "Come on up here."

Inside the cabin, he directed her to the seat next to the pilot's wheel. It was warm and musty. She was glad when he opened the portholes.

"How can you tell where you're going?" She asked, peering through the windshield into the blackness.

"I've made the trip often. You get used to it."

A silence enveloped the cabin then, and there was only the rhythmic chugging of the engine as they proceeded out of the harbor, up the lake. They had been traveling for several minutes when suddenly the moon emerged briefly from behind the clouds, casting a whitish glow on the water. Something off the starboard bow caught her eye. As the moon disappeared, she glimpsed a great black mass of rock.

"What's that ahead?" she asked.

"Pulpit Rock."

She was uneasy as she felt the boat shift slightly to the right. "Do we have much farther to go?"

"We're almost there. See those lights up ahead? That's the camp."

Squinting through the windshield, she saw several yellow lights that seemed to emerge from the darkness and come toward them. She made out the shape of a long dock and boathouse. As they drew closer, Dave reduced speed and edged toward the landing. Despite several dock lights it was difficult to see. Designed more for navigational assistance than for illumination, the lights did little more than cast an eerie yellow glow in the dark.

She felt a slight impact as the craft came alongside the landing. Dave turned off the ignition and moved quickly from the cabin. She followed and watched him as he tied the boat to the dock. When finished, he turned to her and smiled. "That wasn't too bad a trip, was it?"

"No, not at all. But it's so quiet."

They stood for a moment listening to the deep silence of the Adirondack Forest.

"Don't you get lonely out here?" Ann asked.

"You get used to it. I don't spend that much time here. Just to sleep."

Suddenly, a soft, flutelike sound came from the darkness behind the landing.

"What was that?" said Ann quickly.

"What?"

"That noise. It was like . . . I don't know . . ." She paused, listening.

Again the same trilling sound; a rapid succession of high notes that floated from the blackness.

"There! There it is again," Ann said in a hushed voice. "Hear it?"

"Oh. That's a loon."

"A what?"

"A loon. A bird."

"Really? Why that's the oddest thing I've ever heard. It sounds like . . . like a funny little laugh. Like a girl laughing."

Dave nodded. "Sally Wood's laugh."

"What?" When he did not respond, she looked at him closely. "Sally Wood's laugh? What do you mean?"

"Oh, nothing." He smiled and patted her arm. "I'll be back in a second."

"Where are you going?" she asked.

"Up to the main house. I have to get a flashlight to show you the apartment. I'll be right back." He disappeared into the darkness.

Ann thought of climbing out onto the dock but decided against it. She could see little in the murky surroundings except the boathouse. Behind a narrow balcony above the boathouse she saw what she assumed was the apartment Dave had mentioned earlier. Beyond the boathouse was the black contour of the dock stretching off into the darkness. It was still except for the water lapping against the side of the boat and the creaking of the wooden pilings. Then it came again: the same strange, quavering little laugh. She folded her arms and hugged her chest, wishing Dave would return. She felt very much alone.

But she was not alone. Overhead in the apartment a curtain moved, and a pair of eyes watched her intently.

Several yards away, a large silver lake trout suddenly broke from the water and snapped an unsuspecting insect from the night. It plunged back into the lake, its slender form twisting and turning into the depths.

The splash startled Ann. She turned and looked out at the lake, but there was nothing. Faraway, barely visible in the blackness, tiny lights flickered from the Dancehall.

◊   ◊   ◊

PART
II
Tarrytown, New York
June 1982

CHAPTER 4

Not far from the prison wall at Green Haven—no more than forty miles as the crow flies—was another wall. In some ways it was similar to the one at Green Haven. It had been constructed during the same period, was of similar shape and length, and, like Green Haven, it enclosed a large tract of land with a meadow facing its entrance. But whereas the wall at Green Haven was a concrete slab rising thirty feet, this one was antique brick less than ten feet high, covered with ivy and climbing roses. Most suggestive of the difference, perhaps, were the sounds. At Green Haven, the noise of institutional living was harsh and relentless; the sounds that drifted over the wall in Tarrytown were happy ones: a piano playing, a child's laughter. On evenings when the wind blew hard against the grim guard towers at Green Haven, the same breeze sang softly in the tall trees behind the wall on Meadow Lane.

Meadow Lane was a peaceful rural road whose main purpose was to service the estate nestled behind the wall. At this particular moment, shadows had lengthened and, as always with the approach of evening, the road was hushed. Then, inperceptibly, the low-pitched purring of an engine broke the stillness as a sleek Rolls-Royce limousine came into view and rolled smoothly down the lane toward an entrance in the wall.

At the wheel was a chauffeur in dark gray livery. In the rear was David Powell. Now in his early forties, he had retained the trim, lanky appearance of his youth. His hair was thinning somewhat at the crown but still hung boyishly on his forehead. The chipped incisor had long since been capped, but the shy, uncertain smile of earlier years remained.

Sitting beside him, playing cards, was his seven-year-old daughter Dana. Suddenly the girl's face lit up. "Too bad, Daddy," she said, pouncing on a card that he had just laid on the seat between them. "I won again." She spread her cards on the seat. "That's three times. I'm still champ."

"Well, *darn* it." Dave dropped his cards, pretending disappointment. "I'm still in second place, though. I can still beat Lindsay." He nodded toward a doll—a flaxen-haired plaything that accompanied Dana everywhere—propped on the seat between him and the door.

"She's getting much better, Daddy. She almost beat me this afternoon while I was waiting for Dr. Heming."

"You're kidding," Dave said, feigning surprise.

"Uh huh. She did, Daddy," nodded Dana solemnly. "Almost."

As the limousine slowed and prepared to turn into the entranceway, Dave leaned forward and spoke to the chauffeur. "Tom, why don't you drop us here? You can go ahead and handle those errands for my wife."

"You don't want me to take you up?"

"I'd rather stretch my legs. I've been sitting all day."

"Will we be going to Lake Placid tomorrow, Mr. Powell?" the chauffeur asked.

"No. Empire is having its annual meeting in New Jersey Friday morning. We'll go up afterwards."

"Can I wait and go up with you, Daddy?" Dana asked.

"No, you'll be going back in the morning with Sam," Dave replied, referring to the caretaker who had brought Dana down earlier that day for her doctor's appointment. "Besides, if my meeting doesn't go well, I may not be able to make it up at all."

"But Daddy, you *have* to come up." Her eyes widened with concern. "It's Grandma's birthday, remember? You promised Mommy you'd—"

"I know, I know." The thought of Lake Placid brought a tinge of uneasiness. "Don't worry, honey, I'll be up." He patted her knee reassuringly as the car came to a stop.

As he opened the door to get out, the doll fell to the ground. The impact activated a mechanical device within the toy that mimicked a crying sound.

"Good grief," said Dave, climbing out and retrieving the wailing doll. He shook it a few times, trying to stop the crying, but once activated it had to run its course. "We'll have to listen to this for the next—"

"Daddy! Be careful with her." Dana jumped out quickly and took the doll. "Poor little Lindsay," she soothed, cuddling it while eyeing her father accusingly. "He didn't mean to do it."

"Do what?" Dave asked, defensively. "I didn't do anything. The thing fell out when I opened the door."

"Lindsay isn't a *thing*, Daddy." She looked up at him reproachfully as she hugged the doll, whose wailing was now a mechanical sob. "She's a little girl, and little girls cry when they're hurt. It wasn't her fault she fell out. She gets dizzy sometimes. Don't you understand?"

Dave understood. He felt the emotion take hold as he gazed down at his daughter's distressed face. She was a pretty child, with large brown eyes, a small nose, and dark, curly hair. She resembled her mother, and it already seemed probable that, like Sue Powell, she would be beautiful. But for an instant, Dave saw a lifetime of sorrow in her momentary sadness.

He reached down and lifted her into his arms. "I'm sorry, darling. Of course, little girls should cry." He kissed her gently. "Crying is a very important part of a little girl. Here, I'll give you and Lindsay a ride up to the house." He raised Dana and the doll onto his shoulders and started toward the entrance. "Tom," he said, looking back, "Don't forget to mail those invitations. And call Mrs. Hunter's office in the morning. She mentioned that she may want to ride back to the city with us after the meeting Friday. Let's hope she doesn't," he added softly to himself.

"What did you say, Daddy?" Dana asked.

"Nothing." Dave adjusted her on his shoulders.

"You said you hoped Mrs. Hunter wouldn't come."

"Shh! No, I didn't."

"You did, Daddy. I heard you. Why don't you like Mrs. Hunter? Mommy likes her."

Dave's dislike of Emily Hunter was common knowledge in the Powell household. He had met her years previously, shortly before his marriage to Sue Dickerson. A close friend of his wife, Emily had owned the Empire Container Corporation, a New Jersey manufacturing firm. After their marriage, Dave and Sue had learned from Emily about a similar plant for sale in Stamford, Connecticut. A loan from Sue's father had enabled Dave to buy the plant, and the venture had led to a partnership with Emily—a partnership that, from Dave's standpoint, had been unfortunate.

"Of course I like Mrs. Hunter," Dave said, walking toward a Tudor gatehouse and garage complex that guarded the entrance to the estate. "It's just that sometimes we see business differently . . ."

The gatehouse was artfully constructed over the roadway, affording access through an underpass. Ivy covered the base of the structure, and from the leafage peered the gnarled faces of several granite corbels. Replicas of grotesque heads used in ancient times to frighten off evil spirits, they had been inserted in the wall as decorative art by the estate's original owner, Amelia Dickerson. Sue Powell's Great-aunt Amelia had been inclined toward such things. She had never been fond of people, and objects that manifested inhospitality could be found throughout the estate. Dave rarely passed the gates that he did not sense the heads peering reprovingly from the ivy, as though questioning his right to be there.

"Daddy," came the voice from atop his shoulders, "Will you stay up at the lake for a while?"

"Just the weekend."

"Oh, *why?* You *never* come up and stay—you always leave right away."

Not answering, Dave moved through the underpass into a cobblestone courtyard where carefully landscaped walks connected the gatehouse with a garage, adding to the old-world atmosphere. Here they were greeted by two St. Bernards—Huff and Puff, who served as security for the estate.

"Lindsay's stopped crying," Dana said, as they paused next to the dogs. "I think she likes the ride."

"Well, maybe Lindsay likes it." Dave lowered his passengers to the ground and then rubbed his neck. "But I think Lindsay may be putting on a little weight." He took a moment to straighten Dana's dress; then, taking her by the hand, he started up the drive.

In the distance, he noticed a bird hovering like a black kite in the evening sky, at times almost motionless. Although he had seen it frequently—often it perched on a chimney at the front of the main house—he could not classify it with accuracy. It was a corvid, he'd thought—perhaps a raven. A few had been observed in the nearby sanctuary.

Birds had been important in Dave Powell's life. It had been in an ornithology class in college that he'd met Sue Dickerson. It seemed almost providential, therefore, that Sue should have a great-aunt like Amelia Dickerson. For Amelia had been a dedicated bird lover. It was the reason she had donated a portion of her magnificent five-hundred-acre estate to the government—with the provision that it be kept forever wild as a bird sanctuary. Almost as an afterthought, she had willed the remainder of the property—the main dwellings and about a hundred fifty acres—to her favorite niece, Sue.

It was one of these recipients of Amelia Dickerson's generosity that Dave now observed. As they approached, the bird flew lower, finally settling in an enormous elm tree that towered over a hundred feet near the main house. For Dave, the elm was the focal point of the estate. A summer's afternoon might find him lounging in a chaise with a pair of binoculars, looking for birds in the labyrinth of branches. In fact, it had been in this position the previous spring that he had been dismayed to see the first telltale signs of Dutch elm disease—a slight premature yellowing of some leaves. At the moment, though, no untrained eye would have seen that the tree was dying. With beams of the setting sun embracing its thick verdure, it looked as if it would be around (as they used to say about Aunt Amelia) "for another hundred years."

As they approached the house, Dave glanced toward a weathered fence that enclosed a cutting garden. Here Sue Powell spent much of her time. Bird feeders and rows of brilliant summer flowers neatly arranged around a large marble birdbath attested to her interest in both ornithology and horticulture.

"Shall we pick some flowers for you to take up to Mommy?" Dave asked, pausing near the entrance.

"Oh, yes." Dana's brown eyes sparkled. "Here, you hold Lindsay. I know the kind Mommy likes." She handed him the doll and ran ahead.

Dave followed her inside the enclosure and waited as she gathered a bundle of peonies. He rested Lindsay on the birdbath, and as he did he noted the doll's deteriorating condition. The flaxen hair was thinning from constant brushing, and the blue dress was faded and worn. The eyes, however, were still wide and clear, belying Lindsay's worsening state.

A few lingering sunbeams drifted through the shade trees that bordered the far end of the garden and created patchworks of radiant color among the flower beds. He stood for a moment, watching his daughter gather the flowers. She would fade soon, he thought. Like the color in the dwindling light.

Suddenly, Dana's face appeared over an armful of flowers, her expression one of joy. "I'm so happy." She paused, her brown eyes searching his face. "What's the matter, Daddy? You look sad. Did I pick too many?"

"No, no. That's fine." Bending over, he drew her close and pressed his cheek against her forehead. "They're perfect."

Straightening, he walked to the center of the garden. Here he selected some daisies and tiny pink roses from which he fashioned a small bouquet. "How do you like it?" he said, holding the flowers appraisingly at arm's length. "This is for someone very special."

"For Mommy, right?"

"No, someone else I like very much."

"Oh, you mean me."

"No, someone else."

"Someone else?" She knitted her brow and the small nose turned up questioningly. "Lindsay?"

"No. Mrs. Hunter."

Dana hesitated, her eyes large with wonder. "Mrs. Hunter? Really?" But then she saw his playful smile. "Oh, Daddy," she squealed. "You're only joking. And I believed you."

He picked her up, flowers and all, and squeezed her tightly. Laughing, they left the garden and crossed a cobblestoned drive leading toward an immense Tudor manor house. As they entered the house, the bird rose and began circling high above the stricken elm. Here it floated in the evening sky, its eyes locked in a black stare as the shadow of the elm crept across the drive and engulfed the house.

With nightfall, the wall on Meadow Lane tightened about the estate. Off to the northeast, behind another wall, strings of yellow lights blinked on.

◊ ◊ ◊

CHAPTER 5

Many Rolls-Royce motorcars have been manufactured since Charles Rolls and Frederick Royce brought out their legendary Silver Ghost in 1907. But the Phantom Five limousine that Tom Lucas threaded cautiously through the Tarrytown traffic was one of the finest. The classic James Young chassis was painted a deep garnet on the sides. The hood, roof, and trunk were jet black. Two large circular headlamps of the type from earlier models had been custom-built on the front fenders. Perched above the hand-sculpted radiator grille, reflecting brilliantly in the morning sunlight, was the Flying Lady. It was a car of classic beauty, and the chauffeur was deeply aware of his responsibility.

At a traffic light he brought the car to a gentle stop. He used the interlude to take a soft cloth from a compartment and carefully remove a film of dust above the dash. When the light changed he looked in both directions and then moved forward, keeping a good distance from the car ahead.

Tom Lucas was a tall, amiable man in his early thirties, with clean-cut features and thick sandy hair that curled becomingly around his chauffeur's cap. A Vietnam veteran with a permanent leg injury, he had taken the chauffeur's job with the Powells until he could find something better. That had been four years before, and he found the job entirely satisfying. He particularly liked Sue Powell.

At the outskirts of town, Tom pulled off the road into a gas station. It was a modern, immaculate place, but the young man who emerged from the building to greet the Rolls was anything but immaculate. He looked as if he had just climbed through several feet of smokestack.

"Hi, Commander," he said affably, gazing at Tom's uniform. "New threads, huh? Not bad. You look like Captain Kangaroo." He nodded toward the front seat. "What's with all the boxes?"

"They're invitations."

"Invitations?"

"Right. The Powells are having a party."

"I'll just take mine." The mechanic reached into the car. "Save you the trouble of mailing it."

"Keep your grimy paws out of here." Tom opened the door and got out. "What the hell happened to you? Christ, you're dirty—even for you."

"I've been wrestling with a goddamn transmission." Taking up a gas hose, he inserted it in the tank. "When you going to get me a job up there on the hill? This place is killing me."

"Are you kidding?" Tom said with mock disdain. "What do you think they're running, an Irish potato farm? You gotta have a little class to work up there."

"How would you like a four hundred pound injection of high octane up your ass?" He pulled the hose from the tank menacingly.

"Easy! Easy!" Tom said, worried lest the nozzle scrape the fender. "And don't get too close to the car. I just washed it."

"So where you heading?" the mechanic asked.

"The city. And I'm running late," Tom added.

"I thought you were going to Lake Placid."

"Tomorrow afternoon. Mr. Powell's got a meeting down in Jersey."

"What's Powell up to now?"

"I don't know. He's been in Chicago all week."

"Maybe he's got a chick out there?"

"If you were married to Sue Powell, would you have a chick anywhere?"

"Yeah, man."

"Besides, he doesn't fool around."

"How do you know? All his dough. He's probably got something in every city."

"I don't think so. I'd know if he did."

"How would you know? You think he's gonna blab everything to you—his *flunky!*" He said "flunky" with as much contempt as could be conveyed in one word.

"I'd know," Tom replied.

"What about that blonde I see him driving around with?"

"What blonde?"

"You know the one. I saw you driving them a few weeks ago. She's not bad. The one with her nose stuck up in the air."

"Oh, Mrs. Hunter. She's his business partner."

"Business partner, hah!" the attendant snorted. "I guess that's what you call 'em when you're a millionaire."

"No, no. You've got it all wrong, as usual. She's a friend of Mrs. Powell. A widow. A real bitch. Mr. Powell can't stand her. Say, I'm running late. Can't you hurry that up?"

The attendant ignored the question. "You reading a book?" He nodded toward a small volume resting on the front seat next to the invitations.

"What? Oh. That's Mr. Powell's. It's a book on etiquette."

"Etiquette? What's that?"

"Etiquette, dummy. Manners. Your trouble is you don't even know what it *means*."

"So why is he reading up on etiquette?"

"He's not. Mrs. Hunter gave it to him for his birthday. I guess she was needling him. It really pissed him off. The book tells you how to have class. You wouldn't know anything about that. People with class have rules for everything. What the upstairs maid does. What the butler says. Who answers the phone. They even got rules on how I drive the car. I'm not supposed to put my hands on top of the steering wheel."

"Powell makes you drive that way?"

"No, I read it in the book. Mr. Powell gave the book to me."

"He's probably trying to tell you something."

"No, no. Not him. He's a great guy." Tom paused. "I shouldn't be telling a sieve like you their business."

"Maybe I should drop up and pay Mrs. Powell a visit while he's gone." The attendant wiggled his brows suggestively.

"Wouldn't do you any good. She's up at Placid. Anyway, she's a hundred percent."

"Boy, what a shape," said the attendant appreciatively. "You think maybe she plays around . . . just a little?"

Tom shook his head emphatically. "Dana, their daughter, that's all she cares about. Dana, flowers, and birds, that's it. She spends a lot of time with the kid down in the garden. One day last week I hear Dana screaming, so I go running down and there's this snake in the flower bed. I'm telling you, the fuckin' thing was two feet long. I wouldn't of touched it with a pole. So what does Mrs. Powell do? She walks over to it real cool, picks the thing up by the tail, and wacko! Slams the fucker against the side of the birdbath. Now, I ask you, how many women would've done that? That's the way she is. She doesn't like something, she doesn't fool around."

The automatic pump sounded a full tank. The mechanic leaned over, grasped the nozzle, and sighed. "Goddamn, that's my kind of woman. The more I hear about that broad, the more I'd like to bang her. She's really pretty tough, huh?"

"No, I don't mean that. It's just she's kind of funny sometimes. But she's real nice. Everyone else blows their cork now and then. Not her. She's always happy. C'mon, I gotta go. Charge the gas." He climbed into the Rolls.

"Relax, will you?" said the attendant. "How's Doris?"

"How the hell should I know?" responded Tom. "When I get divorced, I stay divorced."

"Divorced! You were never even married. You call three weeks a marriage?"

"You know, if Dear Abby was a ratty-looking grease monkey, I'd swear I was talking to her." Tom turned the key in the ignition and the Rolls came to life with a deep, quiet hum.

"Listen to that," he said. "Did you know that at sixty, the loudest thing in a Rolls is the clock?"

"Yeah, you told me that," said the attendant, hanging up the hose. "For that kind of dough, you'd think they'd give you a better clock!"

◊ ◊ ◊

CHAPTER 6

David Powell was relieved when the Rolls turned onto Fifth Avenue and approached the offices of the Hunter Management Corporation. An hour with Emily Hunter could be trying, and when spent in the confines of a limousine, it was unpleasant indeed.

Emily had been nervous at the lunch following Empire's Board meeting, and then, during the trip from New Jersey, she had been in a constant state of movement, folding her arms, crossing her legs, stretching her neck. It seemed to Dave she was forever struggling with some inner turmoil that betrayed itself in a continual restlessness.

She was a handsome woman of forty, with graying blond hair drawn severely into a bun. She had a small nose and striking light blue eyes, which in a blink could blaze with contempt. Her expression altered between disdain and boredom. She was wearing a brown tweed suit that fit loosely, suggesting an indifference toward style. Although Emily Hunter was stunning when stepping out socially, her business world was one of balance sheets and operating statements devoid of fashion.

Dave fingered the papers in the folder on his lap, determined to get an answer to a question she had chosen to ignore. He wanted to know why Hunter Management, a company owned exclusively by Emily, was charging their mutually owned Empire a management fee.

"Emily, this management fee—"

"Why are you always complaining?" Emily snapped, rummaging in her pocketbook for a cigarette. "The company turns a profit, doesn't it? Hunter is a management company. It charges all my companies a fee."

"Why are we paying executives salaries in Empire if Hunter is doing the managing?" Exasperation crept into Dave's voice. "It's not reasonable. Unless this fee is reversed, I'm expanding the product line in Stamford."

"I see." Emily lit her cigarette. "You're going to abrogate your agreement."

Dave started to respond but thought better of it. Closing his eyes, he rested his head against the seat. Meetings with Emily had become increasingly difficult. She was arrogant and irritable—communicative only if the conversation had something in it for her. Even when disposed to talk about Empire, she did so with numbing circumspection, as though speaking of secret formulas not yet patented.

"How in the world did you ever become involved with Emily Hunter?" his friends had asked with wonder. How, indeed? It had seemed logical enough when she had first approached him with her scheme for a partnership. But even then he had been wary of the proposal. For Emily's reputation was formidable. She had married shortly after Dave and Sue, but the marriage had been brief. It was said that she had driven her husband first to alcoholism and then to suicide. At his death she had assumed control of his ventures and had demonstrated a remarkable business acumen, expanding the container firm into a multi-million-dollar conglomerate. She was regarded by those with whom she did business as brilliant, eccentric, and ruthless to the bone.

Mindful of Emily's reputation and aware that his own plant in Stamford, being larger, had certain competitive advantages over Empire, Dave at first had declined the offer. But Emily had persisted. Using Sue, with whom she maintained a close relationship, she had pressured Dave into accepting a fifty percent partnership in Empire in exchange for a lesser ownership for Hunter Management in his Stamford plant. As part of the arrangement, Stamford agreed not to expand its product line to compete with Empire. It was now obvious, however, that Emily's intent was to neutralize the competitive impact of Stamford and to siphon off the profits in their mutually owned Empire firm by a variety of devices, the most blatant of which were Hunter Management's fees.

"If you remember, Emily," Dave said, trying again, "the purpose of our agreement was to increase profits in Empire by restricting Stamford's business. Well, hell, if you reduce Empire's profit by making all these charges, where does it leave me?"

"That's nonsense." Emily extinguished her cigarette, grinding it forcefully into the ashtray. "You heard at the board meeting why profits are off. If you'd been listening, you'd know that much of the deficit is attributable to changes in the company's accounting methods. Accelerated depreciation on that new equipment, for example. Would you prefer to give the money to the government?"

"There's a lot more to it than that," Dave said. "I'm not going to stand by and watch a company of which I'm half owner—"

"Half owner, indeed," snorted Emily. "You couldn't have bought half ownership in a Polish whorehouse if it hadn't been for Sue."

Dave felt the blood rush to his face. It was not the first time Emily had denigrated his Polish ancestry, and she was constantly reminding him that it was his father-in-law who had enabled him to go into business. For years she had had the upper hand in their relationship. He had always been in awe of her social background, her spectacular business accomplishments. But the management fee was the last straw.

"Emily," he said firmly, "if the management charge isn't discontinued, I'm expanding in Stamford."

"Then be prepared to defend yourself in court." As the Rolls came to a stop in front of the Hunter offices, Emily pushed a button on her armrest, lowering the glass partition that separated the front seat from the rear. "Tom, see that my bag gets up to my office."

She had started to leave the limousine when Dave said quietly, "Emily, I *am* prepared to go to court."

"*Are* you?" Emily fixed him with an ice-blue glare. "Perhaps you'll want to think about that. Court can be quite revealing." She continued to look at him steadily.

Dave returned the look, weighing her remark. She had made comments of a similar nature during recent months as their relationship worsened. He wondered if there were any connection between her remarks and a conversation they had had a few years before.

They had been drinking, and Emily had admitted to despondency after her husband's suicide. From her, it had been a rare expression of sentiment. Touched by her disclosure, he had said that he could understand; that he had once had a traumatic experience himself. When he had declined to elaborate, dismissing it as an incident that had happened one summer in college, her curiosity had been aroused. It was then that her perceptive intellect had delivered a bombshell. "Well, you weren't in college in the summer, were you? You told me you worked at Lake Placid. Was it something that happened at Lake Placid?"

Perhaps she had seen the fright leap into his eyes, for even though he had dropped the subject, he had known that the words "trauma" and "Lake Placid" had been indelibly stamped on the keen Hunter mind. Had it been anyone else, anyone with less finely honed instincts for perceiving vulnerability, it would have gone unnoticed. But in that fraction of a second as he looked into Emily Hunter's eyes, he had known that he had committed a grave error.

Sometime later, Emily had mentioned it casually. "Didn't you once say something happened to you at Lake Placid?" He had dismissed the question, feigning ignorance, but he knew he had been tested.

Still, he could be overreacting now to her comment about court being revealing. It took little to resurrect memories of that night long ago on Lake Placid: The dark pier . . . Ann Conway's pretty face smiling up at him in the soft yellow glow of the dock lamps . . . the blood . . . the strange, haunting laugh from the woods. . . .

But how could anyone know? Even Emily, with her uncanny perspicacity, could never suspect. Her remark was probably no more than a shot in the dark calculated to put him on the defensive. Yes, that was it. He had observed her often enough with business adversaries. A combination of an ambiguous statement and her piercing eyes could elicit paranoia in almost anyone. More than likely she was alluding to some embarrassing business matter—a tax impropriety, perhaps—that might be divulged during a court action. Of course. It was Emily's style. A little white-collar blackmail.

He must challenge her, though. Before she left the car. Show her that he had nothing to hide. "What's that supposed to mean, Emily? 'Court can be revealing.'"

She nodded ever so slightly. "Some things are better left undisturbed." Her eyes registered a final knowing glance as she rose to leave.

◇   ◇   ◇

CHAPTER 7

Tom Lucas was familiar in a general way with the Powell enterprises. He knew that in addition to the Stamford company, the businesses included a real estate firm and a small insurance company. He also knew that the Stamford operation was losing money and that David Powell was convinced that its only salvation lay in expanding its line of products. Much of this information had drifted from the back seat of the Rolls, where his boss often dictated letters and memos into a recorder.

He was dictating now as they sped along the Adirondack Northway toward Lake Placid. Tom had sensed that his employer was upset when they dropped off Mrs. Hunter. When the memos started, he could see why.

It was a perfect summer day, and the scenic Northway offered a relaxing drive. The Rolls purred quietly along the smooth highway toward the lofty Adirondack Mountains in the distance. After adjusting the speed control, Tom eased his lanky body against the door and stretched his left leg out under the dash. The leg tended to bother him on a long trip.

They had been driving for over an hour when David Powell set aside his recorder and addressed the chauffeur. "It's been a long time since I've been up here—to Lake Placid, that is."

"I guess you like the ocean better than the mountains," said Tom, straightening in his seat.

"That's right. I prefer the shore."

Dusk was settling as they left the Northway and took the pass up through the mountains to Lake Placid. They rode through deep gorges where rock formations climbed vertically for hundreds of feet. On one occasion they passed a waterfall cascading from above, a rush of white foam in the twilight. Even by dusk the scenery was extraordinary, each twist in the road revealing a magnificent new view.

A breeze picked up as they wove their way through the pass, and an almost imperceptible change in the weather suggested an impending storm. Tall trees lining the road began to sway at the tops.

Tom glanced in the mirror to see if his passenger had fallen asleep. It was difficult to see much in the small rearview mirror of a Rolls-Royce limousine. Mrs. Powell had once said they were made purposely small so that nosy chauffeurs wouldn't see too much. He knew she was joking yet suspected there might be some truth to the statement.

"Where are we, Tom?" The voice startled him.

"Going through the Cascades, Mr. Powell. We should be there in another half hour."

A silence came over the car as the last rays of the sun disappeared and the dim outlines of the mountains dissolved into the black sky.

Tom heard a clicking sound and saw the antenna rising out of the fender as Dave Powell turned on the car radio. A few seconds of static ensued until his passenger settled on some soft string music. The chauffeur found the hours of driving catching up with him. He shifted in his seat, struggling to keep his eyes open. When a curve in the road caught him unexpectedly, he had to apply the brakes more forcefully than he would have liked. The experience shook him from his drowsiness.

It was during a break in the music, toward the end of a news report, when he heard it—an announcement that he accorded only casual attention but that was to have a profound effect on his future:

> The body of a young woman was discovered floating in the water off Pulpit Rock in Lake Placid early today. Authorities say the body was probably submerged for over twenty years, but because of the depth and low water temperature, it was remarkably well preserved. It will be several days before final autopsy reports are released. So far there are no clues to the victim's identity. . . .

For a moment, there was a deep silence. Then the music resumed, filling the limousine with sounds of a light melody from the big-band era of the forties.

"What do you think of that?" Tom said. "A body right here in Lake Placid."

There was no response from the back seat. Tom glanced in the tiny mirror, but all he could see was the silent form huddled in the corner.

◊　◊　◊

PART
III

Lake Placid, New York
June 1982

CHAPTER 8

It had rained long and hard during the night, and an early morning mist drifted over Lake Placid. Tumbling low clouds covered the tops of the mountains that ringed the lake, totally obscuring Whiteface, highest of the peaks.

David Powell sat at a desk in an upstairs guest room of the Dickerson summer house. On a good day the view was extraordinary. Now, as he sat gazing out at the bleak scene, there was little to see. Vaporous clouds rising like smoke gave the lake the appearance of a steaming black pool.

He reached for a silver coffeepot on a tray. The handle was hot, and he let go quickly, shaking his fingers. Using a linen napkin from the tray, he tried again, pouring a hot stream of coffee into the cup. His hand shook as he replaced the pot.

He had not slept at all. It had been twelve hours since the news on the radio about the recovery of the body—a body that might be Ann Conway's. From that moment his life had been a nightmare.

A movement down near the boathouse caught his eye, and he saw Sam Wykoff, the Dickerson caretaker, walking toward the end of the dock with Dana. Suddenly she turned and ran back to the house. Within seconds she reappeared skipping nimbly down the dock, this time carrying Lindsay. Suddenly she tripped, and she and the doll went sprawling. Unhurt, she regained her feet and, comforting a now wailing Lindsay, walked toward the waiting caretaker. Tanned and healthy-looking, Dana's appearance belied her insidious neurological disorder. Doctors had diagnosed one of the childhood degenerative diseases that affect the nervous system, and though the disease was in its early stages when symptoms were still latent, the prognosis was not good. The child would become an invalid within a brief time. Her life expectancy was short.

Dave rose and went to the window. He was about to call to Dana, when he saw his mother-in-law join her on the dock. Sam helped them into a launch and within seconds the boat drew away. They were probably going to town to do some shopping, he thought. It reminded him of the birthday present, a small vase, he had brought from Chicago for his mother-in-law. He would have Sue wrap it while her mother was gone. And he would have to make a special effort to be nice to Arlene Dickerson on her birthday—try to make up for the evening before, when he had arrived strained and detached.

Suddenly Dana, in the stern putting on a life jacket, spotted him at the window. She waved energetically and went on waving even as the launch disappeared into the mist. It was then that Dave noticed the other boat in the distance, coming toward the camp. There was an official look about the craft.

◊ ◊ ◊

CHAPTER 9

"How the hell do you conduct a 'neighborhood' on a lake?" Horace Ackerman of the Federal Bureau of Investigation stood in the stern of the launch with a State Police officer, looking in bewilderment at the mountains surrounding Lake Placid. A tall, friendly-looking man with dark, curly hair, he had a swarthy, somewhat Slavic appearance. Probably his most singular feature was his jaw: square and confident.

"Neighborhood?" John O'Brien, a strapping blond State Police lieutenant in his late thirties, was puzzled.

"A neighborhood investigation," Ackerman said. "We'll need to talk to people who lived near where the victim was recovered, preferably someone who lived here twenty years ago."

"The body was found floating over there off Pulpit Rock," O'Brien said. "But . . . well, you can see for yourself, there's no *neighborhood*."

"How about those houses over there?" The agent pointed toward an island up the lake.

"Buck Island? Those camps on the point weren't there twenty years ago. At least I don't think they were. At any rate, I doubt if you'll find anyone who lived there that long ago."

"How about that big place on the other side of the Buck Island point?"

"That's Camp Louise," O'Brien said. "It's been owned by the Dickerson family for fifty years. You might try there, but they're usually only here in the spring and fall. I know their caretaker, Sam Wykoff. Want to try it?"

"Sure, why not?" Ackerman looked again at the desolate mountains as O'Brien went forward to talk to one of his associates.

The agent realized that a neighborhood investigation of a crime committed so long ago was pretty hopeless. But a neighborhood was a fundamental part of any crime scene investigation, and Ackerman always did things other investigators didn't bother to do. It was his style, and he was proud of it. He had already conducted a preliminary investigation at the Lake Placid Police Department and the Essex County Sheriff's Office. Now, with the aid of the New York State Police, he was doing a crime scene.

He knew that in spite of his efforts the Bureau would probably withdraw from the case, providing only technical help under the FBI's law enforcement assistance program. Because of the extraordinary condition of the body and the publicity it had generated, the Bureau had done more than it usually did in such matters, authorizing its Albany office to conduct a preliminary investigation.

"Mrs. Dickerson is here after all," O'Brien said, returning. "Only she's not at the camp. The pilot said he saw her come into the harbor a while ago. Sam may be out there, though."

"Let's try Sam."

O'Brien motioned the pilot ahead. Ackerman leaned against the hull and withdrew a sheaf of papers and some large photographs from a brown folder. "Your divers didn't find anything yesterday, did they, Lieutenant?"

"No, not yet. I checked before we came out. Whoever dumped her knew where the deepest part of the lake was. They say there's no bottom over there."

"Where's your investigator who was here yesterday?"

"He went down to the state crime lab in Albany. He'll be back this afternoon."

"Here's the victim," said Ackerman handing over a sheaf of photographs—several views of the naked corpse of a young woman.

"What's that sticking out of her hand?" O'Brien asked.

"A chain necklace. It's attached to a medallion embedded in her palm."

"Medallion?"

"Yes, shaped like a star. You can't see from the picture, but the lab report says there's a baseball and crossed bats on it with the date 1962. Someone must have had it around their neck."

"You think she pulled it off somebody?"

"Possibly. It could have been a last grab she made. If so, she must have been pretty desperate the way the thing was stuck in her hand."

"How do you feel about the case?" O'Brien asked. "Can we go anywhere with it?"

"Depends on what the lab comes up with. A lot of this stuff is luck."

"Like the body surfacing. That was luck."

"That was a miracle," Ackerman said.

The state policeman returned the photographs. "The lab probably won't be able to identify the body. There's no missing person report or records to compare it with."

"That's the problem. She had no fingerprints on file in the identification division. Twenty years is a long time. We may never identify her."

"How can they be sure how long she was down there?" O'Brien said.

"They conducted tests on the body. The pathologists are pretty good. According to the lab reports, they did some diatom tests on the medallion, too. Diatoms are algae that form on things in water. Apparently they can measure pretty accurately how long it takes to build up. Also, the date on the medallion would indicate that it wasn't down there before sixty-two."

"What did they say about the rope tied to her waist?"

"A good quality hemp, heavy and expensive—the kind you'd maybe find on larger boats. Whoever tied it to the victim wasn't very nautical and used granny knots."

A silence ensued as the launch plowed through the water. Ackerman leaned against the hull and watched the wake of the boat. There was a beauty in the trough, a symmetry to the flying silver spray. His mind turned to his case load back in the office. Half of his cases were delinquent, and here he was spending his weekend on something not even within his primary investigative jurisdiction. But Ackerman knew an interesting case when he saw one.

Few agents were more experienced. He had been assigned to virtually all of the important field offices of the Bureau at one time or another, albeit never longer than six months at a time. There was a reason for this. Midway in his career Ackerman had incurred the wrath of the Director of the Bureau and had been assigned to the Director's "merry-go-round"—travel assignments intended to discourage one from making the Bureau a career. To everyone's astonishment, Ackerman had thrived on the treatment, notwithstanding eight subsequent letters of censure calculated to keep his wages to a minimum.

But after forty-eight years at the helm, the Director had died in 1972, and there had been changes in the Bureau's style and in Ackerman's itinerary. He was assigned permanently to the New York field office. After receiving four letters of commendation and four meritorious awards in as many years, he had been astounded one day to find himself assigned to his office of preference in Albany. A short time later he had been offered the resident agent's job in Plattsburgh, an ancillary office of the Albany division, and he had not hesitated.

As the launch drew near Buck Island, he observed the long expanse of Dickerson waterfront. Several boats were moored at the base of a landscaped knoll that led up to a stately house.

The orderliness about the shoreline and its trim-looking slips impressed him.

As they reached the shore and the launch eased close to the dock, Ackerman noticed the door of the main house open. A woman appeared on the front porch. Even from a distance she was strikingly beautiful. The agent turned toward the state policeman with a smile and nodded toward the figure. "Sam?"

His associate did not respond immediately, but as they stepped ashore and headed for the house the officer emitted a low whistle. "Man," he said softly. "I never realized there was anything like this out here."

Ackerman saw the woman watching them from the porch as they approached. She was a tanned, lithe figure wearing a sleeveless yellow tank top and white shorts. Her legs were long with slender knees and shapely calves. Very special legs, thought Ackerman. He knew legs, and only one woman in a million had them like that. As he drew near, his eyes focused on her face. She had smooth lovely features—a small nose, a confident chin—and black hair that hung in soft curls to her shoulders. He guessed she was somewhere in her mid-thirties, and *damn*, she was gorgeous.

"Morning," said Ackerman, pausing at the base of the porch and displaying his credentials. "I'm Agent Ackerman of the FBI. This is Lieutenant O'Brien of the State Police. We're conducting an investigation regarding the body recovered from the lake yesterday."

The woman looked at them appraisingly for a second. There was something about her manner that Ackerman found fascinating. Perhaps it was her eyes. They seemed almost black, as black as her hair. They were detached, unemotional eyes, seemingly all pupil. They told you nothing.

"Uh . . . do you live here, ma'am?" asked Ackerman.

"Yes," said the woman, regarding him coolly from behind a tilted chin. "I'm Susan Powell."

◊ ◊ ◊

CHAPTER 10

Dave watched the launch pushing through the mist toward the Dickerson landing. When he saw the uniformed officer in the hull, he felt a surge of fear.

He was aware of the presence of the police on the lake. The household had been abuzz the night before about the recovery of the body and the diving activities being conducted by the State Police. Hearing the news, he had fought his impulse to return to Tarrytown, and had decided to stay for the weekend as planned. Nerve-racking as it was, at least he was on the scene, able to observe at firsthand rather than waiting anxiously at home for news.

He had not anticipated a visit from the police, however. Why would they be coming to the Dickerson camp? Maybe it was only a routine contact. It would be logical for them to check nearby camps.

He rose from the desk and stood by the window as the men introduced themselves to his wife. When she invited them into the house, he left the bedroom and positioned himself discreetly on a loft above the living room from where he could hear them talk.

"We can sit over here," Sue said, ushering the men inside.

"Not a very good day to be out in a boat. May I get you some coffee . . . tea?"

"No, thank you, ma'am." The voice was heavy, official. "We'll only be a few minutes. We're interested in talking to people who lived in this vicinity twenty years ago. Would there be anyone here who could help us—someone who lived here then?"

"My parents were here, but my father died a few years ago. My mother is over in town."

"Is Sam Wykoff here?" It was the voice of the other man, more cordial, not as heavy as the first.

"No, Sam went with my mother. They should be back later. Are you sure you wouldn't care for some coffee?"

Dave shifted uncomfortably. Why was she pressing them to stay?

"I'll have some coffee." It was the lighter voice.

"Fine. How about you, Mr. Atkin . . ."

"Ackerman. All right, ma'am, I'll join the lieutenant. If you're sure it isn't too much trouble."

Dave squirmed. As Sue left for the kitchen, the men exchanged inaudible comments, and there was the sound of a short, stifled laugh.

His wife seemed to take forever. Dave strained to hear the muffled voices, but their comments were unintelligible. Finally, Sue returned with the sound of china rattling on a tray. "Sorry to be so long, gentlemen."

"This is very nice of you." It was the heavy voice, Ackerman. "Quite a place you have here, Mrs. Powell."

"It's my mother's," Sue replied. "We're just here for the weekend."

"I see. You say, 'we'?"

"Yes. My husband and I."

"I guess he's not around now?"

"Well—not exactly. That is, I think he's indisposed just now."

"I see."

There was a break in the conversation as the men sipped coffee.

"We don't want to take too much of your time, ma'am." It was Ackerman again. "We believe the body was submerged sometime after the ice went out of the lake in the early sixties, perhaps 1962."

Dave's stomach sank. There was no question now. It was Ann Conway.

"Would you or your family have any information that might be helpful?" the voice continued. "We realize it's been a long time, but we'd be interested in hearing any thoughts you have."

"We've all been talking about it," Sue said. "It's received a great deal of publicity."

"Would your mother remember anything?"

"No. We've discussed it. We spent most of our summers in Newport. Usually we were here only for a few weeks in the spring or late summer."

"How about Sam Wykoff?" the lieutenant asked. "He was here then, wasn't he?"

"Yes, he was the caretaker, but he didn't live on the island then. We didn't build the caretaker's house until 1967."

"Do you know of anyone else who lived around here at the time?" Ackerman asked.

"No, not really. It's been so long . . ." Sue paused and then continued, "Do you mind if I ask a question?"

"No, not at all."

"Why would the FBI be involved in this? I usually think of the FBI—well, you know, doing other things."

"Federal law gives the FBI jurisdiction over certain crimes under an unlawful-flight-to-avoid-prosecution statute. Also, we sometimes become involved through our law enforcement assistance program."

"I see. Have you got any clues? I don't suppose you could say if you did," Sue added with a laugh.

"We're working on it," Ackerman replied noncomittally. "Murder cases are never closed."

The comment stunned Dave. Apparently they had evidence of murder. He closed his eyes as the significance of the statement sank in.

"So you think she was murdered?" Sue asked quickly.

"Well . . ." The agent hesitated. "In our position we have to presume a crime has been committed."

Dave heard the men rising from their chairs.

"Thanks for the coffee," Ackerman said.

"Yes, thanks very much," the other man added.

"You're welcome. I'm sorry I wasn't more help. Good luck."

"Oh, one more thing," said Ackerman. "I was looking at those boats down on the dock. Were they here twenty years ago?"

"Most of them. That's my father's antique boat collection. We've had them as long as I can remember."

"They're nice. Mind if we take a look on the way out?"

"No—I guess not. Not at all."

Dave heard the door close—a deep, solid, thudding sound. He looked out from the bedroom window as the two men made a cursory inspection of the antique boats. Soon they returned to the launch and headed out onto the lake. He watched the boat fade into the mist near Pulpit Rock. There was a dreamlike quality about the sight, almost as though the craft had submerged into the black water from which Ann Conway's corpse had surfaced the previous day.

Dave gazed out at the dismal scene, his thoughts drifting back to the day long ago when he had first come to the camp. It had been a sunny afternoon in early June. Sam had taken him over on the launch from the mainland. Having recently graduated from Cornell University, where he had been dating Sue Dickerson, he had come at her request to meet her parents. He had been nervous about the visit. The Dickersons, well known at the university as a socially prominent Westchester family, had long been generously involved in the school's philanthropic endeavors. Dave had been acutely aware of his own less distinguished roots as the beautiful Buck Island camp came into view. He could remember vividly Sue's voice calling to him as Sam brought the launch alongside the dock . . .

"Hello, Dave!" The voice was exciting; low, but feminine. He looked expectantly in the direction of the greeting but was unable to locate her in the maze of structures.

"Up here," she laughed.

It was an unusual laugh—a melodious strain of light notes that tumbled across the summer air; a happy laugh that evoked the same thrill he invariably experienced whenever he was about to see Sue Dickerson. He followed the sound to a balcony on a wooden boathouse off to the right. She was leaning over a railing, looking down at him. He had not seen her in two weeks, and she was even more beautiful than he remembered. She was wearing a faded light pink shirt with rolled-up sleeves and khaki Bermuda shorts. A pair of binoculars hung from her shoulder.

"Hi, there," Dave called. He smiled, but his greeting was restrained. He glanced toward the main house—a magnificent structure spanning the top of a landscaped hill.

"Mom and Dad are over in town," Sue said, as though noting his uneasiness. "They'll be back in a little while."

Dave was relieved. He turned to the caretaker. "May I help with the boat?"

"No, thanks, I'm going right out." Then, raising his voice, Sam called, "Susan, Leona is planning dinner for seven o'clock. Will you mention that to your mother when she comes back? I'm going over to Saranac." He casually waved as the boat pulled away.

Dave turned to the balcony. "Sorry I'm late."

"I was expecting you an hour ago," Sue said. "I was getting worried."

"It took longer at the club than I planned."

71

"Did they give you a job?"

"I won't know for a few days," Dave said. "I had an interview and filled out the application forms."

"Come on up. No one's here. The stairs are around back. Leave your bag there for the time being."

His bag looked old and battered in the sunlight. He placed it in an inconspicuous spot next to an Adirondack guideboat—a light wooden craft similar to a canoe—resting on the dock. Walking to the rear of the boathouse, he mounted the steps. Sue was peering at the lake through the binoculars, her back to him, when he arrived on the balcony.

"I've been watching some ducks over there near Pulpit Rock," she said. "It's a mother and her babies."

"Probably mallards," said Dave, his interest piqued. She continued to look through the glasses. Her preoccupation with the birds gave him a moment's uneasiness. He knew that she had been seeing one of her old boyfriends, a recent Yale Law School graduate named Bob Turner. She had assured Dave that it was only an old friendship; that it was her parents who were fond of Bob. Still, he was concerned.

He moved closer, so that her head was only inches from his face. "Two weeks is a long time, Sue, I've missed you." As he spoke, he slipped his arms around her waist and kissed her gently behind the ear. He could feel the contours of her body and smell the freshness of her hair. When she rested her head back against his shoulder he was relieved. He leaned forward to kiss her, but she moved her head and drew away. His uneasiness returned.

"Don't you think I should at least show you your room?" She smiled, squeezed his hand affectionately, and drew him toward the stairs.

After getting his bag from the dock, they walked up the promenade that joined the boathouse to the main premises. Dave marveled at the luxury. Adjoining the boathouse on both sides was a vast expanse of dock with covered slips housing several highly polished mahogany boats, their brass fittings gleaming in the sunlight. He estimated there were almost a dozen.

"They're antique boats," Sue said, noting his interest. "My father collects them. It's silly. He never uses them."

The interior of the main house was as impressive as the outside. The entrance opened into a large beamed living room with a massive stone fireplace at one end. Opposite, a staircase led to a loft from which doorways opened to other sections of the house; nearby was an elevator. Under the loft was the entrance to the dining room. The rooms were furnished with antiques as well as wicker chairs and summer furniture. Although it was a warm day, an air-conditioning system provided comfort. It was gracious summer living, an ambience enjoyed by only the rich.

Dave's uneasiness increased. At college they had been on common ground. Here, he was over his head.

"Welcome to Camp Louise," Sue said, leading him through the living room.

"Why is it called Camp Louise?"

"My father. The camp has been in his family since it was built. He says it's named after one of his old girlfriends—just to kid my mother. He's a terrible tease. Actually, Louise was one of his relatives." She moved toward the stairway. "Your room is up here."

The guest quarters consisted of a bedroom with a large four-poster bed, a bath, a sitting room with a desk, and a few easy chairs. On the desk was a vase with zinnias, snapdragons, and lemon lilies. Windows offered a view of the lake and mountains.

"This is terrific." Dave rested his suitcase behind one of the chairs. "I don't know why your folks would go to Newport with a place like this."

"My mother prefers the seashore." Sue walked to the window. "Too many bugs here for her. She's allergic to mosquitoes. That's why we have air conditioning—so we don't have to open the windows."

"How long will you be here?" he asked, following her across the room.

"Until next week. I can come back up anytime, though. And maybe you could come down to our place in Newport. They have wonderful parties this time of year."

"Sounds great." He paused, looking into her eyes. It was her eyes that he found most fascinating. They had a strange magnetic quality. "Gosh, Sue, I've missed you so much."

He moved closer to her, cupped her face in his palms, and tilted her head toward him as her eyes watched him unwaveringly. When he kissed her she was impassive—almost languid. Nor was it different when he gathered her into his arms and kissed her more fervently. Her reaction was more submission than passion. But he was accustomed to her response. It seemed to be as much emotion as Sue Dickerson ever expressed.

As he held her in his arms, a heavy quiet enveloped the room. From outside came the distant strain of a cicada beating its wings. The faint humming sound rose to a fever pitch and then died away into the silence of the late afternoon.

Sue backed away and turned again to the window. "I'm awfully glad you're here, Dave—I've missed you, too."

"You had me worried when I first came."

"Why? What do you mean?"

"This guy Bob . . ." Dave hesitated, uncertain what to say.

"Bob Turner? Oh, don't worry about Bob. I don't see him that often."

"Well, not only Bob. I guess I thought things might have changed. You seemed preoccupied. Don't misunderstand. With the caretaker there I didn't expect you to vault over the banister, but . . ."

"I'm sorry." She looked out at the lake. "I realize I'm not particularly . . . you know, amorous. We've certainly talked about it enough. Nothing's changed, though." She turned and smiled at him. "Not as far as I'm concerned. I'm glad you're here. I want you to meet my parents."

"I'm looking forward to it," Dave said, gazing past her and through the window.

"I bet you are." Her eyes twinkled. "You can hardly wait. I can tell."

"I am, really," Dave insisted. "What have you told them about me?"

"Everything."

"Everything? I might have known. You told them I was Polish?"

"Of course. You should have heard them when I told them your name—before it was changed. They said it in unison. Pol-*lan*-ski! Honestly, it was so funny."

Dave shrugged. "I'm glad it provided some amusement."

"Come on, Dave, don't be silly." Sue put her arms playfully around his waist. "You're too sensitive. Who cares what your name was? Don't you understand? It doesn't make any difference to anyone but you. What's this?" she asked, noting a small necklace he was wearing.

"Just a medal," he said with a trace of self-consciousness. "From the Majestics—the baseball team."

She drew the medal from under his shirt and regarded it closely. "It's handsome—just like you."

She smiled up at him radiantly. Dave might have kissed her again, but he noticed a long white boat headed for the landing.

"My parents," said Sue, following his look. She walked to the door. "I'll tell them you're here. Make yourself comfortable. Drinks are in the library at six-thirty."

Dave continued watching through the window after Sue left. The boat drew up next to the dock. A tall, middle-aged man with gray hair alighted and helped a woman of similar age from the craft. Both were wearing navy blue jackets—she with a skirt and he with white flannel slacks. They proceeded across the dock toward the house. Dave fingered the medallion uneasily.

Sue and her parents were waiting in the library when he came downstairs. Mr. Dickerson was a large, affable man who seemed disposed to take himself and others lightly.

"I used to be a pitcher myself," he proclaimed, following introductions and the usual amenities. "In fact I held the record at Phillips for the most strike-outs in one game. Sixteen! Actually, I gave up that many walks the same game, which was some other kind of record. I was always a little on the wild side, wasn't I, Arlene?" He winked at his wife as he poured a shot of gin into a glass. "Like some lime with the tonic, Dave?"

"Yes, sir. That's fine." Dave glanced at Mrs. Dickerson, who sat assessing him from the far side of the room. She was a large, severe-looking woman with gray hair and strong features. He was glad for Mr. Dickerson's joviality.

"Sue tells me you made quite a record at Cornell," Mr. Dickerson said as he poured a large amount of bourbon into his own glass. "Tell me, how many hits did the pitcher give up in that game you lost to Colgate last spring? Eleven to nothing, wasn't it?"

"Daddy," Sue interjected plaintively. She turned to Dave. "Don't let him bother you. He's a big needler."

"I'm only kidding," said her father. "You did well, Dave. There's a local team here, the Lake Placid Majestics."

"Yes, I know. I played with them last summer. Their manager is trying to get me a job at the Adirondack Club."

"They've elected Dave captain of the team," Sue said.

"You don't say." Her father nodded approvingly. "I'll plan to catch a few of your games. You've got a pretty good build for a pitcher. What are you, about six two? You could probably use a little more meat on your bones for that high fast one. What you need is a good cook. Right, Sue?"

"Daddy, please!"

"Herbert! Really!" said Mrs. Dickerson.

"Okay, okay, I'm sorry. But it's the truth." He paused for a drink. "Before I got married I was thinner than you. Isn't that right, dear?"

Mrs. Dickerson ignored him and directed her attention to Dave. "Sue mentioned that you come from Rochester. Do you live right in the city?"

Dave tensed; she was zeroing in on him. "Yes, ma'am. We used to live in the suburbs, but we sold our house some time ago and moved into—sort of an apartment." Actually, it was a small duplex next to a corner grocery.

"I see. Sue mentioned that your mother is an English teacher."

"Yes, ma'am. She teaches at a girls' school near Rochester. Sarah Parker."

"And she's taught for some time, has she?"

"Yes, ma'am. I guess it must be almost ten years." He glanced at Sue. She was listening with interest. He had rarely discussed his home life with her.

"And you have brothers and sisters?" continued Mrs. Dickerson.

"One older sister."

"She lives at home with you?"

"Yes, ma'am. Just the three of us. My father died some time ago. He was in the newspaper business." Dave took a sip of his drink. He shifted his gaze from Mrs. Dickerson to Mr. Dickerson and then to the fireplace.

As though sensing that her mother's probes were too obvious, Sue changed the subject. "Dave is going to Ohio State to get his Master's."

"Are you, now?" said Mr. Dickerson. "That's splendid. What's your field?"

Dave started to reply, but the maid announced dinner. They stood and followed Mrs. Dickerson into the dining room, where a large rectangular table was arranged with four place settings. It was a dazzling display of silver, linen, china, cut flowers, and lighted candles.

"How's your appetite, Dave?" Mr. Dickerson asked cheerfully. "Hope you like pheasant."

"Yes, sir. Sounds great." Dave had never had pheasant before and had no appetite now.

Mrs. Dickerson walked to one end of the table and directed Dave to the place on her right. He considered holding her chair, but she sat quickly, before he had a chance. Two maids emerged from the kitchen to serve the first course.

"We were talking about graduate school," said Mrs. Dickerson, settling into her role as hostess. "You mentioned Ohio State, David?"

"Yes, ma'am." Dave regarded the puzzling array of silver before him. From the corner of his eye he saw Mrs. Dickerson select a fork. He glanced toward Mr. Dickerson. He was using a spoon.

"What's your field?" Mr. Dickerson asked again.

"Political science. I've been thinking of a job with the government." Dave decided on one of the forks, recalling his sister Ida's saying that you were supposed to start from the outside and work in. Ida knew about such things. Or was it from the inside out?

"Why not take some business courses?" Mr. Dickerson asked. "That's what makes this country go. If you live in a Communist country like Russia, then you work for the government. That's where the power is. But in a capitalist country, the name of the game is money. With it, you're somebody. Without it, you're a bum."

Mrs. Dickerson glanced up at her husband sharply. "Perhaps, Herbert, not everyone shares your view."

"Maybe not," replied her husband, undeterred. "But the sooner Dave understands, the better. Sue understands. She's smart. You knew she was valedictorian of her class, didn't you, Dave? Yes, sir, she'll surprise you. Remember what the psychologist said, Mother? She has the absolute capacity to accomplish whatever she wants." He paused to taste his wine. Dave noticed Sue glance at her mother.

"The best thing you can do, Dave," Mr. Dickerson continued, "is to take some economics courses and then get hold of a little business somewhere. Or if you can't do that, try for an equity position in something. Ownership is the thing. Without it you'll forever be making it for somebody else."

"Sure, Dave, mention that to the Adirondack Club next week," chimed in Sue, winking at Dave.

Mr. Dickerson smiled good-naturedly. "Maybe we can put in a word for you at the club. Where will you stay when you get the job?"

"I'm not sure. I'll have to find something."

"Why don't you stay here?" Mr. Dickerson offered. "Sam and the others go home at night. You could keep an eye on the place."

"Well, that's very nice of you, sir, but—"

"Sue," Mrs. Dickerson interrupted, "have you thought of taking Bob, uh, *David*, that is, up to Whiteface?"

It was an awful gaffe—or had it been on purpose? Sue delivered her mother an incredulous look, but Mrs. Dickerson never broke stride. "I think David would like Whiteface, don't you? Perhaps you could go in the morning. Sam could give you a ride over." She took a healthy swallow of her wine.

Either because of her apparent faux pas, or because she had lost interest, Mrs. Dickerson was less assertive after that. As the dinner progressed, however, Dave sensed that her intentions for her daughter lay elsewhere, and not even her husband's affable nature could overcome the mood.

Following dinner there were coffee and brandy in the library, and then the older couple retired to their quarters. Dave and Sue walked down to the boathouse and sat on the balcony in two reclining chairs overlooking the lake. It was a clear night with a strong breeze that stirred a few whitecaps. A large moon sent shimmering reflections across the water toward them.

They hadn't been sitting long before Dave broached the subject that had been on his mind most of the evening. "I'm not sure I went over that well with your mother. I got the idea she kind of likes this Bob fellow."

Sue looked up at him quickly. "Don't be silly. She likes you. They both do." She reached over and took his hand.

"Forget Bob. I told you, I don't see him that often. Besides, he's too darn bossy."

"Frankly, I'd just as soon you didn't see him at all," Dave said. "How would you like it if I started dating someone in Rochester?"

"I never worry about such things." She turned in the chair so that she was reclining sideways, looking into his eyes. "Honestly, I don't. I guess I'm just not the jealous type. Besides, I know you love me, Dave." She smiled warmly. "I guess my only rivals are the birds, right?"

Dave was unappeased. In a firm tone he said, "I like to think that . . . well, that we have a future. I don't like having anyone else in the act. If you're going to continue dating, maybe I should just—"

"Please, Dave. You've got it all wrong. Let's not waste our time on something so silly."

Dave considered pursuing the subject. Instead, he put his arms around her and drew her as close as their chairs would permit. "Do you really love me, Sue? Sometimes I wonder. There are so many other guys with so much more . . ."

"Of course I love you. You're very special. Most men are so aggressive. You're sweet and gentle."

Dave leaned over and kissed her softly. As he did he noticed that her eyes remained open. Her seeming indifference troubled him, but he had come to accept it. It was her style—another one of the things that made Sue Dickerson so different from anyone he had ever known. Of course, he had never really known anyone as rich before. That was part of the attraction, according to his sister Ida. She maintained that he was dazzled by the Dickerson wealth. "Would you like Sue as much if she lived down the block from us on Center Street?" she had asked. "In a *duplex?*"

True, he had been overwhelmed by the house, the boats, the servants. But his love was genuine. Of that he was sure. What about Sue, though? She was accustomed to a style of life that he could hardly hope to provide.

He was about to kiss her again when she turned so that she was looking out at the lake. "Pulpit Rock always looks so strange at night," she said. "During the day it's lovely, but at night it's so black. I used to play out there on the rocks when I was young . . ."

Dave hesitated, considering moving forward to kiss her again, but instead sat back in his chair, frustrated. His thoughts turned again to Bob Turner. What was his background? A rich and prominent family? Probably. He could sense it from Mrs. Dickerson.

From somewhere back in the woods came a faint trill, almost like a light, quaking laugh.

"What was that?" asked Dave.

"That's the laugh of Sally Wood."

"The what? It sounded like a bird."

"It is. It's a loon. There must be a storm coming. They do that before storms. Sometimes they're real loud—almost maniacal laughs."

"What did you mean the laugh of—"

"Oh, it's just one of those weird stories you hear on lakes," she said, dismissing the subject with a wave of her hand.

Dave listened for a repetition of the bird's laugh, but there was only the snapping noise of flags flapping in the wind above the boathouse. Somewhere, a loose halyard beat against a pole, making a sharp metallic sound in the summer night.

He lay back in his chair and gazed out across the water at the moon floating above the peaks. Yes, Ida was probably right about the rich. They had such a great start on things. Even the moon was fuller, brighter, more beautiful at Camp Louise.

◊ ◊ ◊

PART
IV
New York City
June 1982

CHAPTER 11

"It's very simple." Emily Hunter's voice was cool, indifferent. "You discontinue your expansion plans or Empire sues Stamford for ten million."

Dave and Emily were lunching at the "21" Club—a place they occasionally met to discuss business. They were upstairs at a corner table. After two martinis Emily was having eggs Benedict and a glass of Chablis. Dave picked at a chef's salad.

"My lawyers don't see it that way." Dave's jaw was set. "As half owner of Empire, I plan to have a say in whatever legal actions are initiated."

"Listen to me carefully." Emily's voice took on its harsh edge. "You tell your Mackel, Tweed, Harvey, and *Whoever* that I'm prepared to break you on this thing. They know I can keep their entire office busy litigating this affair for as long as I have to. And you know who's going to be footing the bill—David Powell! If you're not up on litigation costs these days, then you'd better have them tell you up front. Because before we're through, I'll have you pledging every goddamn thing you own to defend yourself—including that gaudy Rolls-Royce."

She paused to sip some wine, and when the dining room captain passed, she called, "Jeff! Coffee!"

Dave controlled his voice with an effort. "If you want to discuss the matter in a businesslike way, then I'm prepared to listen. But when you act vindictive and start threatening—"

"I haven't even *begun* to threaten you," Emily interrupted. "And don't give me any of that righteous crap."

Fighting his emotions, Dave concentrated on his salad. He had to conceal his concern. Emily would react like a barracuda if she realized the extent of his vulnerability. Between the Lake Placid matter and his financial problems, he was at his wit's end.

"You should eat more," Emily said. It was not unusual for her to follow something vicious with a casual non sequitur. "You look as though you've been losing weight."

"Thanks," Dave said wryly. "I appreciate your concern for my *physical* well-being at least."

He knew his appearance had begun to reflect his anxiety. It had been almost two weeks since the discovery of the body in Lake Placid; days of anguish as he awaited developments. There had been little more coverage by the media. Beyond the fact that the victim had sustained a fatal blow to the head, nothing new had been reported. Dave tried to convince himself that, even though they had the body of Ann Conway, they had no way of connecting it with him.

A waiter appeared with coffee, and Emily lighted a cigarette. She leveled her eyes at Dave, exhaling smoke in a long, controlled stream.

"Did Sue mention that we had lunch yesterday?" she asked.

"No, I don't believe she did."

"I didn't think she would."

It was a puzzling comment. Dave kept his eyes on his salad.

"We had a long chat," Emily said casually. "She mentioned you'd been up at Lake Placid. I understand you had some excitement."

Fear gripped him. He looked up from his plate, and her blue eyes trapped him. They were steady, searching.

"I'm sorry to appear rude," he said curtly. "But I fail to see what any of these things has to do with the issue of Empire and Stamford."

Emily stubbed out her cigarette. She did it with a finality that suggested she had made a decision.

Without a word, she rose from the table and left the restaurant.

◇   ◇   ◇

CHAPTER 12

"But Sue, how could you do it? You could at least have discussed it with me first."

Dave had returned from a two-day trip to Chicago to find that Huff, the male half of the St. Bernard team, had met a premature death at the hands of the local veterinarian. He had been "put to sleep" at Sue Powell's direction after he had attacked a dog that had strayed onto the estate.

"I knew if I told you, you wouldn't let us do it." Sue left her dressing table and crossed the bedroom to where her husband sat in an easy chair. Moving behind him, she ruffled his hair and kneaded his shoulders gently. "It was the only thing to do. The veterinarian agreed. Huff was too unpredictable. If you'd seen what he did to that other dog's ear. And he really could have injured the Dolan boy a few weeks ago when he jumped on him."

"But he never hurt anyone. He just barked a lot, which is what he's supposed to do. He's a watchdog—or he *was* a watchdog. That other dog had no right on our property."

"Well, it had to be done. I'm sorry." Her tone was sympathetic but firm. "I didn't realize you'd be so upset."

"Why wouldn't I be upset? Honestly, sometimes I don't know what to make of you. And poor Dana . . ."

"You'd feel worse if that animal had hurt Dana or one of her friends." She moved back to her dressing table, where she sat down and began brushing her hair. "The vet said that no one realizes how harmful a big dog can be. He was like a lion. Besides, there's no use discussing it now. He's gone."

"That's precisely my point. He's *gone!* You act too quickly. You make up your mind about something and that's it. Then it's too late to even discuss it." Dave could see from her eyes that she was drifting away. Sue Powell did not argue. She merely withdrew into that mysterious inner world that he had never been able to penetrate, leaving him alone with his anger.

He gazed down at his slippers, frustrated. As he reflected on the matter, his anger subsided. His anger always subsided quickly. Another of his character deficiencies, according to Emily Hunter. She had once told Sue that he didn't even have enough to him to stay mad. Emily was probably right. Certainly when it came to his wife. How could anyone stay mad at Sue? He never ceased to marvel at her cheerfulness, her extraordinary peace of mind.

He stood and walked toward his dressing room, pulling off his tie. "Let's forget it. It's done with. Besides, I've got bigger problems. Emily's lawyers are trying to get an injunction against the Stamford plant."

"How will that affect you?"

"If she persists, she could force us into bankruptcy," said Dave from the dressing room.

"Bankruptcy?" There was concern in her voice.

"That's right. There's no way we can keep losing a million dollars a year in Stamford and survive. Emily has us over a barrel. Incidentally, she told me you had lunch with her last week."

"That's right. We went shopping."

"Be careful with her." Dave emerged from the dressing room in a pair of light blue pajamas and a dark blue robe. "She's wily and she has a mind like a trap. She could draw all kinds of information out of you."

"She's never asked a question about your business."

"But that's it. She's too clever. I've seen her operate. She'll just channel the conversation a certain way and listen. You'll do the rest. Think about your lunch. You apparently told her everything that happened at Lake Placid."

"What's wrong with that? There's nothing confidential about what happened at Lake Placid, is there?"

"It's not that," said Dave quickly. "It's just that there's nothing to be gained by talking to her."

"But how can I avoid talking to her? She's a close friend. I've known her longer than I've known you."

"Well, cool it with her, will you please? At least until I get this Stamford matter taken care of." He walked to the window and gazed acoss the drive at the elm tree outlined against the evening sky. "I hate to see the elm go. How much longer do they think it will live?"

"It's hard to tell. The tree people say it could go quickly. It's very bad on the other side."

Dave shook his head. "When I think of all the birds that have nested there . . ."

"I wouldn't worry about the birds. Heavens, we have enough trees for them. If you don't agree, take a look at the bills from the Harrison Nurseries."

"Yes, but I could always see them from here." He thought of getting his binoculars but decided it was too dark. "It won't be the same with the elm gone."

"It won't be that bad. You're letting things get you down. You should get away from business for a while."

"I wish I could. I have to go back to Chicago on Wednesday." He turned from the window and walked to the other end of the room, where he sprawled on the king-sized bed. It felt good to lie down. He propped the pillows behind his head. "If I can land that Chicago account, it will fit in well with our expansion plans in Stamford."

"Don't forget the party Saturday night," said Sue.

"How could I forget the party? What's the final count?"

"Six hundred and twelve."

"I hope it doesn't rain," said Dave.

"Don't be so pessimistic."

"Is Dr. Heming coming?" He knew it was a provocative question.

"I certainly hope so. John makes the evening."

"As well as some of the guests," said Dave.

"He likes to dance with me."

"I know. I've watched."

"I'm lucky he asks me. You never do."

"You know what I mean," said Dave. "The last two parties we went to, he spent the entire evening with you. I really question the propriety of all this socializing with him."

"Why?"

"He's Dana's doctor, that's why."

"So what? He's part of our social group. You should be glad you have a wife someone will dance with. Think of all the wear and tear he's saved you on the dance floor."

"I don't like him."

"He's so urbane . . . always knows what to do. I think he's elegant."

"Your mother says not to use the word *elegant*," Dave said.

"Oh, well, Mother—"

"And I don't know that he's all that urbane. I was watching him at that dinner party last week. He doesn't seem to know all those rules your mother keeps telling Dana."

"What rules?"

"Like keeping the cutting edge of the knife toward the center of the plate. Or eating with the left hand . . . In fact, I never see anyone eating with the left hand unless he's left-handed. Besides, he's much younger than you and—"

"What do you mean younger?" Sue looked up at him indignantly in the mirror. Then, realizing he was teasing, she resumed brushing her hair. "Actually, he's a year older than I."

"That's what he tells you. He's not a day over thirty-five."

She did not respond.

"Well, he's certainly not over *thirty-eight*."

When she continued to ignore him, Dave rose and walked to the dressing table. He stood behind her, looking at her reflection in the mirror. What other woman could look so appealing with no make-up, he thought. But what if he should lose her? What if things continued to worsen? "You do love me, darling?" he said softly.

"Of course."

"You'd still love me, no matter what happened?"

"What's that supposed to mean?" She stopped brushing her hair.

"You know, if the business failed; if everything went wrong."

"I wish you wouldn't talk like that—" She paused, putting her hand to her forehead. Dave wondered if one of her headaches were coming on. He would have asked, but he knew she disliked talking about it.

"I just think of Dana," she continued. "The care she's going to need. And Mother isn't in any position to help. The taxes on Daddy's estate have been devastating. She needs—"

"I know, I know," said Dave, quickly. "I'm not asking—"

"Can't you patch things up with Emily? There must be some way you can keep her happy."

"Sure, I can keep her happy. All I have to do is keep Stamford inactive so Empire gets all the business, and then let her take my share of Empire's profits. That will make her very happy. The only problem is I'm going to the poorhouse in the process." He paused and ran his fingers through his hair.

"Besides, it isn't only business," he said tentatively. "It seems to be *everything*. Huff. Even the elm tree. There are thousands of trees on the property, yet the one that's dying is the most important. There's something eerie about it all."

Sue prepared to put cold cream on her face. Hesitating, she glanced up at his reflection. "Really, Dave, you must get control of yourself. You've been so nervous lately. What *real* difference does it make if the elm tree dies? You get too attached to things. Life keeps changing. Learn to accept it."

"*You* haven't changed." Bending down, he kissed her gently on the forehead.

As he looked into her face, her eyes caught and held him with their magic. It had happened many times before. Yet it was always unsettling. Her eyes seemed bottomless, void of emotion. But it was momentary, and a smile came quickly. "Cheer up," she said. "Don't take everything so seriously."

Suddenly, before he could draw back, she reached up with a glob of cream and smeared it on the end of his nose.

"Why, you little—!" Dave rubbed the cream from his face as she grinned up at him teasingly.

Reaching down, he grabbed her by the waist and lifted her from the chair. Then, holding her under his arm like a sack, he carried her to the bed.

"Dave, please. I'm sorry." She laughed, struggling. "Be careful, you're hurting me."

He dropped her face up on the bed. Then, holding her by the wrists, he covered her body with his. She was breathing heavily, and he could feel her breasts rising and falling. Reaching down, he slowly drew up her negligee.

"Did you miss me while I was in Chicago?" he asked, kissing her tenderly.

She lay without answering, her black eyes staring up at him impassively.

◊ ◊ ◊

CHAPTER 13

Playland! An enchanting spot. So exciting, so different from any other place. Where else, for only fifty cents, could one float effortlessly through the night astride a wild stallion? Or ascend on a gigantic wheel into the heavens and then plummet to earth like a falling star? Or rocket through dark tunnels, past flashing lights, plunging, swerving, soaring with the clatter of metal wheels and the shrieks of fellow passengers? Or gorge oneself on soft drinks, ice cream, and candy? Where else could one do so many things that would ordinarily be out of the question?

Playland was such a place. A half mile of fun and thrills where small hearts beat to mystery and adventure known only to the very young; where the rattling din of the rides and the labored music of the carousel merged into a throbbing cacophony that rumbled through the still night air.

Dana Powell had made it to Playland, and she had made it against imposing odds. When she had asked her father to take her, it had been almost seven-thirty, the time when she was usually getting into her pajamas. It had been little more than an idle question when she had asked, never thinking he would agree. She had been astonished to hear him say he would go. The fact that he had been in Chicago and had spent little time with her during the past few days was the reason, she suspected.

Although it was never easy getting him to Playland, once there, he was all hers. He was all hers now as she pulled him by the arm toward one of the rides—a spidery-looking contraption on the edge of the park.

There was a flush of excitement on her face. She was wearing white shorts and a navy blue football jersey with DANA emblazoned across the back.

In her right arm was the ever-present Lindsay.

She had already been on three rides. But she had a book of twenty-five! That had been the biggest obstacle once they reached the park—the book of twenty-five. Her father had tried for ten at first, but she knew there would be little trouble getting him to fifteen. Twenty was the test. Once there, the rest was easy, for she knew that her father regarded the book of twenty-five as the most economical.

"We won't use them all tonight, Daddy," she said, drawing him toward the Scrambler, a formidable-looking ride.

"That's what you told me last time. I was sick for two hours."

"Well, this next one is easy. Look, there's another man getting on with his little girl, see?"

"Oh, no. Nothing doing!" her father said when he saw where they were heading. "I told you last time, Dana, I'm not going on the Scrambler again. You go. I'll sit on this bench and watch."

"I can't go on it alone unless I'm as big as that sign." She pointed to a life-sized placard of a small boy that stood at the entrance to the ride. The boy was holding a sign that read: YOU MUST BE AS BIG AS I AM TO RIDE ALONE.

"Why not take the Train or the Worm over there?"

"Oh, Daddy, they're for babies," she said disdainfully.

"All right. But remember, I'm not going on the Whirl-away, the Rocket, or the Zapper. But most of all, I'm not going in the Bumper Cars, understand?"

She decided not to argue. She would take them one at a time. She had him for the Scrambler, and that was by far the most difficult. If she could get him through that without his turning green, she would try the Whirl-away, then the Rocket, then the Zapper.

For the next hour she maneuvered him from one ride to another, carefully measuring each ticket against its expected return. It went much as she had expected. Her father rode with her on everything but the Zapper and the Bumper Cars. He seemed to be happy except for the Scrambler. He had been pale for a time after that.

She loved being with her father, although lately he had been very quiet, and she had had difficulty getting him to play with her. Her mother said he was thinking about business. But tonight he seemed happy, more as he usually was. It made her feel better.

She was sitting on a bench with him, having her second chocolate ice cream, when she mentioned her mother.

"Is Mommy sick, Daddy?"

"You mean her headaches? That's not really being sick. Your mother never gets sick."

"Then why would Dr. Heming examine her?"

"What?"

The sharpness of her father's response frightened her, and she was sorry that she had brought up the subject.

"I only asked if Mommy was sick."

"Yes, I understand. But you said Dr. Heming was examining her?" He sounded more casual now, as though sensing he had frightened her.

"Yes, in the bathhouse. Over by the swimming pool."

"When was this?"

"When you were away."

There was a pause, and from her father's manner Dana was convinced that it had been a mistake to bring up the subject.

"How do you know Dr. Heming was examining Mother?" he asked.

"Well, you know that little hill behind the ladies' bathhouse? I was coming down there and I could see in the window, and Dr. Heming was examining Mommy."

Her father became silent again. He folded his arms tightly over his chest and crossed and uncrossed his legs several times. Then he straightened up. "It's time we were going, honey."

"But Daddy," she said despairingly, "we still have six tickets!"

"No, Dana. It's late. Besides, we agreed we were going to save some tickets, right?"

"Oh, Daddy," she groaned. "Well, look, just one last ride on the merrry-go-round, okay?"

"All right, but that's it. I'll sit here and watch."

"You hold Lindsay." She finished her ice cream as she walked to the nearby ride. After relinquishing one of her remaining tickets, she crawled up on a horse and waved to her father. His head was down, and he did not see her.

The carousel began revolving slowly, and the horse rose and fell gently with the music. She patted the lacquered head and whispered in its ear, "Good, General." General was a horse in a children's book she had read recently. "Good, boy." She let go of the pole in front of her and picked up the reins. It was her last ride. She would enjoy every moment. The whirling carousel gathered speed. The breeze felt good on her face. Faster and faster. Her world became a dizzy blur. She dropped the reins, gripped the pole tightly, and closed her eyes. The grinding rhythm of the pipe organ pulsated in her ears as General floated smoothly through the night.

It was well after ten o'clock when they started across the parking lot toward their car. Dana was the first to see the white card on the windshield.

"Look, I think we got a ticket." Dropping his hand, she ran ahead to take a look.

"Be careful of cars backing out," called her father.

At the car she stood on her toes and withdrew the card from

under the windshield wiper. It was one of the invitations that she had seen her mother prepare for the dinner dance. Engraved in script on a four-by-five-inch card of white Bristol board were the words:

Mr. and Mrs. David Powell
request the pleasure of
your company at a dance
Saturday, the twenty-sixth of June
at eight o'clock
Meadow Lane, Tarrytown

R.S.V.P.

At the bottom of the card someone had printed in bold black letters:

THE JIG IS UP!

THEY DANCE TO A DIFFERENT TUNE IN THE DANCEHALL

Below the words was a crudely drawn picture of an hourglass with the sands running out.

"What is it, Dana?" her father asked, approaching and holding out his hand.

"It's one of Mommy's invitations. Somebody drew a picture on it. Look!"

She watched curiously as her father inspected the invitation.

"What's the matter, Daddy?" Her father did not answer but kept staring at the card. "Daddy, are you all right? You look like you've just been on the Scrambler!"

◊ ◊ ◊

CHAPTER 14

It was the night of Sue Powell's midsummer revel, and a flurry of final preparations was under way. Dave, wearing a dinner jacket, stood at the window of the upstairs master bedroom, sipping a drink and gazing at the festivity unfolding below. The area to the right of the elm tree had been transformed with striped green and white tents. A web of wiring holding colored light bulbs covered the panorama, supplementing the gas lamps that flickered about the grounds.

The largest of the tents covered a gleaming white-oak portable dance floor laid on the lawn for the occasion. At one end of the floor, tuning up in a chorus of dissonance, was a sixteen-piece orchestra. Several other nearby tents sheltered tables bearing place settings, flowers, and candles. Servants in black uniforms eddied between the main house and the tents.

To the left of the elm tree was a yellow-striped hot-air balloon. Tethered by a line attached to its wicker gondola, it basked in the glow of two spotlights, helping to accentuate the French theme that Sue had created. She had billed her dance as a *fête champêtre*, and it was expected to be *the* party of the Westchester season.

Dusk with all its leaden tones had begun to settle over the

grounds. The elm tree and the deep forest behind the cutting garden were now a dark outline in the deepening twilight. A light breeze rustled somewhere up in the elm, causing the branches to groan. Dave glanced in the direction of the sound. There was a glimpse of movement high in the crotch of some branches. Perhaps it was the lone black bird that occasionally showed up in the elm. A movement off to the left caught his eye. It was Puff. The St. Bernard was emerging from one of the tents, a large bone in her mouth.

The sound of a car came from down near the gatehouse, where the gardener Brandon Sheehan acted as sentinel. Dave saw a silver-gray Bentley wend its way up the long drive and come to a stop on the cobblestones in front of the main house. Here Tom Lucas was stationed to assist arriving guests. A freshly pressed dark gray uniform covered his tall frame. Boots polished for the occasion gleamed in the twilight, matching the shiny ebony visor on his cap.

Dave watched as Tom opened the door of the limousine and a tall, slender figure emerged. He was a handsome man in his late thirties, with smooth, deeply tanned features. Dark hair, graying at the temples, blended with his black dinner jacket and white shirt, giving him a crisp, distinguished appearance.

"Evening, Doctor," said Tom, holding the door as John Heming alighted. "Nice evening, isn't it?"

"Hello, Tom." Heming glanced toward the tents expectantly. "Am I the first one here?"

"Yes, sir. I believe you are. Mr. and Mrs. Powell should be down in a few minutes."

"Hilda!" Heming called to a maid passing nearby. "Hilda, would you fetch me a vodka martini on ice? Very dry, please."

A frown crossed Dave's face as he watched Heming disappear inside one of the tents.

"Who drove up?" Sue emerged from her dressing room in a tight-fitting black evening gown with revealing décolletage. "I can't believe anyone is here already."

"Who do you think?" replied Dave. "Your favorite doctor."

"John? Oh, yes." She joined her husband at the window. "He said he would come early to help greet the guests. What's Dana doing down there?"

Dana had come out of the house and was standing next to Tom Lucas. She was in a pale yellow party dress. A small garland of yellow and white daisies, fashioned by Sue for the occasion, adorned her black hair. The chauffeur leaned over to talk to the girl and then, taking her hand, limped toward one of the tents.

"I don't think she should be out there greeting the guests," Sue said with a frown.

Dave did not respond. He sensed that the sight of the hobbling chauffeur with her daughter disturbed his wife. A presage perhaps of what lay ahead for Dana.

"Was John alone?" Sue asked.

"Did he come with a date, do you mean?" Dave left the window and moved toward a chair. "No, he didn't. Maybe he thinks he has one here."

"You're so silly." Sue continued to look through the window at the party scene. "I still can't get over how you acted the other night."

"What do you mean?"

"Just that you'd let something a seven-year-old said bother you that way."

"What would you have thought if she'd told *you* I was examining someone in the bathhouse?"

"I don't know what I would have thought. I know I wouldn't have come home the way you did, threatening to leave and acting as though you were on the verge of a nervous breakdown."

"I had a lot on my mind that night."

"Maybe so, David, but you're going to have to get hold of yourself. You've been so edgy. And the other night—I've never seen you like that before. Talking about leaving to live in Europe and all that nonsense. Anyway, I told you, all John did was look at my ankle. Dana spends a lot of time with doctors. Naturally she'd think he was examining me."

"I know, and I understand how you could have twisted your ankle. What I don't understand is why that doctor was here in the middle of the afternoon playing tennis with three women. Doesn't that strike you as a trifle odd?"

"Not at all. He's a good friend of Carrie Miller, and she asked him to substitute for her." She walked to her dressing table. Suddenly, she stopped and turned toward her husband, her face thoughtful, concerned. "Dave, I know how difficult things must be for you right now. But you've been so paranoid these past few weeks. The phone rings, and you pick up the extension to listen in. A car drives in, and you rush to the window to see who it is. Yesterday you almost knocked Hilda over when she went out to get that registered letter from the mailman. Even Dana has noticed how nervous you are. You simply must control yourself. Everything will be all right."

Dave did not reply. He walked into his dressing room and looked at his reflection in the mirror. His face was haggard. He realized he had overreacted to his daughter's comment. Sue had never shown any romantic interest in other men. But it was the other incident at Playland. The note. *Someone knew.*

"We'd better hurry," Sue called. "I heard another car drive up."

"It's probably Emily Hunter," said Dave dryly. He drained his glass and put it on a bureau.

"In view of your problems, she may not come."

"No one else would, under the circumstances, but she will. Wait and see." Dave returned from the dressing room. "She's oblivious of what people think about her. I remember once when she negotiated a deal behind the back of a supposed friend from Florida. The man flew all the way to New York in his private jet to tell her what a bitch she was. When he was leaving she had the effrontery to ask him if he'd drop her off in Washington on his way back."

Sue laughed. "Well, that's Emily. Did he drop her off?"

"Are you serious? He told her that the only way he'd drop

her in Washington was if they didn't have to land. I wish to God you hadn't invited her."

Sue turned, looking at him intently. "Dave, you're going to have to understand. Emily and I have been friends for a long time. We—" She hesitated. Then, with a toss of her head she said, "The invitations went out almost a month ago. How was I to know that you wouldn't want her to come? Frankly, I hope she does come. She's very handsome, and everyone's in awe of her. She's an asset at any party."

"Just keep her away from me," Dave said quietly.

"I'll take care of her, don't worry. I just heard another car." Sue walked to the window. "Oh, it's that friend of yours from Rochester."

"Jerry?"

"Lord, look at him," said Sue. "He's wearing one of those funny light blue tuxedos with all the frills."

Oh boy, thought Dave. Jerry would be the only one there without a conventional dark tuxedo. It would ruin his wife's landscape. It was not the first time the style of some of his friends had proved an embarrassment in the Dickerson social set.

"I'd better get down there," he said quickly. "Jerry doesn't know anyone. He'll be uncomfortable."

During the next hour a caravan of motorcars descended upon the estate, discharging luminaries from throughout the New York metropolitan area. Among the first to arrive were an eminent publisher and his wife in a shiny gray Mercedes limousine, followed by the scion of a wealthy Westchester family with his pretty date in a red Maserati. Two middle-aged sisters, with sufficient stock holdings between them to influence one of the world's largest corporations, struggled from a Volkswagen Rabbit; while a spectacularly beautiful blonde in a dazzling gold evening gown—the proprietress of a local dress shop—slid easily from behind the wheel of her Ford Pinto. A prominent United States senator had seen fit to make the trip from his apartment in Manhattan.

It was an unusual group of guests of different ages and dissimilar interests. But whatever their station in life—rich or poor, beautiful or plain, old or young—each possessed some singular quality perceived by the hostess as an asset to her party. It had all been planned with the usual meticulous, dispassionate Sue Powell style.

For their part, the guests shared one common feeling. Whether it was a young heart beating with the hope of a romantic new contact, or an elderly personage looking forward to rubbing elbows with other elderly personages, or chauffeurs hoping for good draws at the card game set up in the garage area, there was no one who arrived without a sense of pleasurable anticipation. And though some had come from as far away as Long Island or New Jersey, there was a confidence in even the most jaded of the party-goers that the trip would be worth it.

Each guest received a warm reception from the hostess. Standing in an informal receiving line with Dave and a few close friends, Sue greeted each arrival as though the entire affair had been conceived with that particular person in mind; as if now that he or she had arrived, the party could begin in earnest.

Once through the receiving line, the guests were served cocktails by the staff, who moved efficiently through the throng with silver trays bearing drinks and hors d'oeuvres. Soon the orchestra launched into its first number. The melody spilled from the tent and drifted across the lawn into the darkness. Voices became louder as the pitch and intensity of the party mounted. Conversation, laughter, clinking ice and glasses merged with the music as sounds of revelry drifted out into the clear summer night.

It was near midnight, and the party was at its peak, when a pearl-colored Cadillac Seville approached the gatehouse. Unlike the other cars, which had waited to be checked into the grounds, this one breezed through the underpass without stopping, disregarding Brandon, who had emerged from the gatehouse. The car swept up the drive, leaving in its wake currents of air that lifted tiny blades of grass from the freshly mowed lawn beside the road. It lurched to a stop on the cobblestones, well beyond where Tom Lucas had moved out to greet it.

The door opened almost before the car had stopped, and a handsome blonde woman of imperious bearing, attired in a black evening gown, moved out from behind the wheel. She left the door of the car open and sailed past the approaching chauffeur without a word, as though infinitely more important things were waiting beyond.

The mood of the party was free and festive. Restraint and inhibitions vanished along with champagne bubbles into the air. Leaden feet were light and limber, and traditional fox-trots and waltzes yielded to less constrained contemporary gyrations. Austere personalities were now warm and witty. Plain-looking women had turned alluring. Promises were pledged. Hands held. Strange lips kissed. The sound of music, laughter, and popping corks reverberated from the trees into the black summer sky.

Two women on the fringe of the party moved toward each other. The figures stopped for a momentary greeting. It was a brief exchange, unnoticed by a thousand eyes: a wistful look, a quick whisper, a lingering handclasp—a fleeting encounter of two women in love.

◊   ◊   ◊

CHAPTER 15

Dave, reclining on a chaise longue beneath the elm tree, gazed up through the network of wiring that held the branches in position. Because of the size and weight of the limbs, it had been necessary through the years to install support. From the base of the tree one now looked up into a cobweb of steel strands.

The tree would not last long. It had deteriorated more rapidly than the tree experts had anticipated. Despite injections, sprayings, and pruning, increasing areas had taken on the withered yellow cast of Dutch elm disease. Gaps appeared in the foliage, and where once it had been impossible to see through the heavy leaves, patches of blue sky were now visible.

But Dave's mind was not on the tree. He was thinking of an eight-million-dollar loan for which his real estate company had applied. He desperately needed the financing, and not just for the real estate firm. By means of intercompany charges he could draw off some of the eight million to help offset the cash problems he was having in Stamford.

One of Dave's executives had learned from a friend at Hunter Management that a representative of the lending group had consulted Emily Hunter. She had said that she would as soon loan money to an Iranian rug merchant as to David Powell, and that she doubted he would still be in business in two years unless they bailed him out. It was the kind of endorsement Dave would have expected from Emily.

As he gazed up into the tree, his thoughts drifted once again to the invitation he had found on the car. Upon seeing it, he had been frozen with fear. He had tried to convince himself that it was unrelated to Lake Placid, but the mention of the Dancehall and the nature of the illustration had left little doubt—time was running out.

He suspected that Emily Hunter was paying someone to harass him; exercising psychological pressure to divert his attention from their legal confrontation. If this were her stratagem, it had been successful. He had thought of little else since he had discovered the card. Yet how could she know about Lake Placid? About the Dancehall? About Ann Conway?

Since their lunch, he had had no contact with Emily. He had carefully avoided her at the midsummer party. Their eyes had met once inadvertently, and she had looked right through him without the slightest change of expression, as though he were not there. It was as if she had already written him off—not only was David Powell no longer an issue for Emily Hunter, but he no longer even existed.

The ordeal was taking its toll. Like the elm tree, he seemed to be dying a bit each day. His face was drawn, and he had lost considerable weight. He could see the change mirrored in the expressions of his associates. Their eyes would linger on him as though perceiving a grave illness.

He glanced toward the cutting garden where Sue and Dana were busy with their flowers, Puff lying nearby. There was a look of serenity about his wife and daughter as they knelt among the plants. He wondered what Sue's reaction would be if she learned about Ann Conway. She would cope with it, he thought. She had iron nerves and an irrepressible spirit. But what of Dana?

Suddenly the child glanced up and caught him looking at

her. As though sensing his concern, she rose and ran toward him. "Daddy, what's the matter?"

"How's my little girl?" Dave said, holding out his hands as she approached. Was it his imagination or did she seem a trifle awkward?

She lay down on the chaise with him, and he gathered her into his arms and kissed her on the ear. Closing his eyes, he pressed his face into her dark curls.

"Daddy, I want to tell you something."

"Yes, dolly."

"Now, are you listening? Sometimes I talk and I don't think you're listening."

"I'm listening. Very carefully."

"Well, it's just that lately you always seem sad. Please don't be sad." She turned, her dancing eyes looking up at him.

"I'm happy, sweetie. Honest I am." He hugged her and kissed her loudly on the cheek. "Let's sing our garden song. You start."

"Okay." She began singing in a tiny, slightly off-key voice, and Dave joined in:

Here, look in the gar-den bed.
Some-thing beau-ti-ful is grow-ing.
Bright, shaped like a cup-all-red,
Tu-lips open to the sun.

After finishing the song, Dave leaned back against the chaise and again looked up through the foliage of the elm. Two crows landed on a branch near the top. They reminded him of the larger bird that frequented the grounds. He had not seen it since the night of the party. "I wonder where our big black bird is?"

"I don't think he'll be back," said Dana.

"Really? Why not?"

"Mommy didn't like him. He kept messing up the front of the house, over there where he sat on the chimney. Mommy said she sent him away."

"Oh, he'll come back," said Dave.

A yellow butterfly caught his attention as it beat its flaxen wings among some nearby flowers. He marveled at its quiet, simple beauty as it rose on a voluted course that brought it close to his chair. Suddenly it lighted on his knee. It rested but a moment and then was off again, its gossamer wings disappearing among the flowers.

The incident had taken only seconds, but during the brief interlude he had sensed a lessening of his problems, as though the touch of the tiny creature had infused him with some mystical balm. He glanced at his wife working among her flowers. Apparently she had discovered this secret of nature long ago. He called to her softly, but she appeared not to hear.

"Mommy," Dana yelled.

"Yes, my darling," she answered with mild disapproval in her voice. "Don't shout so."

"We called you once, but you didn't hear us," said Dana.

"I heard you." Absorbed in her gardening, she gave them faint attention.

"Isn't it a beautiful day?" Dave said.

"Oh, it is," she replied.

"I love doing this." She turned to him, her face radiating contentment. "We're so lucky, aren't we?" She paused for a moment, looked into his eyes, and then returned her interest to the garden.

Dave marveled at her tranquillity. He recalled when they were first married how they had discovered among her memorabilia a diary that she had kept one summer when she was a child. Almost every daily entry had concluded, "Today I was so happy." It seemed that there had been little change in her outlook during the intervening years. And yet there was that mystifying side to her personality that he could not fathom—times when her eyes suggested that she was far off in some world known only to Sue Powell. In their early years together he had been intrigued by such interludes, but she would pass off his questions lightly, with a laugh or a bemused look suggesting it was his imagination.

He rested his head against the chaise and cuddled his daughter as he watched the sky. Puffs of white clouds were sailing rapidly eastward. Occasionally one would overtake another and form a larger cloud, only to break into a different form. It was a tumbling, disordered, ever-changing phenomenon. It brought to mind Sue's comment that nothing stayed the same.

His own fortunes had seen great change. He thought of his childhood, when they had moved from a pleasant house in the suburbs to the small duplex in the city. That change had affected his sister Ida more than it had Dave. A pretty girl with a social bent, Ida had refused to date for almost a year because of their plebeian household.

On one occasion he had shared his sister's reservations about their home. It was soon after he and Sue had become engaged. He had invited Sue to Rochester to meet his mother and sister. The day was vivid in his memory. He was with his mother and Ida in the kitchen preparing to go to the airport to meet Sue . . .

"But Dave, she's marrying you because she loves you. She doesn't care where you live." Helen Powell alternated her attention between her son and the dishes she was drying. She dried each piece of china, meticulously polishing it with the towel, and then carefully placed it among the neat rows in the cabinet.

"But Mom, you don't understand," Dave said. "If you could see where she lives. It's bigger than the library down the street. When you knock on the front door a butler answers. I'm afraid it's going to be an awful surprise when she sees this place."

"He's right, Mom." Ida, standing over the sink where she had been washing dishes, shook water from her hands and dried them on a towel. "She's going to be *shocked!*" She said "shocked" with authority, as though speaking from experience.

"It's neat and clean," said Mrs. Powell. "Besides, what does she expect? She knows that you don't have a father; that your mother works. You never told her you lived in a mansion, did you?"

"Yeah, that's probably his problem. He probably told her that he's some kind of heir apparent. You did, didn't you?" Ida turned from the sink and leveled an accusing look at him. "You told her your father helped start Kodak or something." She paused, drying her hands. "That's why he's so nervous. The chickens are coming home to roost."

"Listen to who's talking," retorted Dave. "As though you aren't forever complaining about this place. At least I try to help out when you bring someone home."

"What?" Ida exclaimed incredulously. "What have you ever done? Other than be a colossal pest!"

"Plenty. I painted the alcove for you when that guy from Delaware came. And what about the time you made me stand in the hallway half the night in front of where the plaster was falling off the wall so your date wouldn't see it?" Dave shook his head. "What a fool I was. I waited there almost an hour for the guy to leave while she was in there on the couch necking with him."

"Keep your voices down," their mother admonished, motioning toward the wall. "They can hear every word next door."

"You'd better get going," Ida said, checking her watch. "You said her plane is due at four. If I were you, I'd have a cup of coffee with her at the airport and send her back to New York."

"That's a brilliant idea. I could tell her my sister has some exotic disease, and we've all been quarantined."

"Now, that's enough, Dave," Mrs. Powell said. "Remember, Ida's giving up her room for the night."

"I know," said Dave disconsolately. "I wonder if it wouldn't be better to have Sue stay at some motel. I could say that we've—"

"Dave," his mother said sternly. "Bring the girl here. It's your home. If she loves you, where you live won't make any difference."

Dave thought of responding but hesitated. He knew the conversation was beginning to provoke his mother. Besides, his mother was probably right. Standing, he crossed the room and placed his arm around her shoulder. "Wait till you meet her, Mom. You're really going to like her."

"Of course, I will." She kissed him lightly on the cheek and left the kitchen.

Dave glanced toward his sister, who was now sitting in a chair on the far side of the room, gazing out the window. For as long as he could remember she had been sitting alone by windows, forever watching and waiting for something that never materialized. His resentment gave way to sympathy.

"Ida," he said.

She looked at him quickly, frowning as though expecting a continuation of their bickering.

"Thanks for letting Sue use your room."

"That's all right." She returned to the window. "I wish it were nicer."

Helen Powell had been right. For Sue Dickerson the house was of little concern. Beyond an almost imperceptible arch of an eyebrow upon learning she was to share the upstairs bath with the rest of the family, she exhibited little interest one way or the other. She charmed his mother—even Ida had been impressed—and the following day Dave packed her off to New York in the same good spirits in which she had arrived.

They were married a few months later. The wedding was one of the grand events of the Westchester social season. Dickerson relatives and friends from throughout the New York area and fashionable distant points descended upon Scarsdale. It was a traditional ceremony at the local Episcopal church.

The Dickerson guests continued to come until the final moment, filling the pews behind the bride's family and spilling over to the more sparsely occupied seats reserved for the groom.

Dave stood waiting nervously with his best man near the front of the church. He looked over the assemblage and noted Herbert Dickerson at the rear, smiling at him. The man winked and gave a small thumbs-up gesture. In the front row, Arlene Dickerson wore an expression of resignation. Dave glanced to the other side of the church where his mother sat with Ida. They looked self-conscious.

As he looked over the rows of pews, he noticed the stunning blonde seated a few rows behind Mrs. Dickerson. It was Emily Rhodes, Sue's friend from Newport. He had met her briefly the previous day, and he had noted then, as now, a certain contempt in her pale blue eyes. Sue had probably told her everything about him. The elevated chin and haughty expression said it all—David Polanski was clearly marrying out of his class.

But he knew this—indeed marveled at it. Why Sue Dickerson had agreed to marry him was almost beyond his comprehension. She had so much; he so little. She had told him repeatedly that she loved him, yet sometimes he wondered if perhaps in her pragmatic way, she had simply decided it was time to be married; that David Powell was a convenient choice. She often commented that she was glad he was not the aggressive type. In effect she was saying that he was easy to handle. And he recalled how, on a few occasions, she had referred derisively to the single status of her friend Emily Rhodes. "Emily's going to end up an old maid," she had said.

Yes, for Sue Dickerson it was time to get married, and for whatever reasons, he was the one she had selected. Nevertheless, for Dave it was all a miracle of good fortune—a fairy tale come true.

But they were not married yet. Anything could still go wrong. A rash of possibilities tumbled through his mind. Sue could have an accident on the way to the church. Or the minister could suddenly get sick. He had heard of such things. They would have to postpone the ceremony. Then maybe it would never happen. Sue might have second thoughts. Perhaps her mother would try to resurrect the relationship with Bob Turner. She would if she could. Bob had all the credentials. The Ivy League. Westchester society. Dave wondered idly what Bob was doing. It could hardly be a good day for Bob.

Suddenly the treble notes of the wedding march pierced the air. The music rang from the choir loft across the great ceiling, resounding from the marble pillars and walls, filling the enormous church with its vibrant sound. Until that moment he had not felt the full emotion of the event. But with the peal of the wedding march, reality burst upon him in a glorious surge of relief, triumph, and love for Sue Dickerson.

The bridal procession was now moving slowly from the rear of the church down the white carpet toward the altar. He watched as the bridesmaids appeared two-by-two, pretty girls with wide, nervous eyes. And then he saw her—smiling, poised, confident. Never had she seemed so lovely; her dark hair and tanned, beautiful features in stunning contrast to the white satin and lace. As she neared the altar, her enchanting eyes caught and held him, and in that brief moment Dave Powell felt a touch of paradise.

◇ ◇ ◇

PART
V

Lake Placid, New York
July 1982

CHAPTER 16

Horace Ackerman listened to the chugging of the engine as he leaned against a bulwark in the stern of the launch. It was a strong, constant vibration that he found pleasant, the sound of something performing steadily and reliably.

With him was the State Police lieutenant who had accompanied him on his earlier trip to Buck Island. The weather was better than it had been the last time. It was clear and cool, with a hint of fall in the air. A crisp breeze off the starboard bow sent whitecaps splashing against the hull, occasionally spraying the deck. In the distance was the Dickerson camp, where colorful flags stood straight in the wind and the lawn rolled down to the lake like green velvet.

"You think he'll be there?" Ackerman asked.

"Should be. They saw him going out about an hour ago," O'Brien said. "I don't know how much Sam'll talk, though. He's pretty close-mouthed."

"We may have to put a little pressure on him. We've got to get him on record before this stuff leaks to the press."

"You're sure none of the family's there?" O'Brien asked.

"Yeah, I made a pretext call this morning. The Dickersons are in Newport; the Powells, in Tarrytown."

Ackerman watched the enlarging outline of the Dickerson camp and thought about the people who lived there. If the case continued to go as he anticipated, their lives would soon change drastically.

His drive and tenacity had paid off. So much so that he had spent the better part of the previous morning in the Essex County Sheriff's office checking files to find something that would strengthen the Bureau's jurisdiction in the case. Even though he suspected the subject might have traveled out of state following the crime, which would bring the case under the Unlawful Flight to Avoid Prosecution (UFAP) statute, he wanted something more tangible. He had been lucky to find what he needed. It had come in the record of a Chevrolet Belair found abandoned on the lake road next to Lake Placid on July 2, 1962. The car had carried a Michigan registration and could be presumed stolen. This, in theory, gave the FBI jurisdiction under its Interstate Transportation of Stolen Motor Vehicle statute or ITSMV case, as it was known in Bureau jargon. In view of the proximity of the vehicle to where the body had been recovered, it had been a logical extension of Ackerman's personal authority, as he saw it, to undertake an ITSMV-UFAP-murder investigation. A woman's sweater found in the trunk strengthened the theory. It was not the first time the investigator had used the ITSMV statute to enter a case. Indeed, the former Director had used it repeatedly himself as a convenient entrée to cases of national significance. It had been the ITSMV statute that had given the Bureau jurisdiction in the John Dillinger case.

What was sufficient to get the Bureau into the Dillinger case was certainly enough to justify Horace Ackerman's role in the Lake Placid murder investigation. In fact, who was to say that the car was *not* related to the case? Under different circumstances Ackerman would not have expended such time to cover jurisdictional matters. In this instance, however, because of the publicity, he wanted to be certain that the

Bureau, and more specifically Horace Ackerman, received appropriate credit without challenge.

"You deserve a lot of credit," O'Brien said, with near-clairvoyance. "You say the medallion was the big break?"

"That and the guideboat. When the divers brought up the boat, we knew we were close. The rope in the boat matched the rope on the victim. We asked the boat manufacturer in Saranac to check their records and find out who had bought it. They said it wasn't necessary. The name of the owner was always under the brass plate that holds the oarlock. We unscrewed the plate and there it was—'Dickerson.'"

"And the medallion came from the local ball club?"

"Right. We showed it to one of the men who used to help manage the team. He said they awarded them to the team captains. In 1962 the captain was Dave Powell. The team used to hang out in that restaurant over there on the pavilion. They called it the Dancehall then. Anyway, the rest was pretty easy. We found out that Powell worked at the Adirondack Club. The club records showed that he and the girl were discharged the same day. When we checked out the girl, we found a missing person report had been filed on her in the New York City Police Department. The lab made a positive identification based on dental records."

"Didn't they try to trace her twenty years ago when she was reported missing?"

"The records showed a routine investigation. Nothing special. There were no leads. Apparently no one knew she was in Lake Placid. Her mother died a short time after the girl's disappearance. No one pushed the thing. Besides, they get thousands of missing person reports in the city. Teenage runaways. There's no way of checking them all out."

"You've got enough for an indictment?" the lieutenant asked.

"An indictment, yes. A conviction, no. You can run anything past a grand jury and get an indictment. Proving it in court is something else. Right now it's pretty circumstantial. All we know for sure is that the subject and victim were dismissed at the same time. The subject listed his address on the club records as Camp Louise, and the victim was found over there with the Majestics' medallion in her hand. It's damned incriminating, but it *is* circumstantial. I'm doing a few things that might help, though. Which reminds me." Ackerman pulled the folder from under his arm and withdrew a yellow legal pad. After making a few notes he returned the pad to the folder. "I'm exerting a little pressure on the side," he said almost more to himself than to the State Police officer.

"What do you mean?"

Ackerman did not respond. There were certain things an agent did not discuss with local law enforcement.

"I hope this caretaker talks," O'Brien said after a pause.

Ackerman shrugged. "The constable thinks he might know something."

"Charlie Welsch? Why, what did he say?"

"Just local scuttlebutt—that the Dickerson caretaker might know something. It may be nothing."

"Maybe Mrs. Powell will be here after all," O'Brien said. "It would be worth the trip just to see her."

With the mention of Sue Powell's name, Ackerman's thoughts returned to the interview he and O'Brien had had with her. Her eyes had gripped him in an odd, hypnotic way. He had watched her intently throughout the interview. There was something about her manner. Something he sensed but couldn't put his finger on. It had been almost as though she were doing the interrogating. Horace Ackerman was a man who prided himself on his ability to control an interview, and the encounter with Sue Powell had left him uneasy.

◊   ◊   ◊

CHAPTER 17

Sam Wykoff was apprehensive as he saw the police launch draw near. He had feared they would return. It seemed inevitable.

He had been cutting flowers for the house, and he placed his shears down next to a basket of gladiolus. Slowly, reluctantly, he started toward the dock. He reached the landing as the boat came alongside. The state policeman stepped nimbly ashore before it stopped and tied one of the lines to a large brass ring in the dock.

"Have a few minutes, Sam?" he asked. "This is Agent Ackerman of the FBI." He nodded toward the tall man climbing out of the boat. "He wants to ask you a few questions."

The comment sent a shiver through the caretaker. "Sure. What can I do for you?"

"Can we sit down for a few minutes?" Ackerman asked, looking around.

"We can sit up there." Sam motioned toward the balcony of the boathouse.

They followed him to the rear where the stairs led to the upper deck. With each step Sam felt himself drawn closer to an involvement he wanted to avoid.

"Feels almost like fall, doesn't it, Sam?" O'Brien commented genially.

"Yes, it does. Unusual this time of year."

They mounted the stairs to the balcony, where the caretaker motioned to some porch furniture overlooking the lake. The wind had increased, whipping up whitecaps that came and went like tips of tiny icebergs.

"Bit breezy up here," Sam said, his breathing labored. Settling into a rocking chair, he glanced at the FBI agent, who took the chair next to him. The man seemed austere.

"We appreciate your taking a few minutes, Mr. Wykoff," Ackerman said, displaying his credentials.

"Call me Sam. Everybody does."

"All right, Sam. We're investigating the body found in the lake. We thought you might be able to help us."

"Will if I can." Sam thought that was the reason they were there, but the confirmation increased his anxiety.

"We believe the body was submerged after the ice went out of the lake in 1962—sometime between May and November. I understand you were the caretaker then. Ackerman paused to level a penetrating look. "We'd appreciate it if you'd tell us some of the things that were going on at Camp Louise at that time. You know, who was here, what they were doing. Anything at all you can remember. We'd also like to hear any ideas you have about how that girl ended up in the lake."

Sam adjusted himself in the chair and withdrew a pipe from his breast pocket. "Don't understand why you'd be asking me."

"We're contacting anyone who was in the area at the time," O'Brien said.

"We know you were working here that summer," the agent added.

Same shifted again in his chair and averted his eyes. "That's a long time ago. Summers have a way of running together when you get to be my age."

"You must have thought about that particular summer though, haven't you?" asked Ackerman. "With all the publicity, you must have thought quite a bit about it."

"Can't say's I have." Sam lit his pipe, taking longer than usual. His hands trembled, and he wondered if the men noticed. "I don't think I could tell you anything about any particular summer that long—"

"This was a very special summer," Ackerman said, with a trace of irritability. "And that body was right over there by Pulpit Rock. We have reason to believe that you may have information that could be helpful."

The comment stunned Sam. They must know. His wife must have let something slip to her mother or sister. With only twenty-five hundred people in town you couldn't afford to say anything. Suddenly he needed a drink. He thought of the bottle of Jack Daniels under the eaves on the front porch. He should have taken a nip when he first saw the launch. "Not sure I know what you mean." He avoided the agent's eyes.

"Sam, we have evidence that within the past month you made a comment to the effect that you might know something about this case."

Sam felt the nerve drain from his body. He remembered making the statement to his brother on the telephone a few weeks before. As soon as he had said it he had realized it was a mistake. He felt a wave of hopelessness come over him and began to rock in the chair. Seconds elapsed as the pressure mounted. He had not wanted to become involved. He had never been in trouble, and he attributed it to the fact that he minded his own business.

"I'm just the caretaker here—" he began.

"Now, Sam." Ackerman's voice was measured and coldly official. "This is serious. It's my duty to remind you that withholding information of a felony, or aiding or abetting a crime, or furnishing false information to a federal officer are all violations of federal law and have severe penalties."

Sam was listening. Why did it have to come to this? "Can I, uh . . . Can I be kept out of this?" he asked, turning toward the agent. "I would just as soon you didn't tell anyone you talked to me, understand?"

"I can't promise you anything. Not now."

There was another long pause as Sam rocked. "Well . . . I guess I don't have much choice." He glanced anxiously at the lieutenant and then back to the FBI agent. The agent withdrew the legal pad from his folder and prepared to take notes.

"Go ahead, Sam," Ackerman said. His voice was softer now. "We're listening."

It was Tuesday, July 3, 1962, and Sam Wykoff was celebrating Independence Day early. He had already visited a few of his favorite bars in town and before going home had decided to make a quick stop at Camp Louise to check things out. The truth of the matter was that Sam planned to take some whiskey from the Dickerson liquor closet, and he always felt more comfortable waiting until dark when removing things from the camp.

After landing his small skiff in its usual slip at one end of the pavilion, he proceeded to the main house, where he took four bottles of Jack Daniels bourbon from the closet. He opened one of the bottles and took a long swallow. Then, turning out the lights, he left by a side door and started down the walk toward the waterfront. Although he carried a flashlight, visibility was poor. The only other light came from the soft yellow lamps on the boathouse pavilion.

As he reached the slip where his skiff was tied, he heard a quivering little laugh. Sam had never liked the sound. Stories involving the loon's laugh abounded on the lake. He had started to untie his boat when he heard the motor of the Dickerson launch. He assumed it was Dave Powell, who was staying at the camp at the invitation of the Dickersons.

As the craft drew near the dock lights on the landing, Sam saw Dave standing with a girl in the cockpit. The caretaker hesitated, considering going to greet them. But after considering the delicate nature of his condition, and the four bottles of bourbon he was carrying, he decided to remain out of sight. He put the bottles carefully in the bow of the skiff and then quietly paddled out onto the lake. From somewhere near the landing, once again came the sound of a loon. Or was it the girl with Dave? No, it was a loon. Only a loon had that crazy, wild laugh. Some distance from shore, he started the engine and headed for the harbor. He looked back several times, but no lights came on in the house. Whatever Dave Powell and his friend were doing, they were doing it in the dark.

The following day Sam awakened to one of those cold, foggy, rainy days that occasionally hang over mountainous regions. It had started to rain late the previous night and had continued intermittently through the next morning. The weather held up Sam's morning activities at a local nursery where he bought several shrubs he intended to use to replace some burned-out plants at Camp Louise. It was almost noon when he arrived at the harbor terminal. Looking down the rows of slips to where the larger craft were moored, he saw the launch Dave had used the day before. It was in its usual berth, and he assumed that the young man had gone to his job at the club. After loading the shrubs into the skiff, he cast off and headed for Buck Island.

Visibility on the lake was poor. Rain squalls swept over the small craft, beating against Sam's foul-weather gear and stinging his face. The trip took longer than usual, and he was glad when the waterfront came into view.

As he brought the boat into the landing, he noticed that the Adirondack guideboat was missing from the dock where it had been the day before. Dave and his friend must have been using it, he thought, or perhaps it had been stolen. It was not unusual for light boats to disappear from island camps.

Deciding to wait until the rain abated before removing the shrubs, he started toward the flagstone walk that led to the main house. It was then that he noticed the dark brown spots on the canvas-covered deck. A particularly large patch appeared below the balcony of the boathouse and was smeared, as though someone had tried to remove it. His first reaction was that someone had spilled paint. It annoyed him, since he had installed the canvas only that spring. He walked over to inspect the large patch more closely. With a chill he realized it was probably blood.

It was raining harder now, and the water beat down on the rubberized hood of his foul-weather gear, creating a loud crackling in his ears. It ran into his eyes and off the tip of his nose, and it pounded onto the dark brown stains. He stood motionless, staring at the spots, as though hoping that the pounding rain would drive the marks from the canvas.

But it was blood, or it sure looked like it anyway, and there had been lots of it. Judging from the smeared marks, someone had gone to considerable lengths to try to remove it. Because of the absorbency of the canvas, however, it was indelibly cast.

A slamming noise came from the balcony. Sam looked up and saw the door of the studio apartment was open, banging in the wind. He felt instinctively that something was wrong. He wondered if he should contact Charlie Welsch, the local constable. Better not to, he thought. Charlie was a sarcastic type. He had a brief vision of Charlie arriving on the Dickerson dock, remarking in his mocking tone, "Discover some blood, Sam?" No, short of finding a body to go with the blood, he wasn't about to call Charlie.

He knew he would have to look in the apartment, though. He walked toward the stairs to the upper deck. Once on the balcony, his uneasiness intensified. One of the panes in the upper section of the door had been shattered. Sam hesitated, then steeling himself, moved down the balcony to the entrance. Gazing inside, he saw nothing unusual. Cautiously he pushed open the door and entered. A bath towel lay on the floor near the door. Otherwise, nothing was out of the ordinary.

As he stepped back out the door and again saw the blood on the deck beneath the balcony, he began to reëvaluate his reluctance to call the authorities. He walked back down the balcony, surveying the area as he went, mystified by what he had seen. Descending the stairs, he made his way up to the main house, where he sat down in a rocking chair on the porch. It was here that Sam spent many of his caretaking hours, sipping Jack Daniels while observing the tranquillity of Lake Placid, making sure that things were in order at Camp Louise. For over ten years things *had* been in order. Now, in the space of ten minutes, everything had come apart.

Sam rocked harder as he considered his alternatives. He could either call Mr. Dickerson in Newport and explain what he had seen, or he could get Charlie Welsch out there. Either way, there were bound to be embarrassing questions. Why had he come out to the camp at night? Why had he avoided Dave Powell when he arrived in the launch? What was his own risk, alone at the scene with no one to support his story? How deeply might he become involved?

He got up and walked to the eave where he stashed the bourbon. Returning with it to his chair, he unscrewed the top and took a long swallow. As the liquid warmed his gullet, he began to see the merits of forgetting that he had noticed anything unusual. Why not wait a while to see what happened? At least wait to hear what Dave had to say. Dave or his guest might have been cut accidentally. The window was broken. Although there *was* an awful lot of blood for an accident of that type. Still, if it were some harmless incident and he called Mr. Dickerson or Charlie and made a big fuss about nothing, he would look pretty silly. If he hadn't noticed the marks in the first place, he wouldn't have the problem.

The more he considered his alternatives, the more slowly he rocked. He had never had any serious problems because he never went looking for them. Why change now? Besides, he was a caretaker, not a detective.

◊ ◊ ◊

PART
VI

Tarrytown, New York
July 1982

CHAPTER 18

Tom Lucas stood next to the Rolls-Royce in front of the main house. The morning sun reflected off his polished boots and the glossy visor of his cap. He had opened the rear door of the limousine in anticipation of Sue Powell, whom he was driving to Manhattan.

Tom looked forward to the trip. He was practical enough to realize that the closest he could ever be to Sue Powell's beauty was in the limousine. He never drove her anywhere that he did not enjoy a feeling of intimacy, and he valued the trips.

She was almost twenty minutes late—a rare deviation from her usual punctuality—and Tom had begun to wonder if there had been a change in plans. He folded his arms across the top of the opened door and watched the workers from the Harrison Nurseries cover a large hole where the base of the elm tree had been. Having filled the hole, the men were carrying mats of rolled turf from a nearby truck and sodding the ground. They rolled the mats neatly into the soil, blending them with the lawn as though patching an enormous green carpet. Soon there would be no trace of the once magnificent elm.

The change wrought in the landscape by its removal was dramatic. Tom saw trees that he had never noticed before. To the right of where the remains of the elm were being interred, a large horse chestnut stood as heir apparent. To the left was a gnarled old sycamore that hovered over the spot like a priest administering last rites, while from behind the cutting garden peered a cluster of twisted crab apple trees like poor relatives paying their last respects to a once mighty member of the family.

Tom wondered what David Powell's reaction would be when he returned from Chicago. Earlier in the week, his wife had made up her mind to remove the elm and had then handled the matter with her customary dispatch. When Tom had suggested, a bit uneasily, that perhaps she might want to discuss it with Mr. Powell first, she had been adamant. "Oh, no. He'd never let us take it down. He'll just sit around and watch it die a little each day. It's not going to make it. The sooner we get rid of it, the better." The Harrison people had been summoned forthwith.

As the chauffeur stood reflecting on the change, he heard a door open behind him.

"Good morning, Tom."

Sue Powell emerged from the house wearing a suede suit and carrying gloves and a brown leather pocketbook that matched her high-heeled shoes. She swung the pocketbook as she walked, and her carriage was confident and sprightly, as though pleasant things awaited her.

To Tom she was dazzling as she walked across the cobblestones toward the car. The sight filled him with a yearning he knew could never be fulfilled.

"Isn't this a lovely morning?" She smiled and her dark eyes flashed. "Haven't they done a splendid job?" She looked toward where the men were busy repairing the lawn. "I don't think we'll miss the elm, do you?"

Tom raised his eyebrows as he followed her gaze to the workmen. "Maybe *we* won't . . ."

"You mean my husband? Oh, he'll get used to it." She stepped into the limousine. "He can sit over there under the beech. In time, he won't even know the difference."

Tom closed the door and walked around the car to take his position behind the wheel. Once out on the main road, he adjusted the rearview mirror so that by raising his eyes he was able to catch an occasional glimpse of her face.

They drove down the long hill that led to the business district of Tarrytown. Tom glanced frequently in the mirror at his passenger, who stared pensively out the window. He would have liked to start a conversation but restrained himself.

It was several minutes before Sue spoke. "Summer's passing so fast, isn't it, Tom?" She straightened in her seat so that she could see him in the mirror. "I always feel a bit sad this time of year. I hate to see summer end, don't you?"

"I suppose so," he said. "I like the fall though."

"But there's nothing like summer. This one has been so beautiful. Such glorious days. And the flowers . . . Wouldn't it be terrible if there were no more—if this were the last summer?"

"The last summer?" Tom was curious.

She hesitated as though she might speak further but then returned her gaze to the countryside and fell silent.

Traffic was light by the time they reached the Saw Mill River Parkway. Most morning commuters were already in their offices, and the highway was now a wide-open expanse. Tom set the automatic speed control at sixty and settled back in his seat. The hum of the heavy tires on the pavement was the only sound in the car. They sped through shadows cast by large pines lining the road, and the Flying Lady atop the glistening chrome radiator flashed intermittently in the sunlight. Occasionally a car passed, its occupants craning their necks to view them.

As they approached the outskirts of the city, Sue leaned forward to give directions. "Take the Major Deegan, Tom. I told Mrs. Hunter we'd pick her up at her house. We'll be lunching at the Four Seasons, so you'll have a few hours to do as you like."

Aware of the hostility between David Powell and Emily

Hunter, Tom was baffled by the continuing association between the women. On the previous week he had picked Sue up at the Hunter townhouse, and he knew that she received frequent calls from Hunter at home.

He took the Major Deegan to the East Side Drive. Traffic was heavy and soon became a continuous stream of metal. At Ninety-sixth Street he left the drive to avoid the congestion and headed down Second Avenue. Turning right at Seventy-third Street, he proceeded west and brought the limousine to a stop before an attractive red-brick townhouse just beyond Park Avenue. He carefully backed into the empty space in front of the driveway leading to the garage and turned off the engine.

"Should I call for Mrs. Hunter?" he asked.

"I don't think it will be necessary. She'll be right out. Ah . . . Tom." Sue leaned forward, her manner suggesting that she had something important to say. "Tom," she repeated tentatively, "I'd appreciate it if you wouldn't mention my lunch with Mrs. Hunter to my husband. Do you understand?"

"Yes, of course."

Just then the front door of the townhouse was opened and held by a small, timid-looking butler. He stood looking anxiously back into the house as though he expected some momentary explosion inside might blow him and the townhouse into the far corners of Manhattan. Suddenly, Emily Hunter strode through the entranceway, according the butler no more attention than if he'd been a fixture on the door. She was wearing a fawn-colored suit that matched her hair, and a kelly green scarf. In spite of his dislike for her, Tom had always had a grudging admiration for her good looks. Today she seemed particularly attractive. As he watched her breeze down the steps, he thought how deceptive her appearance was. Rarely was a brutal personality so well camouflaged. He slid from behind the wheel to open the door as she approached.

"Good morning, Mrs. Hunter," he said, tipping his cap.

She nodded briefly and entered the car. "Hello, dear," she said, patting Sue on the knee as she settled beside her.

Tom closed the door and returned to the driver's side. As he climbed into his seat, Emily delivered a few curt directions and then abruptly raised the glass partition.

En route to the restaurant, Tom discreetly observed his passengers through the rearview mirror. They were animated throughout the trip and appeared to be enjoying each other's company.

"Pull over behind those cars."

He had not seen Emily pick up the intercom, and her voice startled him. He stopped behind several cars that were waiting to discharge passengers at the restaurant.

Sue leaned forward and pushed the button that lowered the glass partition. "We'll get out here, Tom. Why don't you plan to come back at two o'clock."

"Sure, Mrs. Powell. Just a second, I'll get that door for you."

"That's all right." Opening the door, she slid out to the sidewalk. She stood, straightening her skirt as Emily Hunter joined her, and the two then started toward the restaurant.

Tom watched them walk up the street, admiring the lovely legs and trim figures. Two workmen near an open manhole paused to look after them. They had neared the entrance to the restaurant when Tom saw Emily reach out and take Sue Powell's hand. She held it only briefly before letting it go, but there was something about the gesture that struck him as unusual. A thought occurred to him—a fleeting impression that floated in and out of his mind, nagging, persistent. Could it be? No, never. Not Sue Powell.

A low admiring whistle came from the direction of the manhole as the women entered the restaurant. Tom glanced to where the two workmen had been, but they were gone, swallowed in the black pit.

◇　◇　◇

CHAPTER 19

"There's no way we can sustain these losses in Stamford and survive." Bryan White, comptroller and chief financial officer of the Powell business ventures, was delivering a report to his boss. The two were seated at a large mahogany conference table in David Powell's spacious Park Avenue executive offices. "Even if they'd approved the real estate loan, there would have been so many restrictive covenants it's doubtful we could have channeled much into Stamford."

Dave listened quietly. It was apparent that the pressure of trying to stay afloat was taking its toll on his associate. Bryan looked weary, and his tumbled mass of thick, wavy hair seemed grayer. A large, affable man, with steady gray eyes, he had been a source of stability through the years. Rarely did he show emotion. Bryan said it was because at the office he was resting; that the pressure didn't start until he arrived home in the evening where eight children awaited him, seven of whom were girls. He inspired confidence in almost everyone. Even creditors who had begun to nibble at the heels of the Powell corporations had faith in him. When Bryan White said a check was in the mail, they knew it to be a fact. But now, what previously had been only whispered at bank executive committee meetings was discussed openly. Powell was in trouble.

"We have a cash deficit of three million," Bryan continued, "and you can see from the forecast it's going to be close to five million by January."

Dave studied the report the comptroller had spread on the table in front of him. "That eight-million-dollar loan would have helped," he said ruefully.

"No question about it," Bryan replied. "But even if they'd approved it, it wouldn't have bailed out Stamford. The only way Stamford can make it is to put on new products. I've got some figures here on the proposed expansion. Give me a second to correlate them with that cash flow, and I'll leave them with you."

A silence fell over the room as the accountant worked on his report. A rubber band that Dave had been playing with snapped. He tied the ends together and resumed expanding and contracting it nervously about his fingers. If only his father-in-law were alive, he thought. Herb Dickerson might have had the answers. Dave remembered how his father-in-law had helped him start the business years before. It had begun in the Dickerson library, where Dave and the older man had gone one evening after dinner.

Dave and Sue had been married for over a year, and his relationship with her father had become more that of a son than an in-law. Still, Dave had been uneasy when he first told him of his plans to purchase a container plant. As always, Herb Dickerson had been understanding. Dave remembered his kindly face and his head nodding sympathetically as he listened . . .

"It's an older plant near Stamford." Dave carried a brandy snifter across the room and handed it to his father-in-law, who was sitting near a freshly lighted fire. He returned to the bar and made himself a weak Scotch and soda, adding a touch of bitters to give it a darker cast. The drink held little appeal for him, but he knew that the older man enjoyed his brandy more when someone drank with him. Drink in hand, Dave sat down next to him. "They've been in business since 1926. We first heard about it from Sue's friend Emily Hunter. Her husband died and left her a similar plant in New Jersey. Apparently she's been remarkably successful with it."

Herb Dickerson lifted his glass. "Here's to the container business." He took a swallow of the brandy and gazed thoughtfully into the fire. "Well, you've got to begin somewhere, I suppose. You say the equipment is old?"

"Yes. In order to expand and make it profitable, we'd have to have new machinery. The bank has made the mortgage and our credit line contingent on the investment for new equipment."

"And that's two million?"

"That's right, sir. Two million three, to be exact."

The older man studied the blazing fire, his head cocked as though listening for answers to problems in the crackling logs. After several seconds he looked at Dave. "When Sue first mentioned it, I told her I didn't understand why a big outfit like United Industries would sell off a plant if it can make money. It isn't like those conglomerates to do something like that. Why don't they install the equipment themselves?"

"They're going out of the container business. I don't know why. Emily told Sue that they're selling a couple of their other plants in Maryland and Pennsylvania. Apparently she's already negotiating to buy another one, or she'd buy Stamford herself."

Herb Dickerson returned his gaze to the fire. The glow lit his face, emphasizing the many lines and giving his skin the appearance of a russet fabric that had been crinkled into a ball and then smoothed out. Sue and her mother entered the room followed by a maid bearing demitasses. Dave stood, intending to bring some chairs closer, but his mother-in-law motioned him back.

"Don't bother, David. We can sit here." She took a chair

behind the two men where she could observe them. Her presence made Dave uncomfortable.

"We've been talking about this container plant up in Stamford," Herb Dickerson said, turning toward his wife.

A silence greeted his words. Dave was aware that Sue had discussed the plan with her mother and that Mrs. Dickerson had been exceedingly cool to the idea. The reason, of course, was the two million three hundred thousand dollars.

"I think it's a wonderful idea," said Sue, attempting to fill the awkward void that followed her father's comment. "Don't you think so, Daddy?"

"Yes. I've told Dave many times that he should do something like this. I guess the least we can do is lend them some money to get started, right, dear?"

Again, the silence. Dave felt increasingly uncomfortable. He knew his mother-in-law would take her husband to task after he and Sue left. It was common knowledge that she could be severe with him. According to Sue, however, her father rolled with the punches, laughing off his wife's rebukes.

The venture had been launched shortly thereafter with a loan from Herb Dickerson, which he insisted was not to be amortized until the plant was a "going, flourishing concern." And a going, flourishing concern it had become—until his father-in-law died, and Emily Hunter had decided to inject herself into the Stamford operation.

"Here it is." Dave's reflections were interrupted by Bryan White, who handed him the accounting report. "You can see it works out pretty well with the new figures."

Dave glanced at the statement. "But there's no way it will work with Hunter in the picture. She'll do everything she can to keep us from adding new products."

Bryan began gathering up his papers. "Well . . . there is one thing we could try." He spoke hesitantly, avoiding Dave's eyes.

"What's that? I'm ready to listen to anything."

"We could try to strike a deal with Hunter. Get her to lift that injunction on Stamford. With more business we could turn things around in a hurry."

Dave knew Bryan was right. He'd considered some peace proposals to Emily. But it was a bitter solution, not only because of his ego. He knew Emily would be brutal in her demands, exacting every penny from a crippled adversary.

"How do you make a deal with a cobra?" Dave asked. "She'd devour us."

"You're right. But you've got no choice. She's our only way out."

Dave lowered his eyes once more to the operating statement. The stark specter of bankruptcy was hovering, waiting for the first major creditor to bring suit. He knew that, not only for the sake of his family but out of consideration for those who had helped him build the company, he would eventually have to swallow his pride and approach Emily.

"Why don't you have the lawyers feel out Hunter's counsel about a meeting of the principals?" he said with resignation. "I suppose that's the place to start." He rose and walked toward a gleaming mahogany desk. "I can just see her face when her laywers tell her we've sent up the white flag."

Bryan nodded and walked slowly from the room.

His associate gone, Dave considered the ramifications of an overture to Emily Hunter. Her demands would be dispiteous. And there was always the question of Lake Placid. He still felt that Emily might suspect something, although with the passing weeks he had accorded the matter less significance. Perhaps the note on the windshield had been nothing more than an odd prank—a mischievous, unrelated act. After all, there had been no further developments in the case. Although the status of his business affairs was deplorable, he could at least take heart that with each passing day the torment of Lake Placid was diminishing.

"Mr. Powell!" The intercom on the credenza behind him interrupted his thoughts.

Turning, he pushed a button that connected him with his secretary. "Yes, Anna."

"Mr. Putney is calling."

"Okay, I'll take it." He lifted the receiver. "Hello."

"Good morning, Mr. Powell. I'd like to make an appointment to discuss our recent assignment. Would you be available tomorrow morning?"

"Yes. Yes, of course. What time is good for you?"

"Would ten o'clock be satisfactory?"

"That's fine," Dave answered. "Ah . . . How is it going? Did you come up with anything? Anything interesting?"

"Well . . . yes. But I'd prefer to talk to you in person, Mr. Powell."

"Fine. I understand. I'll see you in the morning."

Dave replaced the phone. Eric Putney was the head of a private detective agency that Dave used occasionally for corporate personnel matters. Several weeks before, he had asked the investigator to compile personal information on Emily Hunter. After his rift with Emily, his lawyers had counseled him to develop whatever background data were available in anticipation of litigation.

Dave jotted a note in his diary. "Putney—ten." He wondered what the agency had discovered. Probably little he didn't already know. The usual stuff from magazines and newspapers.

Dave spent the remainder of the morning trying to devise a strategy to serve as a basis for negotiation with Emily Hunter. He had little inspiration, however, and left for lunch no closer to a solution.

After a sandwich at a nearby men's club, he returned to his office. As he entered the outer chamber, his secretary looked up from her desk and reached for a spiral notebook. "Only one call, Mr. Powell." She flipped through the pages, consulting her notes. "Mr. White said to tell you that Mrs. Hunter is unavailable. However, her lawyers are willing to meet with you next week if you'd like."

Dave knitted his brow. He was not surprised. Emily would let him cool his heels; force him to deal with her lawyers for a while. Time was on her side.

Preoccupied, he didn't notice the letter that the secretary tried to hand to him as he passed her desk. "Excuse me, Mr. Powell. This came for you while you were at lunch."

"What's that? Oh, thank you," Dave said, taking it from her hand. Roughly inscribed on the envelope in large block letters was DAVID POWELL—PERSONAL. There was no address or postmark.

"Where did this come from?" he asked, turning to his secretary.

"We don't know. It was on the receptionist's desk."

"Well, someone had to bring it. Did the receptionist see anyone come into the office?"

"No. She left her desk for a few minutes, and when she came back, there it was."

Dave entered his office and closed the door. Walking to his chair, he sat down, placing the letter on the desk in front of him. As he looked at the inscription on the envelope, he felt uneasy. He tried to shake off the feeling as he opened the letter, but then he saw the contents—a slip of lined yellow paper with a sketch of an hourglass similar to the one on the invitation. Beneath the sketch, inscribed in the same block letters that appeared on the envelope, were the words:

THEY'RE WAITING IN THE DANCEHALL.

◊ ◊ ◊

CHAPTER 20

More suicides are committed when it is overcast rather than when it is sunny. Dave had heard this somewhere and it seemed reasonable to him that one might feel more despondent on a gloomy day. How much the weather affected his own mood, he was unsure. But as he stood peering through the rain from a window in his office high above Park Avenue, suicide was on his mind.

It had been raining steadily since dawn. He knew because he had been awake at dawn. He had heard the patter of the first drops against the pane of his bedroom window shortly before daybreak.

Bryan White had called him the previous afternoon to inform him that a bank, one of their largest creditors, had served notice of their intention to call notes totaling almost three million dollars. The action threatened to topple the entire Powell business structure. This, coupled with the anonymous letter he had received, had left him drained.

After analyzing the note he had decided that by itself it was not that significant. The reference to Dancehall was as enigmatic as it had been in the previous communication. Actually, the letter did little more than confirm his earlier suspicion that Emily Hunter was having someone harass him. The most confusing aspect was whether the allusion to time running out, as suggested by the hourglass, referred to the Lake Placid matter or to his business affairs. With the first note he had felt certain it was the former, but in view of what was happening at Stamford, it could be suggesting that time was running out with his business.

But why the reference to the Dancehall? He had thought constantly about it, to the point that the word was now firmly rooted in his weary brain. From somewhere outside, amid the clatter of Manhattan, came the noise of heavy construction equipment—a pile driver or steam hammer. Subconsciously he adjusted the meter of the two syllables in dancehall so they conformed to the rhythmic pounding of the equipment. *Dance-hall! Dance-hall! Dance-hall!* The word pulsated unremittingly in his mind as he gazed down some twenty-five floors to where lines of traffic inched along the avenue.

It was not the first time he had considered suicide. It had been on his mind often during the summer. One evening he had toyed with the loaded revolver he kept at home in a bureau. By merely squeezing his forefinger, he could have ended the agony.

Yet in spite of these fleeting impulses, he had never really believed he would perform the act. Dana was the main reason. Just the thought of her reaction when told that her father was gone had been enough to banish such inclinations.

The events of the previous day, however, had plunged him to new depths. He was unable to set aside the deepening conviction that there were distinct advantages to his death. Not the least of the benefits would be two million dollars of life insurance held by the company, and there was an additional million of personal insurance. Odd, he thought, three million was the amount needed to satisfy the demands of the bank.

As he looked down from the window, he was overwhelmed by a feeling of intense despair. What if he *were* to jump? Simply close his eyes and slip away. The misery would be over.

All he would feel was the air rushing past as he dropped into eternity. Suddenly, he felt dizzy and leaned against the windowsill for support. His mind's eye saw his body hurtling toward the black pavement; far below, a flurry of activity—traffic stopping, hundreds of umbrellas, like black dots, rushing and clustering about a spot where a form lay on the bloody pavement. Panic gripped him.

"Mr. Powell!"

He turned and glanced over his shoulder at the intercom. His forehead was wet with perspiration. Again he looked out the window. Traffic was normal, the body on the pavement was gone. He had had an hallucination, he thought. He was cracking up! He stared down the endless rows of windows narrowing to the ground. The dizzying sight left him nauseated. Taking a linen handkerchief from his pocket, he wiped his brow.

"Mr. Powell! Are you there, Mr. Powell?"

He walked to the credenza and flipped the switch on the intercom. "Yes, Anna." His voice seemed peculiar, distant, belonging to someone else. Maybe he was dead . . . down on the pavement . . . no longer a part of the real world.

"Mr. Powell . . . Mr. Putney . . . delayed . . . rain . . ." The words came vaguely, in pieces.

Dave flipped off the switch and sank into his chair, shaken. Gradually he recovered. He reached for the coffee he had been drinking earlier. After tasting the cold liquid he returned it to the desk. The cup rattled against the saucer.

He glanced at a photograph on the credenza. It was a picture of Sue and Dana on the lawn in front of the main house a few years before. The occasion had been Dana's birthday party. It had been one of the many happy days. With the memories his eyes began to fill. He was falling apart, he thought; he *had* to control himself.

Swallowing with difficulty, he turned to the intercom. "Anna, bring some fresh coffee, will you please?" He rested his head against the cushion of the chair and closed his eyes, exhausted. As the minutes passed, his anxiety began to dissipate. He picked up the morning paper and forced himself to read. With the arrival of the fresh coffee, he felt better. After scanning the paper, he relaxed in his chair. Finally, he returned to the reports he had been studying the previous day in anticipation of the meeting with Emily Hunter's lawyers.

It was almost eleven o'clock when a call announced the arrival of Eric Putney. As he had done the previous evening, Dave considered the advisability of mentioning the two anonymous notes. Perhaps Putney could devise some way to determine their source. But it seemed remote. Moreover, just mentioning them to anyone was expanding the awareness, or at least the suspicion, of some liability on his part. He was still undecided about whether he should disclose the matter when his secretary appeared in the doorway with two men.

The first to enter was Eric Putney, a tall, distinguished-looking man with silver hair, in his early fifties. He walked erect, and carried a soft leather briefcase bound by two leather straps. Affixed to the clasp of the bag was a small brass padlock.

After shaking hands and exchanging greetings, Putney turned to the man with him. "Mr. Powell, this is one of my associates, Jim Delaney."

The man who stepped forward to shake hands was anything but distinguished. He was a dour-looking man about Putney's age but shorter, more heavy-set. His hair was thin and was combed laterally across a pink scalp in dark, slick streaks. Sagging jowls pulled down the corners of his mouth. His attire was nondescript—that of any middle-management executive—until he took the chair offered in front of Dave's desk. Once he was seated, his trouser legs were drawn up to reveal light blue socks that were discolored where they disappeared into a pair of worn black shoes.

"I'm sorry we're late," Putney said, "We were delayed because of the rain."

"Cabs!" Jim Delaney interjected. "Forget 'em when it rains!" He spoke with a Bronx accent, and his voice was harsh.

"We had trouble finding a cab," Putney continued, as if the other man had not spoken. His voice was subdued, and his hesitant delivery indicated he was not altogether comfortable with himself, his associate, or the impending meeting.

"Has your firm completed its investigation?" Dave knew from previous contacts that Putney referred to what he did as the "firm's work," as if wanting to put as much distance as possible between himself and the shadowy world of dossiers.

"No, sir. The case is still open." Putney balanced the briefcase on his knees as he withdrew a key from a vest pocket and opened the padlock. "You requested a full-field investigation, and it's going to take longer than the usual background checks. However, our research department has already compiled a substantial amount of information." He took two paper volumes from the briefcase and handed them to Dave. "You'll see that much of the information was obtained from public records, Mr. Powell. The subject has a prominent business profile, as you know, and there's quite a bit about her in the newspaper morgues.

Dave leaned across the desk to take the files. "I hope you have something more than what's been in the newspapers. Were you able to come up with anything I don't already know?"

Putney shifted in his chair and glanced at Jim Delaney. "Well, they were able to develop some information of a confidential nature . . . It has to do with the subject's private life." He glanced again at his associate.

"Where is it?" Dave asked, looking through one of the files. "It's not in there."

"No, it's not there," Delaney echoed. "It's part of the verbal report."

"Verbal report?" Dave looked from one to the other.

As Delaney started to respond, Putney cleared his throat, gently interrupting him. "Maybe I should answer, Jim." He recrossed his legs and fingered his tie as he spoke. "Some of the information is quite sensitive."

"Sensitive?"

"Sensitive in that it was developed through . . . ah . . . confidential techniques." Putney again shifted in his chair. As he spoke his eyes roved the wall, searching for something on which to focus other than David Powell.

"You mean through illegal means?"

"I did not say that, Mr. Powell," said Putney, straightening. "The Putney Research Agency operates one hundred percent within the law, and any conclusions to the contrary would be—"

"What Eric is sayin'," Jim Delaney interjected, "is that his firm doesn't specialize in certain types of investigations. That's why he's asked me to handle parts of this case. Right, Eric? We're more equipped to handle surveillances and that sort of thing. We've got more manpower and equip—"

As though afraid he might be losing control of his associate as well as the meeting, Putney leaned forward in his chair and interrupted the speaker. "Excuse me, Jim. Ah, Mr. Powell, when certain things came to our attention, I—that is, our firm—thought it best to bring in Mr. Delaney. Jim has worked with our firm on special cases in the past and—"

"Well, what *is* this information?" Dave interrupted.

"Of course," Putney said quickly. "But first, I just want to say this. Ah . . . it's my understanding that the results of the investigation are for your own personal information and that no record will be made of any verbal report—is that correct?"

"I understand," said Dave, impatiently. "Any information you provide will be kept strictly confidential."

Apparently satisfied, Putney settled back in his chair. "Very well, sir. I trust you'll understand after I tell you this why we were concerned. You see, even though our information is accurate—and the truth is an absolute defense against libel, of course—there's no way we could substantiate the charges if we were called upon to do so. Simply because of the way the information was developed. Do you understand?"

"Yes, yes," Dave replied. "What *is* it?"

"Well, Mrs. Hunter apparently leads a rather unusual sex life."

"Unusual?" Dave leaned forward. "What do you mean?"

"She has a girlfriend with whom she's been having sexual encounters."

Dave stared at him. "*Sexual* encounters?"

"That's correct."

"I find that hard to believe. You must be mistaken."

Putney turned to his associate. "Jim?"

"No question about it," Delaney said, straightening in his seat. "She's a lesbian. We've observed her in the act," he added, matter-of-factly.

"But that's incredible!" Dave leaned back in his chair. "Emily Hunter! I can't believe it. Who's the other woman?"

"We haven't had time to establish her identity," Putney said. "We do know she's married. One of our investigators overheard her express concern to the subject that her husband might learn of their affair. We know of two definite encounters the subject had with her. Isn't that correct, Jim?"

"Right." Delaney produced a worn pad from a breast pocket and consulted it. "They had two meets here in midtown. Both times the subject departed the Hunter office on Fifth Avenue shortly after eleven hundred and walked to Grand Central, where she met her contact. They had lunch at a nearby restaurant and then rented a suite at the Waldorf. We covered the second meet pretty good. Had a man in the elevator with them."

"But how could you be certain it was a—a sexual encounter?" Dave asked. "People rent suites in the afternoon; it could be for anything."

Delaney turned to his associate as though looking for direction, but Putney kept his eyes on the floor. "I told you before, Mr. Powell, we *observed* them."

"How could you observe them? They weren't doing it in the elevator, were they?"

"Technical surveillances."

"Technical surveillances?"

"Right. Confidential investigative techniques."

It was obvious that Delaney did not want to elaborate, and Dave did not press the point. He had heard of complex reflective lenses used to look around corners of buildings and assumed it was something similar. It didn't matter. The main thing was they had stumbled on some extremely compromising information, and he was quick to see its value as a possible counterbalance to the notes he had received.

"Will you be able to identify this other woman?" Dave asked.

"Yeah, no question," the detective replied. "If the subject keeps meetin' her, we'll make her eventually."

"That's important," Dave said. "Particularly since this other person is married. Find out what you can about the husband while you're at it. It might come in handy."

"We might be able to make an ident on her this week if the subject contacts her," Delaney said. "Only thing is, you got to understand you risk heatin' things up with fizurs."

"Fizurs?"

"Physical surveillances. You got to tail her and once you do, you risk blowin' it. Don't get me wrong," Delaney added. "I personally don't think she's tail conscious, and I doubt if she'll make us. But there's always the chance."

"We have to take that chance. It's important that I know who it is—as soon as possible, too. I'm sure you'll be discreet."

"Absolutely! We're sure not hired to blow surveillances."

"Mr. Powell," Putney interjected himself softly into the conversation, "I'm sure you understand what's involved in these physical surveillances. They require a good deal of manpower, particularly a case as sensitive as this one. And, well . . . This could be quite an expensive undertaking."

Dave wondered whether Putney had heard of his financial problems and was concerned about being paid. Or perhaps he was looking for a larger retainer. "I don't believe you've ever heard me complain about your fee, have you, Mr. Putney?"

"No. No, of course not." Putney shifted uneasily in his chair and pulled on the tip of his nose with his thumb and forefinger. "It's just that I thought I should mention it. Ah . . . incidentally, Mr. Powell, while we're on the subject . . . ah . . . my office mentioned that there are a few invoices outstanding from previous assignments. Probably overlooked. I suppose small bills get lost in a big operation like yours." He busied himself buckling the straps on the briefcase, avoiding his client's eyes.

"I'll look into it immediately," Dave said. "Is there anything else?"

"No. No, I believe that's all, Mr. Powell." He seemed relieved. "I should be in touch before the end of the week."

"Very well." Dave rose. "Thank you, gentlemen." Then, impulsively, he pulled out the middle drawer of his desk and withdrew the two notes. "Ah . . . before you leave, I thought I'd get your reaction to these." He handed the notes to Putney. "I discovered that invitation on the windshield of my car a few weeks ago. The one in the envelope was left on my receptionist's desk yesterday. Probably some crank, wouldn't you say?"

Eric Putney studied the two items. Finally he looked at Dave and held up the invitation. "This was an affair at your house?"

"That's right. A recent dinner dance."

The investigator shrugged and handed them to his associate. "What do you think, Jim?"

The other man regarded them quietly for several seconds. With a shake of his head he handed them back to Dave. "Who knows? Could be anything."

"Do you have any idea what they mean by 'Dancehall'?" Putney asked.

"Maybe it means the Dancehall at Green Haven Prison," Delaney said

"Green Haven Prison?" Dave felt his stomach tighten.

"Yeah, it's a holding cell. Where they keep condemned prisoners—just before they strap them in the electric chair."

◊ ◊ ◊

CHAPTER 21

"These shots are really great. Terrific!"

Jim Delaney was talking to one of his associates in his fifth-floor office on West Forty-third Street, not far from Times Square. It was not one of the better neighborhoods in New York City, nor one of the better buildings. Nor was there much to the ambience of the Delaney Detective Agency that was not in dreary keeping with the rest of the locality.

"Come again, Chief. I didn't catch you." The man sitting across the desk from Delaney, having difficulty understanding him, was one of Delaney's three-man staff. Though some fifteen years younger, he resembled his employer in both appearance and style. Delaney had just taken a gargantuan bite from his pastrami, cheese, lettuce, and Russian dressing sandwich. His diction, not good when unimpeded, suffered even more when he was eating.

"These pitchers." He freed a hand from the sandwich and tapped one of several photographs in front of him. "These should be worth three grand."

The photos had been taken during a raid conducted by Delaney forces the previous night. The agency had been retained by an estranged husband to develop evidence of adultery against his wife.

"Man, was she pissed off when she woke up!" the younger man said. "Threw every fuckin' thing but the bed at us."

"What'd *he* do?" Delaney asked. He took another bite of the sandwich and with the help of his free hand was able to wedge most of it into his mouth—all, that is, but a small amount of Russian dressing that lodged on his cheek.

"Hardly moved. Amazin'! Just turned over and went back to sleep."

Delaney wiped his mouth and both hands on his handkerchief while glancing down at the photographs. "This should save our guy plenty." He drew a cigar from his vest and began unwrapping it. "Make sure you collect before you turn 'em over."

After lighting the cigar he leaned back in his swivel chair, propped his feet on his desk, and blew a stream of fresh smoke into the air. He watched it drift up toward the brown water-stained splotches on the ceiling, where it merged with the vapor formed by the residue of previous expulsions.

"Wish the hell Putney would return my call," he mused.

"What's that, Chief?"

"Nothing." Delaney was thinking of the delicate information he had to impart to Eric Putney. Not something he'd discuss with a subordinate. It was the type of thing that might tempt an employee to do a little business on the side. "I been tryin' to reach Putney. I gotta talk to him about that Hunter case."

"Man, that broad she's shackin' up with." The younger man stretched his legs out. He was wearing a round felt hat with the brim turned up in front. He pushed it back and strands of dirty blond hair protruded from underneath. "I seen some good-lookin' chicks. Never one like that, though. And to think she's *queer!* Man, I sure would've liked some time with Charlie and Vito on those mirrors."

"You'll get your chance." Delaney exhaled more smoke. "We're gonna milk that thing for all it's worth."

He fell silent as he reflected on the milking process. They'd really fallen into it this time. Wait till he told Putney. Christ, he thought he'd seen it all, but this had to take the prize!

His thoughts were interrupted by the telephone. Easing his feet off the desk, he removed the cigar from his mouth and reached for the phone.

"Hello, Jim," Eric Putney's voice came over the line. "Sorry for not getting back to you sooner. I've been up in Boston."

"That's all right," said Delaney. "I was just thinkin' about you. I got some news."

"I've got some too. And it's not good."

"What's that?" Delaney returned the cigar to his mouth, prepared to listen.

"I'm afraid Powell's not in good shape—financially, that is."

"Whaddaya mean?"

"We've got it on pretty good authority that he's in trouble. It looks as if he may go bankrupt."

"Bankrupt!" Delaney withdrew the cigar from his mouth and leaned forward in his chair.

"That's right. He's owed us for over four months. We were getting concerned so we did a little checking. It doesn't look good."

"Whaddaya mean it doesn't look good?" Delaney's voice took on a deep croaking sound. "I've got over ten G's in this thing. Countin' the payoffs at the hotel, it's closer to fifteen. What are you tellin' me?"

"Well, I've told you. It doesn't look good."

"Listen Putney, don't give me that horseshit. He's *your* client, not mine! I'm not about to drop fifteen grand on this caper."

"Well, Jim, you know the game as well as I do. You take your chances. I stand to lose almost ten thousand myself. But I thought you should know so you could go easy on those surveillances. I wouldn't invest too much more manpower. Incidentally, what was the news you had? Anything to do with Powell?"

Delaney clutched the phone with one hand and his cigar with the other. His complexion had deepened to vermilion, and a large vein that protruded from his left temple pulsed with rage. There was nothing, absolutely nothing, that could send Jim Delaney into a maniacal fury like the prospect of not being paid for his efforts.

"Listen, Putney, and hear me good!" His voice was deep and deadly. "I ain't about to swallow fifteen grand, Pal. He's *your* client and *your* problem!" With that, he slammed the phone onto its cradle.

"You hear that?" he screamed, turning to his underling. "That no good son-of-a-bitch thinks he's gonna drop that on me." He stood and started pacing, emitting large puffs of smoke. "I been in this business too long to let some smooth-talkin' bastard try to hassle me out of fifteen grand."

"What is it, Chief?" asked the younger man, timidly. "Putney trying to screw us?"

"No, no," responded Delaney with a wave of his hand. He continued to pace the floor in silence, puffing feverishly on the cigar as he tried to cope with a setback of monumental proportions.

The younger man stood and straightened his hat. "I'd better cover that lead at the Coliseum."

"Fifteen grand," mused Delaney, ignoring him. "There's no way I'm gonna drop fifteen grand."

He scarcely noticed his associate leave the office, for the germ of an idea had begun to form in the nimble Delaney mind. Maybe Powell was going bust, but that didn't necessarily mean *she* was. And who had more to lose? Besides, it gave him the chance to up his fee. He was certainly entitled to an increase in view of the chances he would have to take.

He walked across the dingy room to the firm's research department—an old table strewn with a score of worn telephone books. Picking out the Westchester directory, he carried it to a nearby window. Here he donned his glasses and looked up the number. He would have to act quickly, he thought. It was sensitive stuff. He knew from experience that it could be worth a fortune today—tomorrow, nothing.

Returning to his desk, he withdrew a small plastic object from the middle drawer. Then, taking his suit coat from the back of his chair, he walked toward the door. From an old coat tree he picked a gray felt hat and rested it on top of the carefully combed strands of hair. Cigar in mouth, he left the room.

It took about twelve minutes for him to reach the Delaney "branch office"—one of a bank of phone booths at Grand Central Terminal. Here, in a booth at the rear of an aisle, he was able to conduct much of his midtown business—including an occasional untraceable phone call—with relative privacy.

From his breast pocket he produced his notebook and, after considering one final time, placed a call to Tarrytown.

It rang only once before it was answered. "Hello." It was a child's voice, gentle, feminine.

Delaney slipped the plastic device into his mouth. It fit against the roof and altered the sound of his voice. "Is Mrs. Powell there?"

"Hold on, please. I'll go find her." There was a clatter as of something falling on the floor, followed by the wailing sound of a crying infant.

While he waited, Delaney nervously tapped his notebook against the shelf beneath the phone box. It was risky stuff. Although it was not the first time, he never embarked on such a venture without concern.

"Hello. Sue Powell speaking." It was a light, friendly voice, unusually pleasant.

"Mrs. Powell, I want you to listen careful. It's very important. And I won't repeat nothin', understand?"

A silence greeted his comment. "Understand, Mrs. Powell?" he repeated.

"Yes, I understand." Her voice surprised him. It was steady, collected. Ordinarily he found it necessary to field irate questions before he could continue.

"Okay. Listen careful. I can save you lots of trouble, see? I got all the stuff on you and Hunter. Where you meet, what you're doin', times, dates, *pitchers—everything*, understand? There was no answer. "Hear me, Mrs. Powell?"

"I'm listening." Her voice was measured now, and the lack of emotion continued to surprise him.

"I can give this stuff to you, or I can give it to your husband. It don't mean a damn to me, understand? Only, the price is twenty-five grand. Got me?"

Another pause and then, "Is this some kind of joke? I don't know what you're talking about."

Delaney felt better. This was more the reaction he expected. "It's no joke, lady. Believe me, it's no joke. We got it all on you and Hunter. Just for openers, I'll give you this." He cradled the phone between his head and shoulder as he flipped the pages in his notebook. "You spent two hours with Hunter last Thursday afternoon at the Waldorf. To be exact, you came out of the restaurant where you had lunch and checked into your room at 2:08 P.M. You were in suite 1108-1110 until 4:22 P.M. While you were in the room you had sexual relations with Hunter. Among other things, you talked about your husband and worried that he was gonna find out what was going on. Now, I could be a helluva lot more specific, like the mole you were kiddin' Hunter about—and a lot more. It's up to you."

He could hear her breathing. Finally she said, "What you're saying is that you're going to blackmail me for twenty-five thousand dollars."

"Hold it, lady. Hold it right there. Nobody's blackmailin' nobody. Your old man owes me. I'm only collectin' a bill. We're givin' you a chance at the stuff before we turn it over to your old man."

"What do you mean? Why would my father owe you—"

"Not your father. Your *husband!* We got the stuff on Hunter for him. He doesn't know you're involved. We know he's goin' broke. We're givin' you a chance to buy the stuff. To settle his bill, that's all."

Once more the silence. It bothered Delaney. She was doing a lot of thinking for a broad under pressure.

"You say you were finding out things about Hunter for my husband. What are you, a private investigator?"

"Okay, Okay! Let's forget it, lady. No more fishin'. You want it or you don't. It's that simple."

"All right, but how do I know if I give you the money you'll be satisfied? How do I know you won't continue to—"

"I'm tellin' you. All I want is what I got comin'."

"But what about the others? You said 'we.' What's to stop your associates from doing the same thing? You could take the money and disclose the information to anyone."

"Okay, lady, I'm gonna level with you. Nobody knows I'm even talkin' to you. What do you think, I'm crazy? Besides, my boys don't even know who you are. Even if they did, they wouldn't dare do nothin'. This stuff is highly sensitive, understand . . . ?" Delaney's voice trailed off. The bitch was getting too much out of him, he thought. Still, her questions were legit. He had to satisfy her that no one was going to milk her; that it was a one-shot deal and that he'd bury the stuff when paid. If she knew how vulnerable his agency was as a result of the illegal methods used to obtain the information, she sure wouldn't worry about *anybody* talking. "I'm tellin' you, lady, nobody knows nothin' but me. Pay me what I got comin' and you're home free, understand?"

Once again there was a long pause and then, "What do you want me to do?"

"Okay, now you're bein' smart. So here's what you gotta do. Take a cab to Forty-third and Twelfth Avenue. Drop the cab and walk west on Forty-third toward the river. Just before you come to the dock you'll see a warehouse on the north side of the street. You with me? Beside the warehouse is an alley. I'll be waitin' in the alley for you at eleven tonight. Now, get this straight. Bring two hundred and fifty one-hundred-dollar bills. I'll give it to you again. Two hundred fifty one-hundred-dollar bills. Put it in a regular brown paper bag, understand?"

"Yes . . . Yes, I understand. But it might take me a while to get that much money. It's almost two o'clock. And going into a bank and asking for two hundred and fifty one-hundred-dollar bills . . . Perhaps I could call you back and—"

"Forget it! You got one shot. Take it or leave it. I ain't callin' back to have you set me up for somethin' neither. It's now or forget it. Twenty-five grand is nothin' to someone like you. You think I don't know that? Hit a couple of banks if it makes you feel better. So what's a teller care if he gives you some hundreds? You think he's gonna step on the floor alarm?"

There was no answer, and he was beginning to think he was losing her when she finally said, "All right, but I'm not going to Forty-third Street and the river alone at night with twenty-five thousand dollars. You'll have to come to Tarrytown."

Delaney hesitated. She was setting him up. On the other hand, she had a point. Sharp broad. He'd have to be careful. "Nothin' doin'," he said. "I ain't goin' to Tarrytown." He thought feverishly of an alternative. She was being coöperative. He didn't want to blow it. Where else could he set up a meet? It had to be dark. It was important that she didn't see him clearly. "All right. I'll meet you in Central Park at Seventy-ninth and Central Park West. There's a bridge about fifty yards in. Next to the bridge there's a—"

"That's no good."

"Listen, lady, you're in no position to be sayin' what's good."

"I told you I'm ready to give you the money, but how do I know I'm not being led into a trap of some kind—a kidnapping or something?" Her voice was plaintive now, as though it were a mutual problem and she needed his help. It was convincing. "If you'll come here to Tarrytown, I'll give you the money."

"Whereabouts in Tarrytown? I'm sure as hell not comin' to the house."

"No, no. There's a place on our grounds where I can meet you—a place no one will see us. Do you know where we live?"

"Yeah, pretty much. You own most of Tarrytown, right?"

"Come out Old Town Road until you get to the bird sanctuary. Leave your car in the parking lot. Or if you come by cab, have him drop you there. There's a path from the parking lot over to Meadow Lane. Walk down Meadow Lane until you see a gatehouse. It will be on your left. Continue for a quarter of a mile until you come to an old iron gate. There's a road there that leads back into our property. I'll see that the gate is unlocked. Keep walking until you come to a pond. Then take the path to your left—"

"Wait a minute! Hold it right there, lady. I didn't even say I was comin' yet." Delaney hesitated, considering the liabilities of meeting the woman on her own ground. On the other hand, what was the difference? Even if she was setting him up, he had an out. He'd been retained by the Powell family to do a job. Who was to say what the job was? He had every right to be there. It would be her word against his if something went wrong. Besides, she was vulnerable. Life would be tough in Tarrytown if she blew the whistle. He was wearying of the call, and the plastic device was beginning to hurt where it rubbed against his palate. "Okay, okay." He laid his notebook on the shelf under the phone and pulled out a pencil. "Gimme those directions again."

He made notes as Sue Powell repeated the directions. Her manner and precision impressed him but increased his uneasiness. "Sharp broad," he thought.

"Okay, lady. I'll be there tonight at eleven. Make sure you got the paper bag, understand? Remember, you got one shot at this thing."

After hanging up, he removed the plastic device from his mouth with one hand and inserted a cigar with the other. He rested his head back against the wall of the phone booth, considering the advisability of going to Tarrytown. It was less convenient than the city, but for twenty-five grand he was ready for a little train ride. He could understand why she wouldn't want to come to the city. Scared to death. Although you'd never know it. Talk about cool. Christ, she sounded as if she didn't have a nerve in her body. But it was all smoke. She had a lot to lose if the thing ever blew. Still, he'd have to be careful. If the thing backfired, it could cost him plenty.

◇ ◇ ◇

CHAPTER 22

At the same time that Jim Delaney was planning his trip to Tarrytown, Dave Powell was less than a mile away in the luxurious offices of Hunter Management on Fifth Avenue, awaiting a meeting with its chairwoman. His appointment had been for one-thirty; it was now almost two o'clock. He knew that he was being kept waiting purposely, but he had expected that. It would have been unusual for Emily Hunter to see an adversary without some calculated insult. An agitated person was more likely to make mistakes.

Before coming he had been almost sanguine. It would be the first time he had been with Emily when he was not on the defensive. Since the visit from the private detectives, he had laid meticulous plans for a confrontation.

The comment by Delaney reagarding the Dancehall had lent a new dimension to the notes he had received. It now seemed they were a pointed reference to the electric chair at Green Haven Prison. He was still sure Emily Hunter was responsible. Somehow she may have connected him with the body in Lake Placid.

As part of his plan, he had slipped a letter marked "Personal" under the mailroom door of the Hunter offices early the previous morning. It was an anonymous note printed in large block letters on lined yellow paper similar to the letter he had received the week before. The message was brief: I KNOW OF YOUR AFFAIR. Beneath the words he had sketched an hourglass.

Since the note was similar in character to the two he believed she had sent to him, she would know immediately that he was responsible. It was implicit in the communication that there was now a basis for give-and-take in their negotiations. At the very least, she would know she had something to lose. From what he knew about Emily, there was little that would cause her more concern than the thought of executive chambers throughout the city filled with the droll recounting of Emily Hunter's sexual behavior. His one regret was that he had not yet learned the identity of the woman with whom she was having the affair. Since Emily associated only with the elite of New York society, he felt there was a reasonably good chance that the other woman might be from a prominent family. He hoped this was so; it would make Emily that much more vulnerable.

It was after two o'clock when a tall, attractive woman in her mid-thirties appeared at the heavy oak door leading to the inner offices. It was Elizabeth Raderman, Emily Hunter's personal secretary. The very sight of her engendered dislike in Dave. She did her best to match her boss's arrogance.

"Good afternoon, Mr. Powell." As she spoke she walked to the receptionist's desk and proceeded to go through some papers, according him only token attention. "Mrs. Hunter has been delayed at lunch. She'll be along."

Dave, having glanced up from a newspaper, returned to the paper without comment.

After a word with the receptionist, the secretary turned and walked back toward the inner offices. Just before she disappeared, Dave said quietly, without looking up, "Tell her I shall give her precisely three more minutes."

Three minutes passed, and Dave thought he was going to

have to make good on his threat, when the oak door opened and the secretary reappeared. "Mrs. Hunter will see you now."

Dave rose and followed her down a wide passageway, lined with abstract paintings and statuary, that opened into a large, elaborately decorated anteroom that served as the secretary's office. It was a room most corporations would have found adequate for the president of the firm. Since Emily Hunter was better known for her penuriousness than for frills for her subordinates, Dave never entered the office without wondering about Elizabeth Raderman's position in the Hunter hierarchy. The knowledge of Emily's affair made him speculate anew about the relationship between the two.

"You may go in, Mr. Powell." She motioned toward an archway leading to the inner rooms.

Dave passed through the entrance into a spacious and lavishly furnished office. Soft wool and subdued leather fabrics blended with the deep mellow tones of cherry paneling. An expanse of windows on the far wall was covered with filmy curtains that muted the sunlight but still permitted a spectacular view of the Manhattan skyline. Probably the most notable quality of the room was its silence. High above the din of midtown Manhattan, the office seemed to muffle all sound.

At the far end of the room, seated at a large antique desk, was Emily Hunter. She was in a gray silk suit adorned by a black and white scarf. She was writing and did not look up. Dave sat down in one of several chairs near her desk. He had expected a cool reception, but her insolent disregard for his entrance was irritating. He was about to make a comment when she spoke.

"Your secretary insisted that you had to talk to me. I'm listening." She continued writing as she spoke.

"Perhaps we both should do some listening," he said quietly. "To begin with, you might accord me the courtesy of not writing while I'm talking."

Emily looked up, surprised. "Very well, David." She put down her pen and leaned back in her chair. "Go ahead."

Her indifference confounded him. He wondered whether she had received the note. Or, if she had, whether she realized it had come from him. His confidence began to waver.

"I think we have some things to talk about, Emily," he said, maintaining a subdued manner. "We both have some serious problems."

"I know *you* certainly do. You're going broke. And it's your own fault. You're the one who started all the mess in the Stamford—"

"Pardon me, Emily, but I happen to know that *you* have some problems also."

"What's that supposed to mean?"

"Exactly that. *You* have some real problems."

Emily leaned forward in her seat quickly as though exasperated. "David, why the hell don't you just say what's on your mind instead of talking in circles? You didn't have your people badger my secretary for this meeting out of consideration for my problems. I'm sure you came here for a reason, or you—" She stopped talking in midsentence. A look of surprise surfaced in her blue eyes. It was fleeting. "I see." She leaned back in her chair, her voice barely audible. There was a moment of silence. Then in a resigned tone she said, "*You* sent it."

Dave said nothing. He could feel the tension mounting as she came to grips with the reason for his being there.

"Well, I must say you surprise me." Her voice was no longer harsh. "Most men would have reacted differently."

"What do you mean?"

"Oh, nothing. Only I think some men would have reacted more . . . well . . . directly, rather than through an anonymous note."

"Why?"

She didn't answer, but her eyes focused on him intently, searching for answers. Dave marveled at the change. It occurred to him that it was the first time he had ever observed a helpless look on her face. She seemed prettier, younger, perhaps as she might have looked as a girl.

"You did send that note, didn't you?" she asked, almost plaintively.

Dave nodded. "Yes, I did. I'm aware of your affair." Then he added somewhat defensively, "And you arranged to have those notes sent to me, didn't you?" She continued to gaze at him without replying. "Didn't you?" he repeated.

Her vacant expression made him wonder. He waited for her to speak, but he knew she was too clever. She would wait for him to elaborate.

Finally she said, "What about them?"

Dave hesitated. Her remark was calculated to draw him out. It was better to drop the subject for the time being. "Bryan White said you sent some notes regarding Stamford last week. Perhaps it was your lawyers." She continued to watch him closely. He knew she was not satisfied.

"David, why don't you tell me what you want? I'm sure you came here with something in mind."

Her manner was more conciliatory now, and he knew he had struck pay dirt. "It's very simple, Emily. I want to rescind our original agreement regarding Stamford. I'm prepared to work out a reasonable settlement."

She regarded him through curious eyes and then said, "Excuse me." Rising, she walked to the other end of the room to Elizabeth Raderman's office. The secretary appeared in the entranceway, and the two conversed in low tones for a moment. As he watched, Dave's suspicions regarding their relationship increased. He would have to tell Eric Putney.

"Hold my calls," said Emily, closing the door. She returned to her desk and leveled her eyes at Dave. "What about this other matter? This so-called affair. Would you care to elucidate?"

"I know everything about it," he bluffed. "Where you two meet. Your lunches. The afternoons at the Waldorf—suite 1108-1110, to be precise. Times. Dates. *Everything.*"

Emily sat fingering her pen, her face drawn and pale. Finally she looked up. "You don't seem all that concerned."

"Concerned?"

"Our affair."

"I don't give a damn about the affair. All I want is to put an end to our business relationship."

Emily raised her eyebrows. She began to tap the pen lightly against the edge of the desk. "Have you discussed this with Sue?"

"No, I haven't." There was another pause.

"Let me see if I understand this correctly," Emily said, straightening in her chair. "You say you're aware of the affair and you don't care? That all you want is an end to our agreement? I find that hard to believe."

"Emily," Dave said, with a trace of impatience. "I'm sure you realize I'm on the verge of bankruptcy. My only concern is to strike a deal on Stamford. Beyond that, I don't give a damn what you do. Can't you understand that?"

"Very well. Have your lawyers draw up a buy-sell agreement for the Empire-Stamford stock. As long as the terms are reasonable, I'll sign it."

Dave stood up. He was elated and hard pressed to contain his delight. "I'm sorry it had to work out this way, Emily. But I think we'll all be much happier."

Emily leaned back in her chair and gazed up at him through wondering eyes. "You're a strange fellow, David."

◊ ◊ ◊

PART
VII

Tarrytown, New York
July 1982

CHAPTER 23

"Here's a twenty. Keep the change. There's another one if you pick me up here in an hour." Jim Delaney handed the bill over the scat to the cab driver. It was a big tip, perhaps too much, he thought. But it was nothing compared to what he would be carrying back to the city. And he had to be sure the cab would be there to take him back to the station.

He had arrived in Tarrytown some forty-five minutes earlier and had waited in a coffee shop. As the time for the meeting neared, he had taken a cab to the parking lot of the bird sanctuary on Old Town Road. It was twenty mintes before eleven, and if the directions were accurate, it would take no more than fifteen minutes to walk to the meeting place.

After leaving the cab he waited for its lights to disappear and then started down the path from the sanctuary to Meadow Lane. It was a cool, damp night, and an occasional gust of wind swirled debris in his path. He pulled his hat down low on his forehead and turned up the collar of his raincoat to ward off the chill. The taste of coffee lingered in his mouth. He wished he had brought a container with him. Coming up on the train there had been a few showers, and though it was misty in Tarrytown, he was relieved that it was not raining. From the directions, he expected some rough terrain.

When he reached Meadow Lane he went north. Soon he came upon a high brick wall, which extended down the road as far as he could see. He assumed it enclosed the Powell estate. As he walked along the wall in the darkness, a sense of uneasiness came over him. He was sorry he had not held out for a meet in the city. He knew the city. Up here he was out of his element.

In the distance he saw the lights of an approaching car. He moved closer to the wall. As the vehicle approached, he drew his collar up over his face. The car swept by, leaving a vaporous cloud in its wake.

As the sound of the engine faded, the night was quiet. Now and then the wind rustled the leaves of trees beyond the wall, but other than that the only noise came from Delaney's labored breathing and the scuffing of his feet against the pavement.

He had walked well past the prescribed quarter of a mile when he finally came to the gates referred to in the directions. They were set in the masonry beneath a narrow portico. A chain used to hold the gates together where they joined at the center hung from one of the crossbars, an open padlock dangling from one end. Beyond was a curtain of blackness. He pushed open one of the gates, and it creaked loudly. The strident noise was unsettling in the stillness, a signal to anyone waiting, he thought.

He walked inside and took out a pencil flashlight. The tiny beam was little more than light from a keyhole streaming into a dark room. The outline of what had been a dirt road lay before him. He hesitated a moment and then followed it onto the grounds. According to the instructions, the road would lead into woods some fifty yards ahead.

As he pushed his way through the darkness, his uneasiness increased. The road was nothing more than a path. Finding his way to the meeting place was one thing. Getting out could be more difficult.

Eventually Delaney came to the trees. What small spirit he had for the venture faded once he walked into the dense woods. A shroud of darkness enveloped him. And now there were sounds. Relentless, high-pitched, creaking sounds—everywhere. Delaney hesitated, listening to the indefinable hum of nocturnal life in the forest.

The road was lined with trees and heavy brush on both sides. As he pushed down the narrow corridor, his misgivings increased. If it hadn't been for the twenty-five thousand dollars, he would have turned and left. The Delaney avidity for money was greater than the doubt in his heart, however, and he pressed on. Besides he was almost there. In a few more minutes he should reach the pond. Then, according to the directions he would see a path leading to the left. Some thirty yards down the path was an old farmhouse where she would be waiting. She might be tough at first. Try to negotiate. Accuse him of blackmail. It wasn't blackmail. He was only collecting a debt. He sure as hell wasn't going to take five cents on the dollar awarded by some lousy bankruptcy court.

Thoughts of the money bolstered his spirits—until he saw the pond. There it lay ahead, between the trees, a slick pool stretching off into the darkness. There was a portentous quality to the still, black water. To the left he saw the path leading into another part of the woods. As he turned onto the path, he heard it for the first time, a soft rustling somewhere behind him. He wondered about it but kept walking for several yards, when he heard it again. This time it was closer, more pronounced. He hesitated, listening. The strange cadence he had heard upon first entering the forest seemed to intensify, and from high overhead came the sound of wind in the treetops.

He resumed walking, slowly now. Where the devil was she, he wondered. He was sure he had gone over thirty yards. And then he saw it. To the left of the path. A large black hole. It appeared to be an abandoned well. Next to it was a pile of heavy stones. At first his reaction was one of anger. God almighty, he could have fallen in the damn thing. Then he heard another noise immediately behind him. This time, the sound was unmistakable—a twig snapping underfoot. Something was stalking him. He froze.

Suddenly, an explosion! Something ripped through his shoulder—a terrible burning. He reeled on the edge of the well, clutching his wound. Again! This time in his abdomen. Agony! And then a vague feeling of falling, bouncing from one side of the shaft to the other to the bottom of the pit. He landed on his back over thirty feet below, his body twisted and broken, still conscious.

"My God! Oh, my God!" he cried. He tried to move but was paralyzed. There was no pain, only numbness. Then he heard them. One by one. The heavy stones as they came whining through the air down into the pit and thudding into the soft earth next to him.

"Lord, Jesus," he screamed. "No! Please, God! No!" The muffled bleats from the shaft were suddenly silenced as a rock crushed Jim Delaney's skull.

It was quiet then, except for the strange, soft, rhythmic hum of night creatures in the forest and the muted thudding of rocks as they piled up at the bottom of the well.

◊   ◊   ◊

CHAPTER 24

It had been a glorious day. And it was not over. Although shadows from the grove of trees near the gatehouse lengthened along the drive, there was still plenty of time. She had until nine o'clock before she had to be in bed—well past the usual time. But this was a special day, and Dana Powell was making the most of it, eking out every bit of enjoyment. It was her birthday, and she was eight years old.

She thought about the special things that had happened during the day, reliving the most enjoyable moments. There had been a party on the lawn near the teahouse, with ice cream and a big cake. She had made a wish before blowing out the candles. It was the same wish she always made—that her father would get her a horse. Several of her friends had brought presents. They had been having a good time until Jane Bennett fell, hurt her knee, and started to cry. Then it seemed everyone had been nicer to Jane than to her. Finally Jane's mother had come and taken her home. Dana had been glad to see Jane leave.

After dinner had been fun, too. She and her father had played jungle. They had turned out the lights in the drawing room, and she had climbed onto the elephant's back. Then they had padded through the jungle, encountering all sorts of wild animals. Her father had been so good to her. He had played with her lots the last few days.

She reviewed in her mind the presents she had received. There were the games, the stuffies, and the books. But the best one of all she was riding. A new two-wheeler, light blue with red and white stripes and shiny chrome fixtures. Her father had given it to her. She knew her mother was not too happy about it.

The seat was a bit high and threatened her balance. Her control was further compromised by Lindsay, whom she balanced on the handlebars. When she rounded the curve and saw the man getting out of a car beyond the gatehouse, she tried to wave. It didn't work. First Lindsay, then the bicycle, and then Dana came to a clattering heap on the cobblestones. The shrieks that ensued brought an anxious Horace Ackerman hurrying through the gates.

"It's going to be all right," he soothed, extricating the crying youngster from the bicycle. "Where does it hurt?"

"My arm," Dana sobbed, holding up a scraped elbow.

"Here, let's take a look." Ackerman took her arm and examined it gently. "Well, it isn't too bad. It's just a scratch. See, it isn't even bleeding."

The sobs subsided and Ackerman brushed some dirt off her shorts. Then he reached down and picked up the crying doll. "I think this little girl is going to be all right, too." he said, straightening its dress. "What's her name?"

"Lindsay."

"Lindsay? That's a pretty name. Can we stop her crying?"

"No, she always does that. She's sick."

"Sick?"

"Yes, sick. She's never going to get better." Dana rubbed her eyes and reached up for the doll.

Ackerman hesitated, regarding her quietly for a moment, and then stooped to hand her the doll. As he did, she caught a glimpse of a gun under his unbuttoned jacket. "Are you a policeman?"

"Why, yes. How did you know?"

"I can tell. Are you going to arrest me?"

"Of course not. Why would I arrest you? In fact, I'm going to give you a piece of gum for being so brave." Ackerman took a package of gum from his pocket and gave her a stick.

Holding Lindsay under one arm, Dana unwrapped the gum. "Thank you," she said, doubling up the stick and putting it into her mouth. It tasted good and offset the sting that was beginning to throb in her elbow. She considered crying again and might have done so if the man hadn't asked her name. "Dana Powell," she replied. The man seemed nice. She liked his eyes with all the wrinkles in the corners and the way he smiled. "Would you like to play with Lindsay and me?"

"Of course. Only right now I have to go to see your father." He glanced over his shoulder toward his car. "I wonder if my car is all right there? Is there anyone in the gatehouse?"

"Brandon's probably there. He's the gardener. Only he's probably in bed. He hurt his back again—filling up the old well."

"The old well?"

"Yes, it's over that way." She shifted her doll to the other arm and pointed in the distance. "Over in the woods by the old farmhouse."

"Why is he filling it up?" Ackerman said, following her line of direction.

"So nobody falls in. Children might take the top off and fall in."

"Well, that makes sense. You wouldn't take the top off, though, would you?"

"Course not. It's too heavy . . . I've tried, lots."

Ackerman laughed. "Well, it looks like you're all better now. How about that chin? You've got a few scratches there, too."

"They're from Brandon's cat. He scratched me. It's almost all better, though."

Ackerman leaned over, took the bicycle by the handlebars, and stood it up. "Shall we see if we can get you going again? Why don't you climb on, and I'll help you steer up to the house? I think we're going to need a Band-Aid for that elbow."

He helped her onto the seat. After balancing the doll on the handlebars, he guided the bicycle up the drive.

Horace Ackerman considered his interview with David Powell of paramount importance. He was confident that he had sufficient evidence for a murder indictment, but to get a conviction for first degree murder, he needed a statement from Powell admitting he had been on Buck Island with Ann Conway. It was a substantive point, since the evidence linking him with the victim, including Sam Wykoff's statement that it had been Powell who had come out on the launch, was largely circumstantial. And how well twenty-year-old evidence would stand up in court, particularly if it were testimony from an elderly man, was a matter of conjecture. Although there was no statute of limitations barring prosecution for capital crimes, old evidence made convictions difficult. If Powell denied having seen the victim following their discharge from the Adirondack Club and remained mute, then the government's case could start to crumble.

Under different circumstances, Ackerman might have invited Powell to his office for the interview. There he could have had other agents to act as witnesses, as well as the benefit of an interrogation room with its technical supplements. But inviting Powell to the office would only alert him to the gravity of his position. It would be tantamount to inviting his lawyers. There was nothing quite so inhibiting while trying to elicit statements as having a subject's attorney on hand. No, the only way he could lead Powell into the compromising statements he needed was to meet with him in his home under the guise of a routine interview.

As he walked up the drive, steadying Dana on her bicycle while carrying his folder under his arm, he contemplated the importance of what lay ahead. He had planned the interview carefully and was relying on the psychological condition of the subject. He knew Powell was a nervous wreck. Ackerman had seen to that. The messages he had put on the car and in Powell's office had been designed to intensify the uncertainty that he must have experienced with the recovery of the body. It was Ackerman's intention to prolong this uncertainty to the point at which a confrontation would have devastating impact. Under such pressure he believed there was a chance Powell might crack.

When they rounded the bend in the drive and the house came into view, Ackerman was taken aback by the beauty of the dwelling and the grounds. The fading rays of the sun shone through the leaves on the trees bordering the turrets and reflected off the blue slate roof. He noticed the new sod, where the elm had been, and wondered about it. At the entrance to the house he helped Dana off the bicycle; turning to the large arched doors, he looked for a doorbell.

"You have to pull that," Dana said, pointing to an iron rod extending from the wall.

Ackerman pulled the rod, and soon the door opened. A matronly woman in a dark green uniform smiled at them.

"Hilda, this man wants to see Daddy. He's a policeman."

"Good evening, ma'am," said Ackerman quickly. "Would you tell Mr. Powell that Agent Ackerman of the FBI is here to see him, please?"

The woman looked startled. "Yes, of course." She spoke with a German accent. "Won't you come in, please. I'll see if Mr. Powell is at home."

Ackerman knew he was. He had called at dinner time, representing himself as an investment consultant.

The agent stepped through the doorway into a large, sparsely furnished foyer made elegant by a highly polished oak floor and travertine marbled walls. The woman closed the door and led the way through the foyer, down three steps into an exquisite drawing room. He felt as if he had walked into the chambers of a medieval monarch. The room was furnished with Tudor and Stuart pieces and was softened by long sofas and easy chairs resting on large Oriental rugs. Oak-paneled walls rose three-quarters of the way to the ceiling, where heavy beams extended the length of the room. At one end was a fireplace framed by a great antique marble mask. At the other end were three large leaded-glass doors bearing brilliantly colored intaglios cut into the panes. The doors opened onto a terrace, where lawn furniture and garden statuary were fitted into the landscaping.

The maid invited Ackerman to sit on a Jacobean settee near the fireplace and then left the room. Dana crawled up on the settee with him and balanced Lindsay on his knee.

Suddenly, she straightened. "Here comes my mother. I'll be right back." She dropped the doll in the agent's lap and ran onto the terrace.

Ackerman felt a tingle of anticipation when he saw Sue Powell walk across the terrace. She was clad in blue jeans and a dark blue sweater. A red scarf was tied around her hair. He watched through the partially opened doorway as Dana intercepted her. The girl pointed toward the drawing room as she spoke. He caught a glimpse of Sue Powell's lovely face as she glanced in his direction. Taking the girl firmly by the hand, she moved across the terrace and out of sight.

Ackerman wondered how much she knew of her husband's involvement in the Ann Conway case. Probably nothing. It would be one hell of a shock. He reflected on the incident in the drive with their daughter. The Powells had their share of problems ahead. The thought evoked a measure of sympathy in the agent. He took the doll from his lap and placed it beside him so that its head was resting on the arm of the settee. From there it gazed up at him with a look of innocence found only in little girls and their dolls.

Several minutes passed. A clock chimed from somewhere

off the drawing room. Ackerman shifted impatiently. Powell couldn't have the maid say he was not at home. He would know that his daughter would have said he was there. Besides, right now Powell must be desperate to know why the FBI had come. He was probably considering how he should act; what he should say. That was bad. The more time he had to think, the less chance of an unconsidered remark. Maybe he was calling his lawyer.

As the time elapsed, Ackerman's patience began to wane. He stood up with the intention of walking to the glass doors to look out on the terrace. In doing so he accidentally knocked the doll from the settee onto the floor. The impact started the mechanism that made Lindsay cry. He quickly retrieved the doll and placed it on the settee. The forlorn sound of the crying was disturbing. Again he glanced at his watch. He was considering going to the front door to ring the bell when he heard something behind him. He turned to see Dana Powell peering from the doorway.

"My father will be down in a few minutes," she said.

The girl stood eyeing him, and Ackerman sensed that her manner had changed. She seemed less friendly. Perhaps a reflection of her father's reaction to his visit, he reasoned. "How's that elbow?" he asked jovially.

She hung in the doorway, ignoring the question, her dark eyes watching suspiciously. "Why is Lindsay crying?" she asked.

◊   ◊   ◊

CHAPTER 25

Dusk spread over the wall on Meadow Lane. The ivy and climbing roses had lost color with the passing day, leaving a long expanse of umber-colored masonry that stretched off into the deepening twilight. It was still, except for an occasional breeze that bent the tall grass in the meadow facing the wall. Suddenly, two shafts of light split the darkness, illuminating the pasty faces of the corbeled heads imprisoned in the wall. They glared out in reproachful anticipation as the steady hum of a perfectly tuned Rolls-Royce engine grew louder. Soon, the long, gleaming chassis rolled into view.

Inside the limousine, Tom Lucas took his chauffeur's cap from the seat beside him and set it squarely on his head. As he neared the entrance, he noticed a sedan parked near the gatehouse. He stopped and was about to get out to open the gates when Brandon Sheehan appeared from behind the building. The gardener motioned Tom to remain in the car as he walked slowly to the gates and opened them. Tom noticed that the older man moved with difficulty. Nodding his thanks, Tom drove through the entrance and parked on the cobblestones in front of the garage. He got out of the car as the gardener approached.

"What's the matter, Brandon? You look stiff."

"It's my back. They've got me to filling in that old well."

"Why do they want it filled?"

"It's so damned silly." Brandon shook his head. "They're afraid some kid will pull the top off and fall in. It'll take me forever to fill that hole. I'm too old for this type of work."

"You'll feel better in the morning."

"You going up to the house now?" asked Brandon.

"Yes, I've got to deliver this package to Mrs. Powell."

"Would you give these to somebody up there?" The gardener handed Tom a small notebook and pencil flashlight. "Somebody must have dropped them. Found them up by the well."

"Sure." Tom took the items. "I just have to stop up in my apartment a second. Say, whose car is that?" He motioned toward the sedan.

"I don't know. I dozed off and didn't see anyone come in."

"Take care of that back."

As the gardener limped toward the gatehouse Tom walked behind the garage and mounted the stairs leading to his quarters. Once in his apartment, he laid the package, notebook, and flashlight on a table and went to the bathroom. When he returned he picked up the items, preparing to leave. As he did he flipped through the notebook and noticed the address stamped on the inside of the front cover:

James J. Delaney Associates
143 West 43rd Street
New York, New York

He riffled through the pages quickly. The book contained penciled notes in a peculiar combination of printing and shorthand. Their legibility indicated that the writer had taken pains in making them. Curious, Tom began thumbing through the pages. There were numerous names, addresses, telephone numbers, and dates with notations such as "physical" or "technical" and the names of city detectives with their precincts and telephone numbers. Toward the end of the book, he saw several references to "Powell" and "Hunter." The last entry carried directions on how to get from the bird sanctuary to the farmhouse on the Powell estate and bore the notation "Thurs. 15th 11:00 P.M."

As the importance of the notes registered, Tom pulled a chair from the table and sat down. He reread the pages where the first references to Powell and Hunter had appeared. "Goddamn!" he murmured. He reached into his breast pocket and withdrew a package of cigarettes. Tapping the package against the table until one of the cigarettes projected, he drew it out with his lips. After lighting it he inhaled deeply; then, leaning back in his chair, he blew a long stream of smoke toward the ceiling. He sat for several minutes, smoking and tapping the package of cigarettes against the table. Finally he stood and, gathering the items, left the apartment.

As he descended the stairs to the courtyard, he noticed the kitten near the garbage can—a new pet acquired by Brandon to replace an older cat that had disappeared a short time before.

It was almost dark as he started up the drive toward the house. He continued to think about the significance of the notebook as he walked. There was no doubt that someone was conducting an investigation. The question was whether the person was working for the Powells or investigating them. And why would a flashlight and the notebook be left by the well? Deep in thought, he was startled when a voice called to him from the shadows of the pines beside the road.

"Is that you, Tom?" It was Sue Powell.

"Oh, hi, Mrs. Powell. I was on my way to drop off your package." As he walked toward her, he quickly stuck the notebook and flashlight inside his tunic. He would keep them overnight, he thought. It might be well to have another look. In the morning he could give them to Mr. Powell.

"Here, I'll take it, Tom," she said as he drew abreast of her. "Save you the trip up."

"Sure, here you are, Mrs. Powell." He handed her the package. "Nice evening, isn't it?" He turned, preparing to go back down the drive.

"Don't you have some other things?"

"I beg your pardon, ma'am?"

"I was talking to Brandon on the intercom about his back. He said you were bringing up some things he'd found. I believe he mentioned a notebook." She spoke casually, but Tom detected a firmness in her voice.

"Oh, yes," he said quickly, reaching inside his tunic. "I almost forgot. Here you are." It was awkward. She would know he had not intended to give them to her.

"What are they, do you know?" She took the items and glanced at them curiously. "Brandon said he didn't bother to look at them. Is there a name or anything?"

"I don't really know." He could sense that she didn't believe him. It would have been better if he had leveled with her.

"Thank you, Tom. Hilda's going to stay in town with her sister tonight. Would you take her down? She's ready to go."

"Sure, Mrs. Powell."

"By the way," she said, hesitating as she turned to leave. "Brandon left his pipe over by the well. After you drop off Hilda maybe you could pick it up for him, okay?"

Her white teeth flashed briefly in a smile as she disappeared into the shadows.

◊ ◊ ◊

CHAPTER 26

"I'm not sure I understand." Dave felt warm and would have liked to loosen his collar, but he continued to look the FBI agent in the eye, trying to conceal his anxiety.

"All I said was that you have the right to remain silent or to have an attorney—"

"No. No, I heard what you said. But why would you be telling *me* that? It sounds as though—"

"Excuse me, Mr. Powell. I don't mean to interrupt, but you must understand. I'm conducting a criminal investigation, and I'm required by law to say these things. Really, all I'm saying is that you have a right to remain silent, to have an attorney, and that anything you say may be used against you later in court." Horace Ackerman spoke softly, more softly than he had before Dave had asked the question. "I merely want to ask you a few questions about the Lake Placid matter. We talked to your wife a few weeks ago. Did she mention it—that we had talked to her?"

"Yes, she did."

"Well, then I'm sure you understand why I'm here. We've contacted a number of people in the Lake Placid area, trying to develop information on the body recovered from the lake. As I said, you're under no obligation to talk to me at all, but I thought perhaps you might be able to help—"

"I don't mind talking to you. In fact, I'm glad to be of assistance. It's just that I didn't know why you were saying . . . you know, what you did about—"

"Well, then, if you have no objections, I'll proceed," Ackerman said, passing over Dave's comment. "Mind if I smoke?"

"Not at all." Dave watched the agent take a package of cigarettes from his pocket.

"Care for one?" Ackerman asked, offering the pack.

"No, thanks. I don't smoke."

Ackerman lit up and settled back in his chair as though preparing for a friendly chat. Dave sensed something in his manner that did not ring true—a studied nonchalance, as though the agent wanted to convey an impression of indifference. It did little to allay his concern.

Before coming downstairs Dave had paced the floor, trying to collect his thoughts. He had finally convinced himself that the visit was probably little more than a follow-up to the last one. With this in mind he had been relatively composed as he came into the drawing room. Horace Ackerman's easy smile and general affability had further relieved his anxiety. But after he had invited him into the gun room, and Ackerman had attempted to finesse the statement about Dave's rights, his perception of the visit had changed markedly. Now, as he sat observing what he felt might be contrived indifference on the part of the agent, his suspicions were further aroused.

"This is certainly a beautiful place, Mr. Powell," Ackerman remarked, glancing about the room. "Those figures worked into the glass, for example." He gestured with his cigarette toward several large leaded intaglios in the windows. "That's a hunting scene, isn't it?"

"Yes, it is. It's Diana and the Hunt."

"Diana and the Hunt?"

"Diana was a Roman deity. Goddess of the moon and the hunt."

"Somehow I thought she had someting to do with women."

"Actually, she did." Dave wished the man would get on with his business. "She was also the protectress of women."

"That's interesting." Ackerman exhaled smoke that clouded his features. Then, as though aware of Dave's impatience, he opened the folder on his lap. "I guess Diana must have been out to lunch when that girl needed her."

"I beg your pardon?"

"The girl whose body was recovered from Lake Placid."

"Oh. Yes."

"Tragic thing, wasn't it, Mr. Powell?" The agent gazed at him through the cigarette smoke, a look of compassion on his rugged features. "A young girl's life snuffed out like that?"

"It certainly was." Dave realized he was tapping his foot against the ottoman and restrained himself.

After another drag on his cigarette, Ackerman leaned forward and placed it on an ashtray near the chair. "Our investigation indicates the body was submerged sometime in 1962." He withdrew a sheaf of papers from the folder. "We're trying to locate people who were in the area at the time. Your name came up."

Dave felt a new wave of fear. How had his name come up? Was Emily Hunter behind it? And those papers Ackerman had removed from the folder. There were photographs among them. He could not be certain, but he thought he had seen what looked like an arm. Also, a pad. It was lined and yellow. He wondered . . .

"Didn't you stay at Camp Louise during the summer of 1962?" the agent continued.

"Let's see," Dave mused. "It's been so long . . . I really can't remember where I—"

"Apparently you were employed at the Adirondack Club at the time."

"Yes, I guess you're right. It would have been sixty-two, then. You're right, I was working at the club. It was only for a short time."

"About how long?"

"A few weeks. Maybe three weeks."

"Three weeks? Why only three weeks? Wasn't it a summer job?"

"Yes, it was. I forget now why I left. I think I had to go home to Rochester for some reason. It's been so long that—"

"Yes, I know what you mean." There was an understanding look on Ackerman's face. "I couldn't tell you where I was twenty years ago, I traveled so much. Ah . . . let's see now. How about your free time? When you weren't working, that is? Did you date quite a bit?"

"Not really." Dave thought it an odd question. He caught his foot tapping the ottoman again. "I was about to be engaged—to my wife."

"Oh. Was she at Camp Louise then?"

"No, she was with her family. They spent most of their summers in Newport. She came up on occasion. Not very often though."

"Didn't you play ball with the Lake Placid Majestics?"

"Yes, I did," Dave said, surprised. "You seem to know a good deal about me."

Ackerman ignored the comment. "Didn't you get one of those medallions they awarded to captains of the team? You know, with the ball and bats on it?"

"Yes, I believe I did."

"Didn't you wear it around your neck?"

"I beg your pardon?"

"Didn't you wear it around your neck?"

"Now that you mention it, I do recall that."

"Do you remember what happened to it?"

"I have no idea. I don't remember having it very long. I guess I lost it or misplaced it."

Ackerman regarded him quietly for a few seconds. Dave had the impression that he did not believe him.

"You say you stayed at Camp Louise while you worked at the club. Did you commute each day?"

"Yes, pretty much."

"That view of Whiteface is extraordinary." Ackerman paused to retrieve his cigarette from the ashtray. Dave used the moment to glance at his wristwatch, doing it in a way that would convey the impression that his time was limited. The agent inhaled on his cigarette and then extinguished it hastily in the ashtray.

"Ah . . . ever take anyone out to the camp with you?"

"I beg your pardon?"

"Camp Louise. Did anyone ever stay with you? Did you ever take anyone out to the camp?"

"That would be difficult for me to remember after all this time."

"Are you saying you can't remember whether or not you ever took anyone out to Camp Louise with you, Mr. Powell?" There was a dubious note in the agent's voice.

"Mr. Ackerman, do you mind if I ask why you're asking me these questions? I don't see why my activities should be of interest insofar as—"

"Of course. I'm sorry, Mr. Powell. I hope you don't mind. As I mentioned earlier, you don't have to talk to me at all if you don't want to, but we're really dependent on people like you. You may be able to offer something helpful—something that fits into the case."

"I want to be helpful if I can," Dave said. "It's just that I have plans for the evening."

"I'm sure I can wind this up quickly. Let me ask you again," Ackerman said. "Did you ever bring any young woman out to Camp Louise?"

"Not that I recall."

"That's funny. Someone said they saw you bring a young woman out. The night of July 3, 1962, to be precise."

The statement caught Dave low in the viscera and pinned him solidly against the back of his chair. He looked at the agent quietly for several seconds. The man's manner no longer seemed friendly.

"Perhaps I did." Dave's voice was husky, and he cleared his throat. "I certainly can't remember where I was on July 3, 1962."

"But you do remember bringing a girl out to the camp one night, don't you? This person said you did."

"It's quite—yes, I suppose I might have."

"This person said you brought the girl out in the Dickerson launch—that old Fay and Bowen. The person said it was about nine-thirty."

Dave started to answer but no words came. Panic gripped him. Someone had seen him. The girl, the boat, the date, even the time.

"Would you mind taking a look at these?" Ackerman withdrew several eight-by-ten glossy photographs from the papers on his lap and handed one to Dave. "Ever see this before?"

Dave hesitated and then took it. It was a picture of the medallion.

"Ever see that before?" repeated Ackerman.

Dave nodded. "It looks like one of the medallions we were talking about."

"That's right. It's *your* medallion. And you know where we found it? *There!*" With the word "there," Ackerman abruptly shoved another picture in front of Dave.

Dave took the photograph and lowered his eyes to the corpse of Ann Conway. The impact was staggering. He closed his eyes, but the horrifying picture remained vivid in his mind.

Ignoring Dave's reaction, Ackerman pressed on. "That's Ann Conway, Mr. Powell. Remember? You worked with her at the Adirondack Club. You were both discharged the same day for violating kitchen rules. That night you took her out to the

Dickerson camp and killed her. See, there's your medallion sticking out of her hand. Then you tied her into that guideboat, rowed it over to Pulpit Rock, and sank it in the deepest part of the lake."

Dave sat motionless, his eyes closed. The witness, the body, the medallion. He was being charged with murder. Suddenly he felt cold. He shook his head and opened his mouth to protest, but no words came.

"Would you care to talk about it, Mr. Powell?" Horace Ackerman's voice cut through his thoughts. "How did it happen?"

How *did* it happen? he thought. It had been as unreal then as it was now, sitting with the grotesque photographs, listening to the square-faced stranger who talked in mellow tones about tragedy. He struggled to control his emotions. The agent would never believe him—not if what he had said about the medallion and other things were true. But he had to tell him. At least the torment of living with the secret would end.

"Are you all right, Mr. Powell? Would you care to talk about it?"

Dave opened his eyes and gazed into the dark, inquiring face. "Yes . . . Yes, I want to," he said, his voice a whisper. "You don't know how I've wanted to talk to someone these past twenty years—how often I've thought of going to the authorities and telling them about that night."

Dave leaned forward in his chair and handed the photographs back to the agent. "Here, Mr. Ackerman. You won't need these any more. I'll tell you what happened. But when I'm finished, you won't believe it. No one will believe what happened that night on Lake Placid."

As he spoke there was a movement beyond the door. It was Dana. She was on the far side of the drawing room, looking at her father. She was holding Lindsay tightly to her chest. Her eyes were wide and frightened.

◊　◊　◊

CHAPTER 27

"Captain!" There was a trace of constrained excitement in the husky voice that reverberated from the bottom of the well. "I think we got something, Captain!"

Jeb Olsen stiffened as he watched Jules Shaffer, captain of the Tarrytown Police Department, walk to the edge of the well. The captain leaned cautiously over the pit and peered down to where two men were working to remove the heavy stones and dirt.

"Phew!" Shaffer said. "It sure smells like you hit something. What you got?"

"Probably just the remains of some animal," Jeb said. His comment was more to bolster his own morale than for any effect it might have on the captain.

It had been two weeks since the lawyer had agreed to defend Dave Powell, following Dave's indictment for the murder of Ann Conway. He had accepted the case reluctantly, and only because he and Dave had maintained a casual friendship in a Westchester tennis club. The Powell indictment had come only a few weeks after the conclusion of a case in which Jeb had acted as chief defense counsel for a nationally known rock group charged with maiming a dissonant member of their quartet. The case, although furthering Jeb's reputation as one of the country's best known trial lawyers, had done little for his nerves and still less for his ego. All three of the rock group had been convicted and had received the maximum sentence. Despite glowing reports in the press regarding Jeb's dramatics and oratory, it was the third case he had lost in as many times in court, and no one knew better than Jeb Olsen that he needed a winner.

"I think we got an arm," came the voice from the well. "There's a body down here!"

Jeb reached into his pocket for his cigarettes. It was times like these that contributed to the graying patterns in his thick, blond hair. He was an attractive man whose Nordic ancestry was reflected in limpid blue eyes and smooth tan skin. A stooped carriage made him appear shorter than his five feet eleven inches and accentuated a small paunch that had begun to assert itself at his midsection. He had been practicing law for twenty-eight of his fifty-two years, and if his profession had left any mark on his appearance, it was in an expression that seemed to ask, "My God, what else can happen to me?" At no time had the look been more manifest than now.

"Did he say 'body'?" Jeb asked of no one in particular. His hands trembled as he lit his cigarette.

"It's a body, all right!" echoed the voice from the well. "White male. Looks like he was wearing some kind of uniform."

"Must be Lucas," the captain said. "Probably his chauffeur's uniform."

Jeb exhaled slowly, watching the smoke dissipate in the cold morning air. How had he let himself get into this, he wondered. It had been bad enough the past two weeks trying to develop some kind of defense—particularly in light of the statement his client had given to the FBI and the State Police following the interview at his house. The previous day their weak defense had been dealt yet another blow when Horace Ackerman, who had referred the case to the State for prosecution, had made his final contribution. The FBI agent had suggested to the Tarrytown police, who were searching for the missing Tom Lucas, that they have a look in the old well on the Powell estate. Early that morning, search warrant in hand, Jules Shaffer had appeared with two of his lieutenants. After a cursory inspection had shown the well to be partially filled, three workmen with excavating equipment had been summoned. Jeb had arrived in time to see the defense he had been carefully weaving start to unravel.

"You want us to send it up, Captain?" called the voice from the well. "It's in rough shape!"

"Yeah," Shaffer answered. "Be careful with it."

Jeb, waiting at the edge of the well, grimaced as the body was cranked into view. Although the corpse was badly deteriorated, it was obvious from the uniform that it had been Tom Lucas.

"Want us to keep digging?" the voice asked.

"Yeah, long as you're there, go down a couple more feet." Shaffer pulled a handkerchief from his pocket and wrapped it around the lower part of his face. Turning to Jeb, who had moved several yards away, he said, "What do you think, Counselor? He was out for a stroll and fell in, right?"

Jeb did not answer. He was looking at his watch and calculating how long it would take to get to the Essex County Jail in Elizabethtown, where Dave Powell was being held to await trial. There were questions he had to ask his client. He was about to leave when he heard the heavy voice call again from the well. This time the the sound of excitement was unrestrained.

"Captain Shaffer! We got another one!"

"What?"

"We've got another body, sir!"

"Jesus Christ!" Shaffer exclaimed. "You sure?"

"Yep! Another one! You sure we ain't in a cemetery?"

Jeb felt the chill of the cold September morning. He pulled the collar of his trench coat up around his neck and plunged his hands into his pockets. He glanced toward Jules Shaffer. The captain's eyeballs bulged from under the visor of his officer's cap. Within a few minutes Jeb saw a badly decomposed body emerging slowly from the well. It was a revolting sight. The body was strapped to the conveyor in a way that made it appear to be sitting or squatting. The dangling skull, with its hollow eyes and grotesque death smile, bumped up and down on the chest, infused with a weird sort of movement that suggested it was alive and happy and nodding approval of its disinterment. Jeb felt sick. The cigarette dangling from his lips dropped further and ashes crumbled off the end and cascaded down the front of his coat.

"Hastings, call the station," Shaffer said to one of his subordinates. "Have them contact the coroner's office. Also, get an ambulance and some bodybags from the morgue. Tell them to bring some masks, too."

Jeb turned away as they removed what was left of the second body from the conveyor.

"Make sure you sift through the stuff and get everything," Shaffer shouted into the well.

"We've just about reached bottom," the voice replied. "We're—yeah, we've hit rock. We can't go much—what?" The man's voice was cut short and a muffled conversation could be heard, and then, "Captain! We got something else here. It looks like a cat."

"A what?"

"A cat. A dead cat!"

◊ ◊ ◊

PART
VIII

Elizabethtown, New York
October 1982

CHAPTER 28

"But they were murdered! Lucas and Delaney were shot—
with your pistol, according to ballistics!"

Jeb Olsen was becoming increasingly frustrated as he sat
talking to his client in the visitors' room of the Essex County
Jail. His voice was still restrained, but the pile of cigarette butts
accumulating in the ashtray on the table was testimony to his
frayed nerves.

"I'm sure you realize what this does to our case." He
glanced toward the sheriff's deputy, who stood out of earshot in
a far corner. "No one in that courtroom is going to believe you
don't know how those people ended up in your well. They
worked for you."

"Delaney didn't work for me," Dave replied.

"You retained him. You were paying for his services. And
that cat. I don't have confirmation yet, but all indications are
that it belonged to your gardener; that it was poisoned. The
whole thing is bizarre. And your story about what happened at
Lake Placid—my God!"

"You don't believe anything I've told you, do you?"

"What *I* believe doesn't mean a damn. My job is to make
sure the *jury* believes you, and I'm trying to tell you our only

defense at this stage is a plea of guilty by reason of insanity. There's still time to bring in the psychiatrists. I've been talking to the prosecutors. It won't be easy in view of the new laws governing insanity pleas, but I still may be able to get them to listen to a deal . . ." Jeb paused as he saw Dave shaking his head.

"Nothing doing," Dave said. "I'm not going to plead guilty. You're asking me to tell the whole world that I killed three people. Think of what it would do to Sue. To *Dana*—her father a *murderer*."

"Dave," Jeb lowered his voice as he glanced again at the deputy, "if you get on the stand and testify to the story you gave those investigators, we'll never make it. Now that the legislature has reinstated the death penalty, you're not just fighting for your freedom—you're fighting for your life. All the publicity will only make it worse. Look at the coverage we're getting, and we haven't even gone to trial. Pressures on the judge, the district attorney's office—everyone connected with the case—will be enormous. The prosecution's all tooled up for the thing. And we're not in New York City, remember. They do things differently up here. Look what happened at the suppression hearing. The judge dictated the stuff right off the bench. Denial of bail, all motions—set the trial for the fall term. He's tough and he's supposedly retiring in six months. This will be his swan song. You won't have a chance. You've got to start listening to me, or you could end up in that Dancehall you keep talking about."

"I'm not going to say I killed those people." Dave paused and gazed soberly into his lawyer's eyes. "I'm going to tell the truth, that's all. Why should I perjure myself—"

"I'm certainly not asking you to perjure yourself." Jeb glanced again toward the guard and pulled his chair closer to the table. "All I'm saying is that you're under no obligation to take the stand. You were under duress when you gave that statement to the FBI agent and the State Police. We can claim a history of mental disturbances and . . ."

Dave leaned forward, placing his elbows on the table and resting his face in his hands. Jeb could see he was getting nowhere. With a sigh he leaned back in his chair. "They're going to interview you again this afternoon. Whatever you do, don't deviate from what you've told them. Stick to your story that you know nothing whatever about the bodies in the well and—"

"There *is* no other story. I haven't the foggiest idea how those bodies got there. Or how Ann Conway ended up in the lake. I've been thinking about it constantly, and I keep coming back to Sam Wykoff. I know it isn't logical, and knowing Sam, it doesn't seem possible. But, as far as I know, he was the only other person on the island that night. He was in Tarrytown several times this past summer. He knew I had that revolver in my dresser."

Jeb was only half listening. Although impressed by the fervor of his client's protestations of innocence, he was convinced that one of two things was going to happen to David Powell in the coming weeks. He would be sentenced either to a mental institution or to the electric chair. Jeb's only hope was to avoid the latter.

"The authorities have cleared Sam," Jeb said as Dave paused. "They've had him on the lie detector; checked out his story. He was in Placid during the period when Delaney and Lucas were killed. It isn't rational anyway. A man his age—"

"What about Emily Hunter?" Dave said. "She had every reason to want Delaney out of the way. As I told Sue, he was investigating Hunter and her girlfriend, Raderman. She could have had him bumped off and his body dumped in my well to implicate me."

"No, no, Dave. They've checked out all the others. Hunter never even knew Delaney. It all comes back to you. Lucas, Delaney, Ann Conway . . . You're the only one who's had a definite connection with each victim. Brandon Sheehan told the police that you told him to fill in the well. Why would you tell him to—"

"Brandon told Sue he found the top off. I was afraid some kids might fall in. Kids are always—"

"All right, I understand. Let's forget the Tarrytown case. You're not being tried for those murders right now. Our immediate problem is this Lake Placid thing. I wish to hell you'd called me before talking to Ackerman."

Dave shrugged. "I told him the truth."

"Well . . . right now, our big problem is selecting a jury. I don't think we could find twelve Eskimos who haven't heard about those bodies in Tarrytown." He picked up his briefcase and moved back from the table.

"Did you see Dana today?" Dave asked wistfully.

"Just for a minute. She's going to stay with Sue's mother when the trial starts."

"How's Sue?"

"She'll be up in the morning. We've rented some rooms in that hotel over in Westport for our headquarters. She can stay there with us. It's only eight miles from here."

"How's she taking things?"

"Amazing. What composure! She has complete confidence that we're going to beat this thing." The lawyer shook his head as though bewildered by her optimism. "She has no question whatever about your innocence. She's a remarkable woman."

"I know," said Dave, staring at the table. "I know . . ."

◇ ◇ ◇

CHAPTER 29

"If Your Honor please, I respectfully move the case of the People against David Powell."

Jeb Olsen sat listening at the counsel table as Karl Berkholtz, Essex County special prosecutor, formally moved to open the trial. Although Jeb had met him only a few weeks before, during the pretrial hearings, he felt he knew him well. He had researched Berkholtz's career as part of his trial preparation and had found him to be a tough, competent trial lawyer whose quick mind and abrasive tactics were his trademark during the many years he had been practicing law in the North Country.

A former district attorney, Berkholtz had been appointed special prosecutor because of the enormous publicity the case had generated, and because it was felt the present district attorney was too young and inexperienced. A bald, stocky man with square, flat features, he spoke with a deep, authoritative voice that carried well in the cavernous old courthouses of upstate rural communities.

"Your Honor," said Berkholtz, "before we draw names from the wheel, may I make a brief opening statement?"

Jeb shifted his attention to the front of the courtroom, where County Court Justice Clarence Overmeyer was ensconced above a large mahogany bench. The judge was a bespectacled, wiry man with sunken cheeks and thin, gray hair. His diminutive frame was cloaked in a billowing black robe. The small head perched atop the oversized gown and judicial bench looked incongruous.

"Proceed, Mr. Berkholtz," the judge said.

The prosecutor moved in front of the rows of prospective jurors assembled on one side of the courtroom. He was poised and confident, his legs firmly planted beneath his square torso like some solid fixture of the courtroom itself. As Jeb watched him, he wished there were some way to avoid the trial. He had sent out feelers to the prosecution to elicit interest in plea bargaining, but there had been no response.

"Ladies and gentlemen," Berkholtz began, "this is the fall session of the Essex County criminal court. The crime charged is murder in the first degree, a class A felony, and the name of the deceased is Ann Conway. When you are examined, if you knew the deceased or the defendant or any policeman intimately or socially, or if you have heard of this case—"

A ripple of laughter went through the courtroom, bringing Judge Overmeyer's gavel into play for the first time. The prosecutor continued, ignoring the interruption. "If this be the case, please volunteer the information both to the gentlemen of the defense and myself so that we may question you about it. Thank you."

"Half of those people are probably related to the police captain," observed George Cousins, one of two associate counsels seated with Jeb. "We need a change of venue."

"We'll never get it," Jeb said. "Besides, where would you hold the trial? Tarrytown? There are two more bodies and two indictments waiting down there. With the press we've had, it wouldn't make any difference where it was held."

There followed a lengthy examination of prospective jurors. By late afternoon Jeb Olsen had used several of his peremptory challenges—dismissals of prospective jurors uncontested by the court—and only three jurors had been selected. At five o'clock Judge Overmeyer peered over his rimless glasses and concluded the day's activities, admonishing prospective jurors not to discuss the case.

Notwithstanding the judge's warning, little other than the trial was discussed in the community during ensuing weeks. For Elizabethtown, it was a prodigious event, almost more than the tiny town could handle. Deputies had to be sworn to help cope with the crowds that assembled each day on the village green in front of the courthouse. A festive atmosphere prevailed. Vendors sifted through the crowd selling their wares, while television crews were busy recording the event for evening telecasts.

A favorite of the crowds and the media was Sue Powell, who traveled to Elizabethtown each morning from Westport. Her arrival invariably drew a hushed response on the green.

Relatively few gained admittance to the trial. The Essex County Courthouse was inadequate for a case of such notoriety. A picturesque red brick building of classic design, it had an arched white door and long, narrow windows trimmed in white. A white portico supported by four tall pillars formed a colonnade at the front. Contributing to its overall stateliness was a towering white steeple.

The interior was similar to most county courthouses, with traditional wooden furniture. On the walls were portraits of previous county court justices—severe-looking men in high square collars—dating back to the nineteenth century. It was a quaint, impeccably neat room—a fitting courthouse for an orderly rural community.

As the trial progressed, motions for dismissal, postponements, and change of venue were all denied by Judge Overmeyer, who was determined to press ahead and bring the case to a conclusion. After exhausting his peremptory challenges, Jeb had ended up with a jury of eight women and four men, each of them thoroughly familiar with the facts of the case as presented by the media. All were aware of the other indictments for murder pending in Westchester County.

It was Monday of the following week that, the jury having been sworn, Judge Overmeyer addressed the prosecutor. "All right, Karl—Mr. Berkholtz—you may proceed with your opening statement."

As Berkholtz strode to a position in front of the jury and began to outline the People's case in his folksy style, Jeb could feel the abyss widen between the Court and the defense. It was a smooth performance, everything the defense counsel had feared—tough and well planned.

Starting with the medical examiners, Berkholtz brought a parade of witnesses to the stand to establish elements of the People's case. Employment records showed that the defendant and Ann Conway had been employed at the Adirondack Club and had been discharged simultaneously. Sam Wykoff testified to what he had observed. Several pathologists and other experts in forensic medicine, including two representatives from the FBI Crime Laboratory, established that the victim had sustained a lethal blow to the head and that the body had been submerged in the lake for twenty years. Over the objections of the defense, photographs of the remains of Ann Conway had been admitted into evidence and displayed to the jurors. Upon viewing the pictures, several jurors gazed coldly at Dave. The former manager of the Lake Placid Majestics testifed that the medallion found embedded in the palm of the victim's hand was of the type awarded to Dave as team captain. Finally, most damaging of all, was the admission into evidence of the signed statement that Dave had given to the authorities following the interview with Ackerman at the house.

For all his legal finesse and courtroom panache, Jeb was able to do little to shake the State's case. His associate counsel fared no better with the forensic medicine people.

It was near the end of the second week of the trial when Karl Berkholtz stood and addressed the court. "The People rest, your Honor."

Anticipating the defense's next move, the judge turned his attention to the counsel table. "Mr. Olsen?"

"Yes, Your Honor," Jeb said, rising. "May it please the Court, the defendant moves for a dismissal of the indictment on the ground that the State has failed to establish a *prima facie* case of murder in the first degree or any other degree."

"Motion denied!" the judge said.

"May I have an exception to the ruling?"

"Exception to the ruling by the Court," intoned the judge. "Now I think that suffices for this afternoon. We'll reconvene tomorrow morning at ten o'clock."

"Ten o'clock, ladies and gentlemen," rasped the clerk as spectators began jamming the aisles toward the doors.

As he gathered his papers, Jeb noticed Sue Powell standing behind the balustrade that separated the court from the spectators' gallery, talking to a woman reporter. She was smiling, and her easy manner belied the fact that she had been undergoing the rigors of her husband's murder trial. Suddenly, she turned and caught Jeb's eye. Excusing herself from the reporter, she approached the counsel table.

"What do you think, Jeb?" she asked.

He shrugged his shoulders. "They did well with what they had," he said quietly. "Very well. The signed statement is what's killing us. But in New York State a defendant can't be convicted on his statement alone. There has to be independent corroboration, however circumstantial. And the corroboration is all twenty-year-old evidence." He paused and shook his head. "Still, I wish we could convince him to change his plea."

"Plead guilty?" said Sue. "Oh, he'll never do that, Jeb. He'll die before he does that. Like everyone else, you really think he's guilty. But he's *innocent*."

"I know," nodded the lawyer. He busied himself closing his briefcase, avoiding her look. "Oh, I forgot to mention that Mrs. Hunter called again. She's quite upset that you haven't been returning her calls."

"Oh, well. . ." Sue gave a toss of her head, and the dark eyes turned cool. "There'll be plenty of time for Emily."

◊ ◊ ◊

CHAPTER 30

POWELL TESTIFIES TODAY

Dave, sitting in the conference room of the courthouse during a midmorning recess, stared absently at the headline of the morning newspaper. Beneath the headline, filling the remainder of the front page of the tabloid, was a picture of Dave, Jeb Olsen, and Sue Powell emerging from a doorway into a corridor of the courthouse. The photograph showed Dave, his head tilted backward, looking as though he were laughing. Sue hung on his arm, smiling up at him.

It was an anomalous expression of joy that Dave found incomprehensible under the circumstances. He could not recall an instant during the past two months that could have induced such mirth. But there it was, a moment of apparent jubilation preserved by the camera. Dave glanced over the article, which summarized the trial and raised the question of whether or not the defendant would testify. He tossed the paper aside as Jeb Olsen entered the room.

"They're ready in there," Jeb said. "We'll be putting you on as soon as we go in. Remember, don't jump the gun on me. Let me lead you through it. Okay?" Although he was outwardly calm, his concern was apparent.

"I understand."

"All right. Now, Dave, I'm going to tell you this one final time—"

"I know, I know. Both you and Overmeyer have made it very clear. I don't have to testify, and I realize the consequences. It was all spelled out in that statement the judge had me sign in his chambers."

Jeb regarded him quietly for a moment and then nodded his head. "Okay. We've been through it all before." He patted him lightly on the shoulder. "Don't be overanxious. Remember, there are things I have to get on the record."

As they left the room and entered the corridor leading to the courtroom, Dave noticed a familiar figure in a dark suit standing with another man outside the prosecutor's office. It was Horace Ackerman. As Dave approached, Ackerman turned away, but not before Dave caught a trace of lingering uncertainty in his eye.

An air of expectancy filled the courtroom as they filed back to the counsel table. Judge Overmeyer quickly brought the room to order. "Is the defense ready?"

"We are, Your Honor," Jeb said, standing. "The defense calls as its next witness the defendant David Powell."

A murmur of relief passed through the courtroom—like an audience that has been advised a star whose appearance had been in doubt was going to perform after all.

Dave felt his heart pounding as he rose from his chair. For an instant his determination wavered. He was facing death in the electric chair. Was it better to be alive in a mental institution as Jeb had repeatedly said? What of Dana? He was no use to her dead. The agony of his decision weighed heavily as he moved forward.

The low bantering that customarily drifted from the spectators' section dropped off until the only sounds in the room were Dave's heels on the wooden floor and the drone of conversation from the crowd outside on the green.

After being sworn, Dave took his place in the witness chair and looked out at the packed courtroom. It was a disturbing view: row upon row of somber faces. He knew there were few who were not convinced of his guilt. A glance toward the jury box did little to allay the feeling. To his left were the prosecutors, watching intently, waiting their turn. He looked at Sue, who was in the first row behind the counsel table, a position she had occupied throughout the trial. The sight of her across the broad expanse of courtroom filled him with a sense of estrangement. He was parted from her. Perhaps forever. Yet her dark eyes showed no emotion, as though Sue Powell were a mechanical observer of life's passing events, rather than a participant. Dave's loneliness intensified as Jeb Olsen approached the witness stand.

"Please state your full name for the court," Jeb began. The lawyer moved swiftly through preliminary aspects of the direct examination, skillfully developing background material beneficial to his client and setting a credible tone for the coming testimony.

"Now, you stated you had been working at the Adirondack Club since June 10, 1962," Jeb continued, well along in his examination. "When was the first time you saw Ann Conway?"

"It was in the kitchen of the club," Dave replied. "She had just come through a swinging door that separated the kitchen from the main dining room . . ."

Although it had been twenty years ago, Dave could recall precisely that first moment when he had exchanged glances with Ann Conway. The pretty face. The brown eyes. There had been a trace of sadness, perhaps fright, in her eyes—a suggestion that they had seen sorrow in the past and expected more in the future. Later that night he had mentioned it to her when they were alone on the lake. They had just taken a swim to cool off. The lake had been dark that night, almost black; as only a still, bottomless lake can be . . .

"Sad? But I don't feel sad." Ann Conway rubbed her dark hair briskly with a white Turkish towel, and her tiny wet curls glistened in the soft light from the dock lamps.

"I mean your eyes," Dave said. "They have kind of a frightened look. You're not scared, are you?"

"Of course not." She was sitting cross-legged on the dock, clad only in the brassiere and panties that had served as a bathing suit. "To be honest, I was a little scared when we first came out. Well, maybe not really scared, but I didn't know you all that well or where we were going. And then that bird's scary laugh . . ." Her voice trailed off as she began to rub her curls once again with the towel.

Dave was lying next to her in his wet undershorts, his chin cradled in his fist. The girl's face was covered by the towel, and he was taking the opportunity to gaze at her body. It was a lithe, athletic figure, with large, firm breasts, a narrow waist, and long, slender legs. Her wet undergarments clung to her, and in the dim light he could make out the outline of the nipples on her breasts and the dark pubic hair under her silk panties.

When they had landed at the dock a half-hour before, he had no idea he would now find himself lying there with his heart pounding. They had sat in the stern of the launch, sipping gin and tonic and talking about the heat. When he had mentioned a swim to cool off, she had said she had no bathing suit. Half jokingly he had suggested their underwear would be adequate in the dark. Although hesitant at first, after another drink she had surprised him by disrobing and following him into the water.

Now, as she sat drying her hair on the dock, she appeared relaxed and not especially self-conscious about her skimpy outfit. She was probably unaware of how transparent it was, he thought. Or maybe the drinks were getting to her, although she didn't appear high.

As he lay looking at her, he considered moving closer. He had to be careful though. He didn't want to frighten her. Noticing a small scar on her thigh, he was about to rub it lightly with his finger and ask her how she had received it when her voice came from under the towel.

"You're sure no one's here, Dave?"

"Positive. The people who own the camp are in Newport. The caretaker leaves at five."

"Who would have thought a few hours ago that we'd be sitting here like this?" She abruptly pulled the towel from her head and caught him staring at her. Quickly, she dropped the towel into her lap. "It's awfully black out there, isn't it?" she said, diverting his attention to the lake. "I wonder how deep it is?"

"The lake?" Dave followed her gaze. "Pretty deep. Supposedly over three hundred feet over there by Pulpit Rock." He nodded toward the black mass of rock jutting from the far shoreline. "Although I guess they don't know for sure. Apparently they've never been able to find the bottom."

"You're kidding! A lake with no bottom?"

"Yeah, it's all part of that Sally Wood thing."

"You mentioned that before. Who *is* Sally Wood?"

"It's nothing. Just a local story."

"Oh, come on. Tell me," Ann persisted, her curiosity piqued.

"Well . . ." Dave hesitated. "I don't want to scare you. You strike me as having quite an imagination."

"Don't be silly. You're treating me like a little kid. Please tell me."

"It's just one of those stories that Sam, the caretaker, tells," began Dave. "Just some local lore. They call it the mystery of Pulpit Rock. Supposedly a young girl was playing on the rocks out there several years ago and disappeared. Apparently they figured she fell in the lake. They never found her body. Not only that, they couldn't find the bottom of the lake over there. Anyway, the girl's name was Sally Wood. Now, around here whenever anyone hears a loon laugh, they say it's the laugh of Sally Wood. It's just one of those silly stories. I shouldn't have told you. Now you'll probably be scared all night when you hear a loon."

"Oh, don't be silly. I don't believe things like that. But it did sound like a girl's laugh, didn't it? I mean it was so . . . so funny. So strange . . ."

She was sitting with her back to the dock lights, and Dave could not see her eyes clearly, but he guessed the frightened look might be there.

"It's just one of those stories you hear on a lake," he repeated. "You know how people exaggerate."

"Oh, I know," Ann said, with a shrug. She regarded the long expanse of dock and covered boat slips that extended in both directions into the darkness. Then, turning, she pointed to the structure over the boathouse. "So that's where I'm staying?"

"Yes. I sleep up in the main house. I thought you might be more comfortable there."

"Well . . . I suppose I should get into some dry things." Shielding the lower part of her body with the towel, she rose to her feet and tied the towel about her waist so that it hung to her knees like a sarong. "Would it be okay to go up there now?" She stooped to pick up her clothes.

"Sure, whatever you say." He tried to keep the disappointment from his voice. "I'll show you the way. Want me to freshen your drink?"

"No. No thanks." She reached for her glass on the dock. "I still have some. I'm not much of a drinker. Although I guess you'd find that hard to believe," she added. "I mean, the way I've been drinking these things." She smiled, rolled her eyes, and made a pouring motion with her glass near her ear. In doing so she swayed slightly. Dave wasn't sure whether or not the movement had been intentional.

"I guess I'll need my suitcase," she said.

"I'll get it. I have to get the flashlight." He moved quickly toward the launch. With one hand on the hull, he vaulted easily over the side into the cockpit. As he did, he heard the trembling laugh of a loon from somewhere in the darkness. It would frighten Ann, he thought. He shouldn't have told her the Pulpit Rock story.

Retrieving the bag, he put it on the dock beside the Adirondack guideboat. Then he returned to the cabin to get the bottle of gin from which he had been making drinks. He groped about in the dark, trying to remember where he had put the flashlight he had taken from the house. It was warm inside. It would be even hotter up in the apartment, he thought. It would be a good excuse to keep Ann outside for a while. He would open the windows and suggest they have a drink on the balcony while the room was cooling off. They could sit in the old steamer chairs the way he sometimes did with Sue. With the thought of Sue he felt a pang of conscience. Here he was virtually engaged and playing around with someone he had known only a few hours.

Unable to find the flashlight, he rummaged in the liquor cabinet and located the gin. Stumbling, he dropped the bottle to the deck, where it shattered. "Damn it!" he muttered. Stepping back, he felt a sharp pain in his heel and knew he had been cut. He emerged from the cabin to see Ann halfway down the dock, a concerned look on her face.

"What broke?"

"We're out of gin," he replied, climbing from the boat and limping toward her.

"What happened? You're bleeding."

"I cut my foot." He paused near one of the lamps to inspect the injury. Balancing on one leg, he lifted his foot and saw a piece of glass protruding from the fleshy part of his heel. "It looks worse than it is. Can I have that towel?"

"Sure." She put her clothes on the dock and unwrapped the towel from her waist. "Here, let me do it." Bending over, she removed the glass from his foot. "It's still bleeding quite a bit. Can you turn more toward the light?"

Hopping awkwardly, he moved directly under one of the dock lamps, where Ann knelt and attended to the wound. In her stooped position her bosom was clearly visible beneath the brassiere. The sight of her round, firm breasts caused him momentarily to forget his injury.

"I don't want to scare you," she said, "but it looks pretty deep."

"There may be a first-aid kit up in the apartment. Maybe you could help me a little . . ."

She gave him the towel. "Let me get my things." She gathered her clothes from the dock and handed them to him. "You carry these. Here, put your arm over my shoulder." She put her arm around his waist, supporting him. "We can get my bag later."

"The stairs are on the other side," Dave said. "We have to go around behind the boathouse."

He was surprised at her strength as she helped him walk. The closeness of her warm body increased his excitement.

"It sure is dark back here," Ann said as they rounded the corner of the boathouse. "I can't see a thing."

"The stairs are right up ahead." They paused at the base of the steps.

"I think you're on your own now." Ann started to move away. "These stairs are too narrow for both of us."

Realizing a more propitious time might not come, Dave turned so that he was facing her, his arm still around her shoulders. He drew her close.

"Oh," murmured Ann. It was an involuntary exclamation, for she quickly raised her fingers to her lips. Nor did she try to move away.

"What's the matter?" Dave asked.

"Nothing . . . I wasn't expecting this, I guess." She looked up at him, her eyes steady. "At least not at this particular moment."

"You don't mind, do you?"

He relaxed his hold so that she could move away. When she didn't he lowered his head slowly to kiss her. She raised her chin, and he felt the contours of her body move against him. He kissed her gently at first and then more ardently.

Just then the eerie laugh of a loon echoed from the forest. Ann drew back. "Gosh, there it is again. I hope it doesn't do that all night." Taking his hand, she gave it a little squeeze and moved toward the stairs. They were halfway up when a noise came from nearby—a slight scraping sound.

"What was that?" Ann asked, stopping.

"What's the matter?"

"That noise, up ahead. Didn't you hear it? You must have heard it."

"I didn't hear anything," said Dave, unconcerned.

"You sure nobody's up here?"

"I'm certain," Dave said, reassuringly. "Let's go."

They mounted the stairs to the balcony, where the lights from the dock offered some illumination.

"This is better," Ann said, relief in her voice. "At least you can see a little bit. That reminds me." She smiled as she reached for the clothes Dave was carrying.

As he handed them to her, he saw that the towel had become intermingled with her garments, leaving blood on her skirt and blouse. "Oh, boy. Sorry."

Ann followed his look. "Gosh. That's really all I've got to wear." Separating the towel from her clothes, she turned and walked to the railing, where she inspected them in the dim light. "It's not that bad. Maybe it'll wash out."

"I'm sorry," Dave repeated.

"Don't worry about it." She draped the clothing over the balustrade and looked out at the lake. "Those lights way down there. That's where we came from?"

"That's right. That's the Dancehall."

"I like the Dancehall. I wouldn't mind going there again sometime. When I don't have to worry about a place to stay."

"Let's do it," Dave said. "Maybe tomorrow night."

"Well . . . we'll see. I have to get settled first. Gosh, it's dark. Frankly, I don't like the dark."

Dave limped up behind her and put his arms loosely around her waist. "It's really nice here when there's a moon."

"Well, the moon's gone. And that funny laugh . . . Pulpit Rock . . . I'd think it was spooky even if you hadn't told me about that girl disappearing."

"Are you still thinking about that? It's only a story."

"But look at it. Isn't it scary . . . the way the rock comes up out of the lake?"

"I guess you haven't spent much time in the mountains, have you?" He pressed his face against her hair. It was damp and fragrant. He turned her around and kissed her. Suddenly, she pulled back. "I know you'll laugh when I tell you this, but somehow I have the feeling someone's watching."

"C'mon, relax," said Dave with a small laugh. He glanced toward the apartment as he spoke. It was then that he noticed the open window. Odd, he thought. Sam must have opened it for some reason.

"What are you looking at?"

Instead of answering he kissed her again. When he felt her relaxing against him, he released the hook on her brassiere. She did not resist, so he pulled the straps over her shoulders, letting the garment fall to the deck. Drawing her close he felt her breasts against his bare chest. He kissed her long and passionately. When he slid his hand inside her panties, she moved away.

"I'm sorry, Dave. Really I am, but . . ." She moved back farther, folding her arms self-consciously over her breasts.

He had begun to perspire, and he rubbed his forehead with his arm. "Shall we go inside?"

"Well . . . would you mind terribly if I went to bed? I've been up since five-thirty this morning and . . ."

"No, of course not." She was uneasy—probably wondering if he would force himself on her. "Here, I'll help you get settled."

"No, you don't have to," she said hastily. "I'll be okay."

"At least let me show you where the lights are." As he turned, his injured foot made him wince.

"Are you all right? Why don't you go and take care of your foot? I'll walk down with you. I have to get my bag on the dock, anyway."

"I'll get it," Dave said. "You wait here."

"No, no. Not with your foot." She picked up her brassiere and, turning her back to him, put it on. Then she wrapped the towel around her waist.

"Let me help you down." Taking his arm, she started toward the stairs. He thought of stopping her, trying once more to persuade her to go to the apartment, but decided against it. She seemed determined.

When they had descended the steps and reached the area leading out to the dock, Ann stopped. "No point in your walking out here. Go ahead up to the house. I'll be okay."

"I'll wait here till you get your bag." Dave watched her move out into the dim light of the dock lamps. The sight of her bare back and the trim hips swaying beneath the towel excited him. When she returned with her bag he said, "I've been thinking, maybe you should stay up in the main house with me. You know, with all the funny noises and all, you might feel better."

She hesitated, glancing up at the apartment. "No, I think I'd feel better here. If anyone ever came unexpectedly or—"

"No one would ever come out here at night. C'mon, you'll be more comfortable."

"No, I'd better stay here." Her voice was firm. She looked up at him and smiled. "I really appreciate your helping me out." She stood on her toes and kissed him quickly. "Thanks, Dave. Remember, we've got a date for the Dancehall."

He watched her turn and disappear into the darkness. It was the last he ever saw of Ann Conway.

◊ ◊ ◊

CHAPTER 31

"But you haven't answered my question!" Karl Berkholtz stepped back from the witness chair, lifting his arms with dramatic frustration. "I'll ask you once again. Did you have sexual relations with the girl?"

"Only to the extent that I mentioned," Dave replied.

"You kissed her? Removed her clothes?"

"I never actually removed her clothes. We'd been swimming and—"

"You removed her brassiere, didn't you? You said so in your statement to the authorities."

"Yes, I suppose so."

"Please speak up, Mr. Powell."

"Yes."

"And when you tried to remove her underpants, she resisted, did she not?"

"Well—as I said, she moved back."

"Mr. Berkholtz, it's five o'clock." A groan rumbled through the courtroom as the judge interrupted the cross-examination.

Berkholtz had expected the interruption. He had been watching the wall clock, hoping for more time. He knew the judge disliked working after five o'clock. "I'm almost through, Your Honor," he said, trying to mask the irritation in his voice.

"I'm not rushing you," the judge said. "You may resume your cross-examination in the morning."

"With the permission of the Court, I'd like to finish."

"Very well." Judge Overmeyer produced a gold pocketwatch from beneath his robe. "You may continue."

The prosecutor returned his attention to the weary figure in the witness chair. Although the defendant met his look with steady eyes, it was apparent to Berkholtz that he was whipped. Now was the time to tighten the screws.

"But didn't you persist?" he continued. "When she resisted you? Here you were drinking with her for a couple of hours. You'd been kissing her. You'd removed her clothing. Then you just suddenly stopped?"

"Well . . ."

"You were sexually excited, weren't you? You're asking this Court to believe that you just forgot the whole thing?"

"I didn't say that I—"

"Or was it that when she resisted your advances you began struggling with her, and then attacked her? Wasn't that what happened, Mr. Powell?"

"Objection!" Jeb Olsen jumped to his feet.

"Sustained," said the judge.

Berkholtz thought of pursuing the point but glanced at the clock. "Now, the blood that the caretaker discovered on the dock and in the main house the following morning," he said, shifting his focus, "you've testified that it was your blood."

"That's right."

"From the cut on your heel?"

"Yes."

"It wasn't from the girl? She didn't sustain some injury while—"

"Objection!" Jeb Olsen shouted. "Your Honor, the witness has already testified that the blood was from a cut on his heel. I object to this continued—"

"Sustained." As the judge delivered his ruling, he once again consulted his pocketwatch. Berkholtz knew he would have to start summarizing. He did not want to wait until morning, when Powell would have had the benefit of consultation with his counsel.

"Mr. Powell, I'd like to review a few portions of your testimony. You stated that after leaving the girl you went directly to the main house and retired; that you slept until almost seven. Doesn't it appear odd that you wouldn't have heard something? A noise, a scream, a disturbance of some kind? After all, evidence shows the girl was murdered, her body tied into a guideboat, and submerged in the lake. Doesn't it seem reasonable you would have heard *something?*"

"I've told you, with the windows closed and the air conditioning, you couldn't hear anything outside. Besides, the boathouse is quite a distance from—"

"All right, all right," interrupted the prosecutor. "Now you say when you awakened you went directly to the apartment only to find the girl gone."

"Yes."

"That you became worried, that you looked all over for her, and when you couldn't find her, you considered notifying the authorities?"

"That's right. I was concerned. I didn't see how she could have left the island. It was raining very hard. Finally I took the launch and went into the harbor."

"But why *didn't* you notify the authorities? After all, you had nothing to hide. At least that's what you're asking us to believe."

"I thought of contacting the police, but the more I thought about it, the more inclined I was to wait. I thought she'd probably show up at the camp or in town. As I said, the guideboat was gone from the dock. I figured she might have taken it and—."

"In the rain?"

"Well . . . I couldn't be sure of anything. I was reluctant to get the police involved."

"Naturally," the prosecutor said, dryly. "Why get the police involved? You knew they weren't going to believe your story. That after getting this poor girl fired, taking her to the Dancehall and plying her with drinks, bringing her to a remote island and trying to seduce her, you suddenly left and went to bed, only to wake up and find her gone. Isn't that essentially what you're saying? That it was such a ridiculous story you knew no one would ever believe it?"

"At the time I thought of a lot of things. I knew if the police became involved there would be publicity. I thought of the embarrassment to the Dickersons, who had let me stay at their camp, and to my mother and sister. Most of all I worried about its effect on my plans to become engaged. I just thought it was better to wait. That the girl would show up."

"So you continued to wait—for twenty years. And you never did anything to find out what happened to that poor girl?"

"I had no way of finding out anything about her. I did call the club, but there was no record of her employment."

"But there was a record. It was introduced into evidence in this Court."

"When I called the club, the girl said they didn't keep records on temporary employees. Maybe she didn't want to go to the trouble of looking it up, I don't know. But I was very concerned about her. I even called Hunter College, although I never really believed her when she said she went there. I couldn't even be sure that Conway was her real name. She wasn't telling me the truth about her age or—"

"Mr. Powell," Berkholtz said, cutting him off. "You testified that later that same day you called the caretaker at the camp and asked him if anyone had been there looking for you. Is that right?"

"Yes, I thought the girl might have come back and—"

"And you told him that you had lost your job, were leaving for Rochester, and wouldn't be staying at the camp?"

"Yes."

"And when he mentioned the blood on the dock, you told him it was your blood; that you'd cut your foot."

"That's correct."

"But he didn't believe you."

"He didn't say he didn't believe me. He only mentioned that there was a lot of blood for a cut foot."

"Didn't you think there was quite a bit of blood yourself? When you came down in the morning looking for her? Didn't that blood cause you to wonder?"

"I never noticed it. The blood beneath the balcony, that is. I guess I might have noticed the blood from my heel, but when I called the caretaker he indicated most of the blood was off to one side under the balcony. I never saw it. That's what worried me most all these years; the blood that he said he'd seen near the balcony. I couldn't remember having been over near the balcony after I cut my foot."

"And the broken pane in the door of the apartment, that didn't concern you?"

"I told you, it was a stormy night. The door was banging in the wind. I thought it broke from slamming. I tried to close it, but it wouldn't shut right, after all the banging."

"And none of this worried you enough to contact the authorities?"

"After I'd waited a few days, I didn't see how I *could* contact them. It would have looked as though—"

"As though you were concealing something, isn't that right?"

"It's hard to explain. In retrospect it was a mistake—not to have reported it, that is. But at the time I couldn't bring myself to do it. Mostly because of the Dickersons. Later, whenever I considered going to the authorities, I'd think, 'Well, I've done nothing wrong. Why resurrect something from the past that could create problems?' And, of course, the longer I waited, the more difficult it was to report it. I certainly paid the price for my mistake over the years. At first I was able to put it out of my mind, but after a while it became a source of anxiety. I began to feel that something had somehow happened to her—not so much at the time but later on as I thought more about it."

"Excuse me, Mr. Berkholtz," the judge said. "It's well past five."

"All right, Your Honor. I'm about through." The prosecutor turned and walked quietly to the other end of the jury box so that the jurors were between him and the witness stand. He wanted to be certain that each heard the defendant's answers. "Mr. Powell, to be sure that all of us understand what you have said . . . You've testified that the medallion recovered in Ann Conway's hand was identical to the kind that was awarded to you by the Lake Placid baseball team, but that you don't know what happened to your medallion; that you lost it. You've told us that you brought Ann Conway to Buck Island on the last night she was seen alive; you swam with her; you drank with her; you tried to have sexual relations with her but were rebuffed; and then you went off to the main house and slept soundly. Is that correct?"

Dave nodded but said nothing.

"Would you answer, please?"

"Yes."

"You did all of these things, but you did not kill Ann Conway. Instead, while you were sleeping, someone else killed her. They stuck your medallion in her hand, tied her body into that Adirondack guideboat, rowed it out to the deepest part of the lake, stove in the hull, and sent Ann Conway to the bottom. You sure you didn't do any sleepwalking?"

Jeb Olsen was on his feet quickly as the courtroom erupted in laughter.

"Order!" Judge Overmeyer brought his gavel down.

"I withdraw the last question, Your Honor," the prosecutor said, walking to his chair. "I'm through with the witness."

It rained the following day in Elizabethtown. It was a cold, continuous drizzle of the sort that made one's thoughts turn to storm windows, weatherstripping, and cut wood. Though the seats in the Essex County Courthouse were filled as always, the crowd under umbrellas outside on the green was thin.

Inside the courthouse Karl Berkholtz listened to Jeb Olsen summing up the defense Berkholtz's eyes were half-closed, his expression one of boredom. Though he exhibited indifference—in fact, was hoping to convey such a feeling to the jurors—in reality he was avidly following every word. There was little he had not anticipated, however. Other than admitting to a certain admiration for his adversary's abilities, he was not concerned. As Jeb Olsen wound to a conclusion, Berkholtz was satisfied that he could go with the brief summation he had planned. Casually, he picked up his notes and began to scan them as he saw Jeb move close to the jury for the defense counsel's final comments.

"Ladies and gentlemen," Jeb said. "I've been talking to you for almost two hours, and I do not pretend to have proved to you that David Powell did not murder Ann Conway. But you must remember that I do not *have* to prove his innocence. If there are any facts consistent with innocence, even though there may be facts consistent with guilt, the law says that you *must* render a verdict of not guilty.

"The real question here is: has the prosecution proved guilt beyond a reasonable doubt? I'm ready to admit that they did as well as could be expected considering what little they had to work with. Mr. Berkholtz is an eloquent gentleman, experienced in the subtle ways of influencing juries. Blood here! Blood there! Suggestions of sexual assault. Implications! Innuendos! But you know the facts, and the facts are limited. I don't know how Ann Conway died. Nobody does. And that's the cold truth of the matter.

"The theory that the defendant attacked the girl is utter nonsense. I'm sure the judge, when he delivers his charge to the jury, will tell you to pay no attention to it. I hope he will tell you this; I'm going to ask him to tell you because otherwise that would require you to base an inference upon an inference upon an inference, which is a violation of a basic rule of the law of circumstantial evidence. It is all pure speculation and, ladies and gentlemen, you simply cannot guess someone into the electric chair."

Berkholtz glanced at the wall clock as Jeb concluded his summation with a few references to the Bible and with an expression of confidence in the moral qualities and judgment of the jurors. The prosecutor would not have minded had his adversary continued longer. It was almost twelve-thirty, and the jurors were thinking of lunch. From Berkholtz's viewpoint, the more the lawyer talked, the more impatient the jurors would become; the more convinced that they were being conned by a lot of legalese. They all knew by then that Powell was guilty of the murder of not only Ann Conway but of the two people found in his back yard.

It was after two o'clock and well past the appointed time for reconvening when Judge Overmeyer took his place at the bench. Following the roll call of the jurors, he addressed the prosecutor. "Are you ready to proceed, Mr. Berkholtz?"

"I am, Your Honor." Berkholtz rose and planted his square frame in front of the jurors. The low murmur of the courtroom died out. "If Your Honor please. Mr. Olsen, gentlemen," he said, nodding toward the associate counsel at the defense table, "Mr. Foreman, and ladies and gentlemen of the jury. My remarks to you today will be brief. You've all been sitting here for almost five weeks, and as of yesterday there were over two thousand pages on the record. I'm not going to stand here and add to your burden. This will be the shortest summation I've given in thirty-four years as a trial lawyer. The reason is that, contrary to what defense counsel has told you, the facts in this case are strong and simple and require no elaboration. We have here a solid case of murder in the first degree. All of the elements are present. Let's review the evidence . . ."

It was as brief a summation as Berkholtz had promised, and less than ten minutes after beginning, he was offering his final comments.

"I ask you, ladies and gentlemen, how else could the defendant have responded to such incriminating facts other than to fashion an incredible story that admits the irrefutable evidence and then denies the ultimate guilt." He paused, shaking his head in disbelief as his eyes roved over the jury. "Well, we all know what really happened. The defendant did not leave Ann Conway and go to sleep that night as he claims. What really happened is that after she rejected his sexual advances, he bludgeoned her to death and then came up with a means by which he could be rid of the evidence of his crime for good. By all the laws of science, that body should have disappeared from the face of the earth forever. There should have been no way this defendant could ever be tried for the murder of Ann Conway."

The prosecutor paused again, assessing the effect of his words. He was making it, he thought. He could see it on their faces. "Certainly the deliverance of Ann Conway's body in near-perfect form from the depths of Lake Placid, after having been submerged for twenty years, is an act of God. It is a miracle beyond miracles. Surely anyone with a modicum of faith would agree that it was divine intervention that preserved Ann Conway's body so that justice could be served. God answered the prayers of that girl's mother, that poor wretched soul who spent her remaining days helpless in a sanatorium, grieving and praying for knowledge of her daughter. By His divine intervention God has thwarted the near-perfect crime and returned to us the victim, holding in her right hand the identity of the person who killed her. And He has chosen each of you, ladies and gentlemen, to see that justice prevails. Surely you will perform this God-given duty and find the defendant guilty of murder as charged."

◇ ◇ ◇

CHAPTER 32

The Adirondack Northway begins in Plattsburgh near the Canadian border and winds down through the Adirondack Mountains to the state capital at Albany. En route it offers glimpses of spectacular peaks, lakes, and streams. The forests are the most striking aspect of the terrain. Dense woods of pine, hemlock, cedar, and birch abound, and in late fall the variety of leaf color is vivid. The alpine landscape is covered with patches of red, yellow, brown, and orange, and on a sunny day there is no more glorious sight.

It was just such a day when David Powell, seated in the rear seat of a police cruiser between two Essex County Sheriff's deputies, was transported down the Northway to the Green Haven Prison at Stormville, New York. Although there were five people in the sedan, little had been said since the four deputies and their handcuffed prisoner had left the Essex County Jail over an hour before. A sober mood prevailed, reflecting a suitable decorum for a condemned man being transported to the site of his execution.

Now and then the driver and a large, heavy man beside him with buck sergeant's stripes conversed in low tones, but from where he sat, Dave could hear little of what they said. Nor did the splendor of the landscape interest him. Slouched in his seat, he could see only the heads of the deputies in front and the broad brims of their campaign hats outlined against the sky beyond the windshield. Occasionally one of the officers would speak to him. Were the cuffs too tight? Did he want a cigarette? But for the most part there was only the sound of the engine and the rushing wind.

Since his sentencing, the words of the judge intoning the death penalty had weighed heavily on his mind:

> The judgment of the court is that you, David Powell, hereby are sentenced to the punishment of death, and it is ordered that you be delivered with the warrant of this court to the warden at Green Haven Prison, Stormville, New York, where you shall be kept in solitary confinement until the week beginning Monday, January 10, 1983, and upon some day within the week so appointed the said warden is commanded to do execution upon you, David Powell, in the mode and manner prescribed by the laws of the State of New York.

Though Dave expected the sentence—the jury had deliberated less than six hours—it had seared his brain. He had been heedless of the pandemonium that followed. There had been only the sound of the judge's gavel followed by the rasping words of the court clerk. "Remand the defendant. *Death!*" He had glanced at Sue. Her dark eyes never flickered. From that moment it seemed that his execution had begun, that he was dying with each passing minute.

Security had been tightened immediately, and a deputy had been stationed outside his cell. Now, as the car rolled south, lack of sleep and the strain of the previous weeks were having their effect. He was numb, near shock, devastated by the course of events, unwilling to accept reality. He felt he had fallen into some imaginary world of horror. A nightmare. Soon he would awaken to a bright morning, the sweet sound of birds, soft pillows, the warmth of a little girl crawling into bed for a story. . .

He began to doze and slumped against the deputy on his right. Catching himself, he straightened quickly, but again his eyes closed, his head nodded, and once more he leaned against the man. This time he remained in a deep sleep as the car turned onto the Massachusetts Turnpike and then picked up the Taconic State Parkway heading south.

They had almost reached Stormville when he awakened. He sat erect and felt the sharp restraint of the handcuffs. Awareness of his position descended with crushing despondency. He raised his manacled hands, rubbed the sleep from his eyes, and tried to brush his hair back from his forehead. Squinting against the sunlight, he looked at the bucolic scene flashing past the window.

"How you feeling?" asked the deputy against whom he had been leaning. "You've been out for an hour."

Dave was about to respond when the sergeant in the front seat spoke. "We take this next right."

They slowed and turned onto a narrow road that passed under an archway of tall oak trees, their leaves glistening a bright yellow in the late afternoon sun. Suddenly they came over a rise, and before them, stretching a thousand feet across the gently sloping hillside, in grim contrast to the brilliant autumn colors, was a dark, turreted wall.

"Boy, some place," said the officer at the wheel.

"Yep," the sergeant agreed. "They say that wall is rooted in a rock ledge ten feet down."

They drove up a narrow road and across an open field to an entrance in the center of the wall. Above the entrance, in white letters, were the words, *Green Haven*.

The deputies assisted Dave from the sedan and guided him through the entrance into a large open room where three prison guards in blue-gray uniforms waited. Papers conveying Dave's custody to the prison authorities were processed quickly. Throughout the procedure, Dave could feel the eyes of the prison guards appraising him.

The sergeant produced a key and removed the handcuffs. "So long, Powell," he murmured. He turned and left, the other three deputies hurriedly following, as though fearful of being left in the depressing place.

Dave rubbed his wrists and moved his arms and shoulders to rid himself of the cramped feeling from the manacles.

"This way." One of the guards took Dave by the arm and guided him to the other end of the room, where he was checked through an electrical screening device. Accompanied by two other guards, he was led through a series of manlocks—double-barred gates with a small open area between them—which slid silently open, then closed with a solid clang behind him. They emerged into a no man's land—a well maintained grassy corridor—that separated the outer wall from the prison compound. A narrow brick walk bordered with yellow and white chrysanthemums, anomalous in their stark surroundings, connected the wall with the entrance to the compound. As they walked up the steps to the building, Dave stumbled. Immediately the hands of the guards closed on his arms. It was a strange feeling—an indication of the tight personal security awaiting him inside.

At the entranceway they paused for the door to open. Dave glanced at the sky, a deep blue dome over the prison. From somewhere beyond the wall came the sound of a meadowlark. As he listened to its fading song, he felt an overwhelming sense of loneliness. There was nothing left. Even the birds were gone.

◊ ◊ ◊

PART
IX

Green Haven Prison
November 1982

CHAPTER 33

"The fact of the matter is, gentlemen . . ." Richard Wallace, superintendent of Green Haven Prison, liked the word "gentlemen." It gave an aura of class to the proceeding. "If we had to execute David Powell the week of January 10 as directed by the court, we'd be hard pressed to do it. We've got no set procedures, no executioner—at least, none that I know of. We don't even have all the parts of the chair, do we, John?"

Wallace sat at the head of a conference table talking to his five-man executive committee. John Pike, the deputy superintendent assigned the responsibility of resurrecting the execution ritual, started to respond, but his superior gave him no chance.

"Fortunately, all death sentences are automatically stayed for six months pending appeal. That means we have until June to get that special housing unit cranked up so that it can do the job. One thing we can be sure of, K Gallery is going to fill up as the death penalty is invoked around the state. There'll be lots of pressure."

Richard Wallace was accustomed to pressure. He had been part of the New York State prison system for over thirty years and had experienced most aspects of prison life, from riots to executions. If the experience had hardened him, it was not evident in his manner. Having been involved so long, he was inured to the unpredictability and tragedy of penitentiary life. Little shook his basic stability. If the New York State Legislature had reënacted the death penalty, and Green Haven was the place designated to perform executions, well then, so be it.

He was a tall, handsome man in his early fifties, with strong, clean features. His brown eyes had a soft, almost sympathetic look, and his face always seemed on the verge of a smile. When he did smile, which was often, it revealed strong white teeth. His hair was curly and black with a sprinkling of gray, neatly trimmed over small, well-shaped ears. Probably the most notable aspect of his appearance was his expression of complete serenity. It was hardly the face one associated with a prison warden.

Nor were his appearance and easy manner deceptive when it came to his administration of the prison. There were few with whom he came in contact—guards, or inmates for that matter—who did not like and respect him. Undoubtedly it was these qualities that had brought him to the attention of the Commissioner of Corrections—a man interested in humanizing the state penal system—and resulted in his appointment to superintendent three years previously. It had been the first appointment of a black man to such a post in upstate New York.

"Incidentally," Wallace continued, "I think all news releases on the Powell case should come from the central office in Albany, don't you, John?"

Pike, on whom a good deal of the prison's administration rested, shifted in his chair. "No question about it. It's going to be bad enough without getting caught between the media and Albany."

"Why don't you review those pre-execution procedures now, John?" said Wallace. "The rest of you should pay close attention. We'll all be involved as the program develops."

Pike looked down at his papers. He was a harried-looking man in his late forties, light complexioned, with straight brown hair and hazel eyes. One would have thought him of average height until he stood up. Then, at six four, with a reed-thin physique, he seemed almost to brush the ceiling. He had been in the prison system long enough to know that if anything could go wrong in a penal institution, it would. The prospects of having to put a person to death in the electric chair had added for him a new dimension of concern.

When, in August of 1970, the execution chamber at Sing Sing, where New York's death sentences had been carried out in the past, had been moved to Green Haven, Pike had watched the construction of the chamber with a certain morbid fascination. Shortly thereafter the death law was repealed and he, like most other officials in the Department of Correction, became convinced that capital punishment was a thing of the past. The execution chamber at Green Haven collected dust, and rarely did Pike find it necessary to visit the place. When the legislature reënacted the death penalty, he had become nervous. He had begun to worry in earnest the previous week when the celebrated Powell case went to the jury and a verdict of murder in the first degree was returned. When the judge imposed the death penalty there had been a flurry on the part of the Executive Committee in Green Haven as it sought to familiarize itself with the execution ritual.

"You all should have received a copy of my memo containing provisions of *Section 650* of the Corrections Law." The deputy held up a typewritten sheet. "It covers the execution procedure pretty well. What it doesn't cover are the problems of keeping inmates in the condemned cells over a period of months. By the time they go through their appeals—living in solitary with all that pressure—some of them are bound to attempt suicide."

Pike consulted his notes, pursing his lips as he contemplated the difficulties ahead. "There's a lot to be done. As

Richard said, we don't even have all the parts to the chair. The death cap that attaches the electrode to the head is missing. How the hell we'll replace it, I don't know. They tell me it was made out of a football helmet. Can you imagine that?"

"Well, if they made one before, they sure as hell can make another one," Wallace said. "Who made the last one?"

"Some people from GE," Pike replied. "I've already sent them a letter. We're also missing the leather face mask and the electrode for the leg."

"How are we fixed for personnel?" the superintendent asked.

"We're all right in K Gallery. They're used to handling the psychos and should be able to handle the condemned cells. Kolder is the only one who's ever participated in executions, though. I've been in touch with Sing Sing. There are two retired guards in Ossining who worked on them. They've volunteered to come up and put us through a dry run if you think it's necessary. I have no idea what we'll do for an executioner. Apparently that's a lost art," he added dryly.

"Well, we won't have to worry about the executioner." Wallace shuffled the papers in front of him. "That's a job for the central office." He was impatient with his deputy's negative approach and fearful of the effect it might be having on the rest of the committee. "Anything else, John?"

"Only that I've sent all supervisors and officers in the special housing unit a list of revised procedures governing K Gallery, which has been designated as the pre-execution area. You should all get a copy in your mail."

Wallace glanced at his watch in a way that suggested they were running out of time. "Very well, gentlemen. Meeting's adjourned."

As the committee filed out, Wallace gathered up his papers and walked to a broad-surfaced desk at the other end of the room. Bending over, he spoke into the intercom to his secretary. "Have they admitted Powell yet?"

"Yes, Mr. Wallace. He's being processed at the hospital now. They're bringing him over here next."

"Let me know when they get here."

Sitting down, he reached for a folder and proceeded to review the correspondence he had received from the central office on his newest inmate. He already knew a good deal about him from the extensive publicity that had attended the trial in Essex County. A full-page picture of Powell leaving the courthouse in handcuffs had appeared in the newspaper that morning. TARRYTOWN MILLIONAIRE TO DIE IN CHAIR had been the headline.

The sentence had surprised him. Millionaires didn't go to the chair. They rarely even went to jail. He was curious to see the man, to see how he was coping. He thought of the mansion he had seen on television. How would a person like that react to living in a condemned cell?

His thoughts were interrupted by the intercom. "They're here, Mr. Wallace."

"Send them in."

Within a few seconds the door to the office opened and David Powell, in gray prison clothes, entered between two guards. Even in the plain, loose-fitting garments he seemed elegant. But he was not weathering his ordeal well. Although he held his head up and looked Wallace in the eye, it was apparent that he was crushed. His face was drawn; his eyes, bloodshot.

"My name is Wallace. I'm the superintendent." He glanced down at the formal-looking document bearing the New York seal that rested on his desk. I'm required to read this to you. It's a death warrant signed by the Governor. If you have any questions, let me know."

The superintendent shifted uneasily in his chair as he picked up the warrant and began to read the document that recited the sentence of the court and prescribed the mode and manner in which the defendant was to be electrocuted.

As he read, Wallace glanced up and saw that the prisoner had closed his eyes. Probably trying to control his emotions, he thought. He had seen men break down from far less severe sentences. He finished reading the warrant and placed it to one side. "Do you understand what I read to you?"

"Yes." Dave cleared his throat.

"Do you have any questions?"

"No, I don't."

"Very well." Wallace leaned back in his chair. "When you leave here you'll be quartered in the special housing unit. Your daily activities will be carefully explained to you. Any variations from the established routine must be approved by the watch commander. However, many of the regulations have been made in accordance with the law, which doesn't provide for exceptions." The superintendent paused once again and looked at him closely. "Do you understand?"

Dave drew his eyes from the floor. "Yes, sir. I understand." His voice was barely audible. "I won't ask for anything."

Wallace regarded his prisoner, wondering how much he should say. He had to be careful. Almost anything he said could be misconstrued by Powell's counsel, by the press. Yet there was something about the man—something likeable. He leaned forward and folded his arms on the desk. "I don't know how much help it is, Powell, but I've been in this business a long time. Years ago, I was assigned to the death house at Sing Sing. From my experience, the best way to cope is to keep as much emotion out of the process as possible. Those who suffer least are the ones who keep busy, who become involved in something, maybe only a hobby." He paused, evaluating the effect of his words. "All I can tell you is that the more active you are, the better. If you lie on your bunk feeling sorry for yourself, it will be tougher. That's the quickest way to a nervous breakdown. And believe me, that won't solve a thing." The dark eyes narrowed slightly as the superintendent regarded his charge. "Understand what I'm saying?"

"Yes. Yes, I do," Dave replied, straightening. "I'll try to remember."

The warden hesitated, wondering if he should comment further, but decided against it. The less emotion the better. He motioned to the guards who moved forward quickly to escort the inmate from the room.

As they guided him toward the door, Dave glanced over his shoulder. "Thanks," he said quietly.

Richard Wallace nodded briefly. When the three had left his office, he picked up a phone and called his deputy. "John, I just finished talking to Powell. They'll have to watch him carefully over there in K Gallery. He could take a dive the first chance he gets."

◇ ◇ ◇

CHAPTER 34

Death row, or K Gallery, as it was referred to at Green Haven, was situated on the third floor of Building No. 2 above the hospital. It was composed of thirteen small cells in which condemned prisoners awaited death in the electric chair. One flight up, directly overhead, was the execution chamber.

Dave's first view of K Gallery came immediately following his meeting with Wallace. The doors of the elevator—a square structure large enough to accommodate an autopsy table—opened, and Dave looked out through a wall of steel bars into a barren reception area. The two guards who had been with him constantly escorted him to a gate in a manlock where yet another guard admitted them.

As they entered, a sober-looking man approached from an office on the far side of the room. He was in his late forties, of medium height, with straight brown hair and rounded features. On his left breast was a small plate with the words "D. Kolder, Watch Commander." He looked at Dave appraisingly as he approached, but made no comment. Instead, he nodded toward the office, which acted as a command post for K Gallery. The guards guided Dave to the room where the only furniture was a chair and a small metal desk bolted to the floor.

On the desk were a telephone, a pad, and a large ledger. The rest of the room was empty except for a bulletin board containing several typewritten notices.

"Sign your name in the logbook." Kolder motioned toward the ledger. As he spoke, the telephone rang and he lifted the receiver. "K Gallery, Kolder speaking. Yes, sir. They just brought him up." He sat down at the desk and began making notes on the pad.

Dave signed the logbook, then stood by the desk waiting for Kolder to complete his call. He glanced at the notices on the bulletin board. One was the memorandum from John Pike advising of the revised procedures concerning K Gallery. It was Dave's first insight into the extent of the security that governed Green Haven's death house:

November 1, 1982

FROM: Office of the Deputy Superintendent

TO: Superintendent, Deputy Superintendents, Officers, Segregation Officers and Officers of Building #2, Third Floor

RE: Area Designated as Pre-Execution Area

1. Every precaution will be taken through direct observation and constant supervision to prevent attempts at suicide.

2. In accordance with the Code of Criminal Procedure, no person may visit a condemned prisoner without an order from the Court, except his counsel, his physician, a priest or minister of his faith, and members of his immediate family. Visits will be supervised at all times.

3. Inmates will be provided with a separate set of clothing for all visits.

4. Cell Inventory: One outfit of wearing apparel, *which will be worn at all times*, viz: 1 pair socks, 1 pair shorts, 1 shirt, 1 pair slippers, 1 pair pants; paper towels, 1 disposable wash cloth, 1 bar soap, writing paper. Inmates will be permitted other articles such as pencil, toothbrush, etc. They may be issued at 7:30 A.M. and will be picked up at 9:30 P.M.

5. Cells will be searched at least once per day.

6. There will be no messages passed between inmates.

7. Inmates will be fed in their cells. The officer in charge will portion and serve the meal. A spoon only will be issued and will be picked up immediately after the meal.

8. Haircuts will be given on the first Tuesday of the month. Shaving will be every day or upon request. The gallery officer will issue a psycholock type safety razor and metal mirror.

9. Inmates will not be allowed to have matches at any time. When an inmate desires to smoke, the officer will provide the light.

10. Hobbies may be approved by the Superintendent. Officers will be held accountable for all hobby equipment such as pencils, etc., and all strings for stringed instruments.

Following the telephone call, Kolder rose and moved toward the door. One of the guards nudged Dave, and they followed the watch commander across the reception area to a room outside the manlock leading to the condemned cells. Here Dave was instructed to undress for a body search. It was personal in the extreme—an examination that he would undergo whenever leaving his cell. After the search, the officer gave him a page of instructions explaining the daily ritual of death row—regulations incorporating much of what Dave had read on the bulletin board—and motioned him to follow the guard.

As the guard took him by the arm and steered him toward the condemned cells, Dave reflected on the absence of conversation that characterized the admission procedure. Other than the brief interview in the superintendent's office, little had been said to him. Communication had been through gestures or by guards physically guiding him. It was a process devoid of feeling. He was, he thought, little more than a commodity being transmitted through the institution on its way to destruction.

The condemned cells, "CC's" as they were called, were located just beyond the manlock to the left of a narrow passageway formed by a blank wall on the right and strands of vertical steel bars on the left. Beyond the wall of bars on the left were the cells, a row of tiny barren cubicles separated from the entrance passageway by a narrow open area six feet wide. The CC's were divided into what were called "tanks," with a row of four CC's to a tank. In each of the small open areas between the passageway and a tank, a guard was posted. It was his duty to maintain continuous observation of the inmates in his tank. In addition to the surveillance from the tank, a narrow catwalk running the length of the gallery above the CC's provided discrete visual checks of each cell. Backing up the visual security were three separate manlocks between the CC's and the elevator. Beyond the elevator was an endless maze of sliding gates in a labyrinth of corridors leading to the perimeter of the prison. It was a foolproof system that discouraged even the most desperate from attempting escape.

Escape was far from Dave's mind. His despair deepened with the sound of each succeeding gate that slammed behind him. The final door on his cell clanging shut seemed a death knell.

After closing the cell door, the guard moved to his observation post in a chair halfway down the tank.

The cell was six feet wide, nine feet long. In one corner was a narrow metal bunk bolted to the wall and floor. A shiny aluminum commode was in the other corner, its brightness anomalous in the stark surroundings. A small sink was built into the top of the commode. Two buttons in the wall provided water. Overhead were a bright light and small vent, both covered by steel mesh built flush against the ceiling. There was nothing else but three bare walls and the strands of steel along the opening in front.

Dave slumped onto the bed, his feet drawn under him, his back against the wall. The impact of the death house settled over him. Until that moment he had been busy with courtroom activity. Now, there was nothing. Only what lay ahead. His feeling of helplessness intensified. It was terrifying. If only he could have it over with. But there was no alternative. This had been meticulously brought out during the orientation program downstairs in the hospital. The rigid restrictions, safety-lock razors, constant surveillance. Until then there had been opportunities for suicide. Now there were none.

A pain began in his lower abdomen. He regarded the small bare commode only a few feet from where the guard was sitting.

As he huddled in the corner, the chilling realization took hold: there was only one way out for him—the agony of a slow wait, and then death in the electric chair.

◊　◊　◊

CHAPTER 35

"But Jeb, you don't understand Sue. She'll never come here. It isn't that she doesn't love me. It's just the way she is. She's pragmatic to a fault. The truth of the matter is, she's written me off."

Dave looked down so that the lawyer would not see his eyes. The two were sitting in a small chamber near the CC's, where meetings between condemned inmates and their visitors took place. The chamber consisted of two small cubicles set side by side, each just large enough for one occupant. The inmate entered through a door leading from the CC's, and the visitor through a door from the visitors' area. Each cubicle consisted of four bare walls and a bolted-down metal stool. The occupants conversed through a bulletproof window, two feet square, set in the wall dividing the two compartments. Sound was transmitted through a speaker in the narrow steel mesh at the bottom of the window. Another larger window on one side of the compartments provided a view of each interior for a guard posted outside. It was much like sitting in a telephone booth and talking with someone in an adjoining booth.

"That's ridiculous," Jeb said. "She needs time to adjust. After all—"

"I've been here a month. By the time she adjusts I'll be dead."

"But Sue says you keep saying in your letters that you don't want her to come; all that nonsense about not wanting to leave her with memories of death row. Now's the time you need her."

"It wouldn't make any difference what I wrote. She won't come. I knew it in Elizabethtown. That last day. I could tell when she said good-bye." Dave paused. "And I certainly don't want Dana here. Look at me. My hair's falling out. I've lost all this weight. It would be a terrible shock for them—particularly Dana. Why put them through it? You think I want them to remember me like this?" His voice broke and his eyes returned to the floor.

Jeb shifted awkwardly and glanced at his watch. "How is everything back there? Are they treating you all right?"

"As well as can be expected. The guards are impersonal. I guess they train them that way. At first it was a living hell. Alone in that cage hour after hour. I say alone, but you're never alone. There's always someone watching to make sure you don't try to commit suicide. You think of it at first, but it's impossible. A few years ago an inmate swallowed part of his bunk—that's right, a piece of steel—trying to kill himself. But they just took him downstairs to the hospital and took it out. One night I figured that if I tied one end of my shirt to the bunk and the other end around my neck, I could turn over a few times until the shirt tightened on my neck. The only problem was I couldn't figure out how to get my shirt off. You see, you have to wear all your clothes. You can't take anything off—"

"Dave—" Jeb passed his hand over his brow. "You won't do anything foolish?"

"Don't worry. Something happens to you in there. Somehow you adjust. You get numb. No matter what happened now, it wouldn't make any difference. It's such a paradox, though. Here I've been sentenced to die—and I'm going to die, everybody knows that—and yet the state automatically delays my execution for six months and then spends enormous sums on security measures to make sure I don't take my own life. But don't worry. I've never killed anyone. I'm not going to start with myself. It'll all be over in a few months—unless you manage to prolong the agony."

"We can't give up, Dave. There's always a chance we can—"

"Jeb, don't drag it out. Even if you were successful on appeal, there are still two *more* bodies. They'd just try me all over again. It's hopeless."

They sat in silence for a moment. Then Jeb said, "I'd better go. I have that meeting up in Albany at three o'clock. Anything I should take up with the superintendent? I was looking at some of those prison menus. They look pretty sparse. Four ounces of this, five ounces of that."

"No. There's nothing you can do." Dave paused. "You know, up until a few months ago I'd had a pretty good life. I try to remember the good times. I'll remember some trip I took with Sue; start right at the beginning and go through every detail. What we said, her expressions. The prison psychologist says it's an escape mechanism." He lowered his eyes. "Sometimes, I think I'm going insane. The bodies in the well . . . Emily Hunter . . . Sam . . . A few days ago I just about convinced myself that Brandon Sheehan was responsible. Sometimes I even wonder about Sue. It drives me crazy. All I do back there is think, and the more I think, the more confused it becomes." He shook his head hopelessly. "God, how I miss Sue and Dana . . . " His voice died off as he struggled for control.

"You have to hang in," Jeb said soothingly. "Sue could be a great help to you now. Why don't you let me tell her you want her to come—"

"No, Jeb. I don't have anything else left, but I still have my pride. I won't let her see me like this."

There was a silence, and then Jeb glanced again at his watch. "If I don't leave, I'll be late for that Albany meeting.

I'll be back Thursday. Anything you want me to do?"

"Some civil liberties lawyers are trying to see me. Tell them I don't want to talk to them. The same for those requests from the media. It's bad enough without all those ghouls wanting to ask me how I feel about dying."

Jeb rose. As he prepared to leave he drew an envelope from his pocket. "I've got a letter for you from Dana. I'll give it to the guard. See you Thursday."

Back in his cell, Dave opened the letter from Dana—a delightful jumble of words in the misshapen style of a child. Imprinted in the upper corner of the notepaper was a picture of two bluebirds perched on a limb. Enclosed with the letter was a snapshot of Sue and Dana sitting on the lawn near the teahouse. Dana was holding Lindsay on her lap.

Dear Daddy,

I love you. I think of you all the time. I want to come to see you but Mommy and Mr. Olsen say it is not a good place for little girls. I thought you would like this paper with the birds. Here is a picture of me Mommy and Lindsay. Lindsay has been sick. Sometimes she gets dizzy. I wish you were here. We could go on the scrambler. Ha, ha. I love you.

Dana
XXXX

Dave read the letter twice and then settled back on his bunk against the wall, focusing on the picture. How wonderful it had been, he thought. Summer afternoons by the teahouse. Little girls, laughter . . . He studied the picture, savoring the memories. It was then that he noticed the eyes. Sue's and Lindsay's—they had the same vacant, unemotional stare.

◇ ◇ ◇

CHAPTER 36

As the weeks wore on, Dave withdrew increasingly into himself. His days were spent daydreaming or writing letters, mostly to Sue and Dana, occasionally to his sister Ida. Sue's mother died in February, her death perhaps hastened by the trauma of having a convicted murderer in the family. Dave slept fitfully, lying awake on his steel cot staring at the ceiling until the early hours. By six he was wide awake, waiting for another grim day of death-house tedium. His only visitor, other than the prison physician and a psychologist who checked on him regularly, was Jeb Olsen. The prison chaplain had come by the first few weeks, but Dave had declined his services. He continued to receive requests for visits from journalists and representatives of groups opposed to capital punishment, but refused to be interviewed.

With the passing months the courts meted out more death sentences, and the CC's began to fill up. By mid-April, two tanks on Green Haven's K Gallery were occupied. The proximity of the cells enabled the four inmates in each tank to converse, although unable to see one another. A camaraderie developed among the three who shared Dave's tank, but he remained aloof. The others pursued their legal remedies avidly and found the silence from the first cell, where the inmate wanted to hasten the process, puzzling.

Dave's physical appearance changed markedly. He continued to lose weight, and his eyes, always deep-set, became dark and sunken. His hair, which had started to thin even before his incarceration, was now coming out in handfuls. Bald patches appeared on the sides and back of his head. The doctor diagnosed it as alopecia, a condition brought on by mental stress.

Ida came to visit one day in mid-April. She had written to him continually since his sentencing. Her letters had been controlled, but it was apparent she was tormented. When she indicated her intention to see him, Dave urged her to remain in Rochester. Nevertheless, a telegram arrived one afternoon informing him that she would be at Green Haven the following day.

While shaving that morning, Dave regarded his reflection in the metal mirror and worried about the impact his appearance would have on his sister. Nervous under the best of circumstances, she was hardly one to cope with a meeting on death row. That afternoon as the guards escorted him from the CC's into the visiting cubicle, he braced himself for what he knew would be a tearful reunion.

It was several minutes before they brought Ida. As she entered, he was surprised at her appearance. He had visited her in Rochester less than two years before, but she had aged considerably. There was a perplexed look on her face as she sat down and peered at him through the window, as though she had been brought to see the wrong person.

Dave hesitated and then greeted her. "Hello, Ida." Although he tried to speak softly, the acoustics of the chamber boomed the words through the steel mesh and startled her.

Her eyes searched his face for a moment and then swelled into a look of horror. "Oh, Dave! Oh, my God! What have they done to you?"

"Easy, Ida," Dave said, soothingly. "Everything's all right."

Ida closed her eyes and her face blanched. For a moment Dave thought she might faint, and he looked toward the guard posted at the window. The guard was watching Ida closely, his expression uncertain. He moved as though he might go to her assistance, but then she opened her eyes.

"Dave. Oh, Dave." She bowed her head, and her shoulders shook as she began to weep.

"Please, Ida," said Dave. "Please, don't. Try to control yourself."

Ida struggled to regain her composure, started to speak, but then burst into tears again. Dave watched, helpless, as the bent form sobbed convulsively. He noticed the white gloves clutched in one of her hands. She had always worn gloves, he thought. Even as a little girl she had been proper. His execution would be devastating for her. Having lived an almost reclusive existence since their mother had died, she would have too much time to dwell on the tragedy. He felt his eyes begin to brim and glanced toward the guard. The man looked away.

"Ida, please . . ."

Finally his sister straightened, dabbing at her eyes with a small lace handkerchief. She took an unsteady breath and exhaled through quivering lips. "I'm sorry, Dave. I wasn't prepared for . . ." She paused uncertainly. "You've changed so." She looked down and shuddered as though she might once again break into tears.

"I know," Dave said. "I was afraid of this."

"I'll be all right. Just give me a minute." She paused, trying to collect herself, and then, stiffening, forced a weak smile. "I'm no help at all, am I?"

"It's all right." He asked about her life in Rochester, hoping she would gain control. As they talked, she improved. She told him how she had followed the trial closely in the press and had stayed in touch with Jeb Olsen. Although Dave sought to direct the conversation away from his ordeal, she insisted on discussing it.

"But what are we going to do?" She looked up at him searchingly. "Mr. Olsen said you won't let him do anything; that you want to get it over with. You can't just—"

"There's nothing Jeb can do. Nothing anyone can do. Even if he were successful with an appeal, which is very unlikely, there are two additional murder indictments outstanding. I'd just have to go through it all over again. You're going to have to come to grips with it, Ida. There's only one way out of this sorry mess."

"But you never killed those people!" She fairly shouted the words. "You could no more kill another human being than I could. How could this possibly have happened?"

Dave shrugged his shoulders. "There's nothing else I can tell you, Ida. I've told you everything in my letters."

As they talked, the emotion he had felt initially began to fade, and the callousness of death row asserted itself.

"The sooner it's over, the better. For you, for me, for everyone. I don't want any cliffhangers."

"But what about Sue and Dana? If not for yourself, what about them?"

Dave watched her twist the handkerchief over and over in her hands as she spoke. He wished he were back in his cell—in the corner against the wall. He could pull his legs up beneath him, sit back, and think of the past. No one bothered him there.

"Mr. Olsen says that Sue hasn't come to see you," Ida continued. "That no one has; that you don't want to see anyone."

Dave shifted on the stool. "There's nothing to be gained by Sue's coming. It would only make things worse. Look what happened today. The sooner she puts me out of her mind, the better. The same for Dana—particularly Dana."

"But she's your wife . . . your little girl."

"They've got their own lives to live. For all practical purposes, I'm dead."

His sister started to respond, but the words choked in her throat. The guard signaled that visiting time was over. Ida bowed her head and began weeping again as he left the compartment.

Back in his cell, he slumped onto his bunk. The meeting had shaken him. The realization that he would probably never see his sister again had brought home the immediacy of his execution. The visit had done little but intensify the anxiety for both of them. It served to reaffirm his feelings about seeing Sue. He could never handle it.

He turned to the wall so that the guard, a quiet black man named Jackson, would not see his face. It was the only vestige of privacy left. Here, with his forehead against the wall, he could blot out the world. There was nothing then. Only the wall. He could make it if they didn't take the wall away. Yes, Sue was right, as always. But he wished he could see her before he died. If only for a few minutes. Just to tell her that he loved her.

He forced the thought from his mind. He had to think about something pleasant. What would it be? Spring! Yes, of course. Outside, it was spring. Robins. Warblers. The tiny wrens that sang so cheerfully. The tulips were probably already showing in the cutting garden. That was it! He would sit in the cutting garden watching Sue with her spring planting. Dana was there kneeling beside her, singing in her funny little voice that he loved so much. Sue would see to it that Dana had a few flowers that she herself could plant and care for. Probably dahlias. They would grow tall and splendid and be most rewarding to a young heart when they burst into color in July. July! Ah, yes, a wonderful month in Tarrytown. He closed his eyes and pressed his head against the cold masonry.

◇   ◇   ◇

CHAPTER 37

"It's only ten steps from the Dancehall, brother, but when you go through that door and see that motherfucker for the first time—that's when your fuckin' blood runs cold. That's when you really shit. Ain't that right, Jackson?"

The speaker was Willie Howell, a black inmate who occupied the third cell in Dave's tank. From articles he had read, Willie had become an expert on all aspects of the execution ritual—information that he freely imparted to those who shared the accommodations on K Gallery.

"And it don't make a fuckin' bit of difference if you're black or white. Whoever goes in that room to die, they's fuckin' gray, man! That's right, yellow gray. Most everyone starts draggin' their feet then, but the guards move you in the chair fast—strap you in real quick. Then the warden asks if you want to say something. Most don't. The fuckin' words get stuck in their throat. Then the man over in the little office on the side there, he pulls the switch and wham! Two thousand volts! You look like you was hit by a fuckin' hurricane. A puff of smoke goes up and it's all over. Man, you done gone out in a fuckin' blaze of glory!"

There was silence as his fellow inmates brooded on the

description. Then the occupant of the cell next to him, an eighteen-year-old white boy, spoke up. "It don't hurt, though. They say you don't feel—"

"Naw, nothin'," Howell continued. "When that fuckin' flame hits you, you're dead, man. They keep frying you for a few minutes so that everybody gets their money's worth. The place stinks up pretty good. Not like Jacksonville, where they got a glass wall you look through. Upstairs here, everybody's in the same room. The witnesses, everybody. They smell that burnt hair and fried shit you're sittin' in, and plenty of 'em gets sick. But it don't bother you none. You're gone, man! It's the getting there that hurts. Those last twelve hours. Waitin' in that fuckin' Dancehall!"

"Why do they call it the Dancehall?" the younger man asked.

"You're always movin' in there. Nobody sits down. Always movin', dancin'. It's like—"

"Hey, Howell, knock it off! Who wants to listen to that shit all day!" It was Jackson, standing the watch over the tank, whose affirmation Howell had sought earlier.

"What you worried about, man?" Howell responded. "You're out there. You ain't got a fuckin' thing to worry about."

Dave, lying on his bunk, turned on his side to face the wall. He put the sound of the exchange from his mind. Like the others on K Gallery, he had become adept at withdrawing from the world.

It was less than two weeks before his scheduled execution. As the time neared, his anxiety increased. Thanks to the other prisoners, he had become acutely aware of execution procedures. At seven o'clock the morning of July 14, immediately following breakfast, he would be taken one flight up to the Dancehall outside the execution chamber. Here he would be issued the execution garments, and his head would be shaved. At five P.M. they would serve him a last meal of his choice. At eight P.M. all visitors would be removed, and the countdown would start in earnest. At ten P.M. the prison chaplain would come, if Dave desired. At two minutes before eleven, the superintendent and another officer would take him into the execution chamber. At eleven P.M. he would die.

He was prepared to die. His concern was that when the time came, he do it with dignity. He had listened for months to the banter of his fellow inmates about those who had walked "the last mile," about their reactions during their final minutes. The stories had caused him to wonder about his own ability to withstand the ordeal. The execution chamber would be filled with journalists and his last moments would be broadcast in lurid detail throughout the world. What if he should become weak and have to be assisted to the chair, as so many others had? One of the doctors had mentioned that those with the least imagination fared best. The comment was of little help. His own imagination was vivid.

As he lay on his bunk, his thoughts were interrupted by the jangling of keys from the passageway; a sound that always brought a stillness to the tank as the inmates waited expectantly to see what was breaking the tedium of death row. Dave turned and saw the duty officer Kolder appear in the passageway. The officer spoke through the bars to Jackson, who then looked toward Dave. It was apparent they were talking about him.

Jackson turned and walked toward his cell, producing a key as he came. "Got some news for you, Powell. Your lawyer's here. You got a reprieve from the Governor—two more weeks!"

The words shot through Dave like an electric current. His initial elation and relief quickly gave way to an awareness that the reprieve would do little to alter things. With mixed emotions he walked into the passageway leading to the visitors' cubicle.

Jeb Olsen was waiting in the compartment, his expression one of restrained delight. "It isn't only that the appellate court has to rule on these trial errors," Jeb said after greeting Dave enthusiastically. "This brings the Governor into the case. Anything can happen. There's always the chance he'll commute your sentence."

Dave shook his head. "They'll never throw out my conviction on technicalities. And how can he commute my sentence? He became governor promising to reinstate the death penalty. It would be political suicide. Not only that, there are seven other guys in there waiting to die, and five of them are black. He'd have every black organization in the country on his back demanding that he do the same for them."

"But we have two more weeks. As long as you're alive, anything can happen."

Dave continued to shake his head. "The entire country is convinced I killed three people. The pro-capital punishment groups have been promised executions. If they don't execute me, who *will* they execute?" Dave looked away, rubbing the back of his neck with his hand.

Jeb sat quietly for a moment. Finally he looked down at a brown manila envelope on his lap. "I'd better go through this with you." Untying the cord on the envelope, he withdrew a sheaf of papers and proceeded to discuss the technical aspects of the reprieve.

Dave listened apathetically. During a pause in the conversation he said, "How are Sue and Dana?"

"As well as can be expected."

There was another pause and Dave said, "Well . . . could you tell me a little more? You know, how's everything going?"

"Everything's all right. Bryan White says the cash flow is improving now that the stock deal with Hunter has been handled—"

"I know all that. I mean the family—Sue and Dana."

"Fine. Everything's fine. I talked to Ida She's sending you some pictures."

"Pictures? Oh, you mean her album—her scrapbook. Yes,

she mentioned it. She's had it since we were kids. It will help pass the time."

"Will they let you have it?"

"Sure. I got those books that Sue sent, remember? They'll take it apart; make sure there's no poison paste on the back of the pictures. They even take the staples out of the magazines."

"Staples? What could you do with a staple?"

"Who knows?" Dave shrugged. "Maybe they figure you could start saving them up. Make a shiv or something. I suppose if you had enough of them you could do *something*. Say, Jeb . . ."

"Yes?"

"Dana's all right, isn't she?"

"Well . . . pretty good."

"What do you mean?"

"It's just that her periods of, you know, unsteadiness. Well, they're more frequent. Dr. Heming's been wonderful, though. Available day and night."

Dave lowered his head. They sat in silence for a moment, and then Dave said, "I don't suppose . . ." He faltered and then continued. "Would it be crazy to ask them to come?"

The lawyer looked at him, surprised.

"I know." Dave said. "After all I've been saying. But I'd like to see them before I go—just for a few seconds."

Jeb busied himself with his envelope, obviously uncomfortable. "Are you sure you'd want that, Dave? It might be tough on everyone at this point."

Dave nodded. "You don't have to say it. I don't even know why I'm thinking like this. It's just that with this thing getting closer—"

"Let me see what I can do," Jeb said, preparing to leave. "Anything else I can do? Any calls you want me to make?"

"No thanks. Don't interfere with the process, though. I want to get it over with."

Jeb nodded grimly. "I'll see you in a few days."

At Dave's next meeting with the lawyer, Dave learned that all appeals had failed, and a new date had been set for his execution. Unless the Governor intervened, Dave would die on Thursday, July 28. There was other news. Jeb had been unable to persuade Sue to come to the prison. She had agreed, however, to let him bring Dana for a last visit. Dave was overjoyed.

He devoted his last few days on death row to putting his affairs in order. His will had been drawn. He went into minute details to keep busy and to avoid thinking of his execution. Despite such diversions, thoughts of the chair were inescapable.

The meeting with Dana took place on a Tuesday, two days before his scheduled execution. To spare the child the ordeal of death row, Richard Wallace had provided a dayroom near his office for a fifteen-minute visit. It was late morning when the watch commander and two guards appeared before Dave's cell to escort him to the superintendent's office. Jeb Olsen was waiting with Wallace at the door of the dayroom when they arrived. Although Jeb was smiling, the strain on his face was evident.

"She's in there waiting for you, Dave." There was a determined cheerfulness in Jeb's manner. "She's in great spirits." He patted Dave on the shoulder. "Remember, she hasn't seen you in a while. It may take her a few minutes to adjust, right?"

The door opened and Dave went in, followed closely by the two guards and the superintendent. Dana was seated in a chair at the far end of the room near a window. She was holding Lindsay on her lap. The sun was streaming through the window behind her as Dave approached, and he could not see her face clearly. When he did, he was startled. She looked older, thinner. The sight struck him with crushing emotion, but he braced himself and forced a smile. "Hello, Dolly," he said cheerfully.

Dana was nonplussed for a moment, regarding him through quizzical eyes. Then her face broke into a radiant smile. "Daddy!" She spread her arms wide. "Daddy, I'm so glad to see you!"

Dave went to her quickly. Bending over, he put his arms around her and buried his face in her hair. She wrapped her arms around his neck and squeezed him tightly. Suddenly, the emotion he had rigidly controlled on death row surfaced. When she tried to draw back, he continued to hold her closely, struggling to compose himself.

"Daddy, you're kind of squeezing me."

Straightening, he took her hands in his and gazed down into her brown eyes. "How are you, darling? It's so good to see you. You're growing up so. Lindsay too. I hardly recognized her."

"Daddy, I almost didn't even know *you*." She looked up at him innocently—more with wonder than with concern. "You're so thin. And your hair . . ."

The superintendent quietly provided a chair and then withdrew to a respectful distance with the others.

Dave placed the chair close to Dana and sat down. The sun poured through the window, which was partially opened at the top. He adjusted the chair so the light was not in his eyes. "How is Lindsay?" he asked, patting the doll lightly on the cheek.

"Oh, she's fine. She doesn't cry any more. She fell out of my bedroom window onto the patio. That's the last time she cried. I guess she's growing up."

Dave laughed, the first time in months. It was inordinately loud, resounding from the bare walls, more a sob than a laugh. He glanced over at the guards waiting nearby, their eyes compassionate but watchful. Reaching over, he lifted Dana from her chair onto his lap. Although she had grown, she was very light. It surprised him. He kissed her again, pressing his face against her cheek, hugging the small warm body and filling his nostrils with the clean smell of her hair. Again he wrestled with his feelings.

They talked, Dave fielding her questions about himself and directing the conversation toward home, school, Puff . . . For a few glorious moments he was able to lose himself in a child's world—a world in which death row was nonexistent.

As they talked, Dave noticed a small bird light on the ledge of a nearby building. He watched it for a second, transfixed by its tiny form.

Dana followed his gaze. "What are you looking at, Daddy?"

"The bird. On that ledge. Maybe it's a yellow warbler, or a goldfinch. See, its wings and tail are dark. Maybe it will sing for us."

They listened for a moment, but the bird made no sound. Soon, with a flutter of its tiny wings, it was gone.

The scheduled meeting time of fifteen minutes had long passed when the superintendent caught Dave's eye. Dave nodded and rose from the chair, still holding Dana. "It's time to go, darling." He kissed her and gently put her back in the chair. "We've had a wonderful time, haven't we?"

"When can I come back?"

"We'll see. Thank Mr. Wallace for being so good to you, won't you."

"I will. You know, I don't think it's so bad here. Everyone's very nice."

"Yes, they are."

"I wish you'd come home soon, Daddy. I miss you so much. When I go to bed I always pretend that you're coming to tuck me in like you used to."

Bending over, he kissed her a final time, anguished; his throat tight.

"Oh, Daddy, before you go. I almost forgot to ask you, I've been wondering about something."

"What's that?"

"Well, when you come home, how will we go on our bird

walks? I can't walk very well any more . . ." She paused, looking up at him inquiringly. "What's the matter?"

"Nothing. It's just the sun." He hesitated, uncertain, then said, "Don't worry. The next time I see you we'll have our bird walk. I promise. I have to go now. Bye-bye, darling."

He had turned to leave when she called after him. "Daddy, you forgot something." There was mild reproof in her voice.

"What's that?" he said turning.

"Lindsay. You forgot to kiss Lindsay good-bye." She held the doll out to him.

"How could I have forgotten?" There was a catch in his voice. He stooped and kissed the doll lightly on the cheek. "Good-bye, Lindsay."

Suddenly, from somewhere beyond the window, came the long, sustained, trilling notes of a songbird. The clear sweet melody rippled along the summer air, filling the room with its cheerful sound.

"Oh, listen, Daddy. It's the yellow bird. He's singing for us."

◊ ◊ ◊

CHAPTER 38

"You still got thirty hours, man. Anything can happen. Supreme Court. A stay from the Governor—only don't count on that fucker. He'll burn every motherfucker in the tank if he can."

It was late afternoon, the day before Dave's scheduled execution. Willie Howell was delivering a monologue from down the row. Dave was not listening. He was sitting on the edge of his bunk reading a codicil to his will that concerned a small trust he had set up for one of the staff at his house. Suddenly, the jangling of keys announced the arrival of the watch commander. Kolder was carrying what appeared to be a large ledger.

"Got some pictures here for you, Powell." He handed the volume through the bars to Jackson, who in turn carried it to Dave's cell. It was Ida's scrapbook.

"Thanks." Dave reached through the bars to take the album from the guard. "I was beginning to wonder if it would get here on time." He opened the book and flipped through the contents. Much of the material was loose, having been separated from the pages during the security check. After a cursory look, he closed the book and placed it on the end of his bunk. It would give him something to look forward to after dinner.

His meal that evening consisted of six ounces of pea soup, one cracker, eight ounces of corned beef hash, four ounces of canned plums, one slice of bread, and six ounces of cocoa. He saved the cocoa to drink while going through the scrapbook.

After dinner, he balanced the cocoa on the edge of his bunk and assumed his usual position with his back against the wall, knees drawn up. Resting the album against his thighs, he sipped the cocoa as he leafed through the pages. The contents, a combination of Ida's and their mother's efforts, were a comprehensive chronicle of the Powell family. There were pictures of Dave and Ida hugging each other as toddlers, their parents at the family house on Chestnut Street, Ida in the uniform of the girls' school she had attended. There were photos of birthday celebrations and graduations, and clippings of Dave's athletic accomplishments. Dave was especially interested in the newspaper clippings of his engagement to Sue and of their wedding.

He turned the pages slowly, meticulously examining each entry, savoring the memories the pictures evoked. How wonderful it had been; a dream world, now as he looked back. As he continued through the album, a strange sense of well-being came over him—a momentary euphoria at which he marveled, under the circumstances. He thought of Ida and the pains she had taken to preserve the memorabilia. He would write to her the next day and tell her how much the album had helped. But tomorrow was the last day. Would they permit him to write in the Dancehall? He must ask Kolder. The thought of going upstairs sent a shiver through him. He put the thought from his mind as he took a sip of cocoa. It was cool but tasted good.

It was well past nine, and he was going through the album for the second time when it happened—a revelation so staggering that at first it was beyond his comprehension. It came in the form of an old clipping from the society page of a New York newspaper—a picture of Sue and her parents among a number of notables attending a sailing regatta in Newport. He noted the date of the clipping—July 1, 1962. Two days before Ann Conway had been killed. Had he been there with Sue instead of at Lake Placid, the nightmare would never have happened.

It was a nondescript picture with the aging, yellowish hue characteristic of old photographs. Dave would have accorded it only moderate interest had it not been for the tiniest of objects. Though only a speck on Sue's neck, barely discernible against the gray background, it leaped from the page—a brilliant gold memory. It burst in his brain with the force of an electrical current, charring the romantic memories of moments before.

◊   ◊   ◊

CHAPTER 39

State of New York
Department of Correctional Services
Green Haven Correctional Facility
Stormville, New York 12582

July 21, 1983

Mr. Thomas L. Lewis
24 Locust Lane
Hawthorne, New York

Dear Sir:

In accordance with Section 507 of the Code of Criminal Procedure, you are hereby invited to be present as a witness at the execution by electricity of:

DAVID R. POWELL GHP #129760

which will occur at this prison on Thursday, July 28.
The hour of 11:00 P.M. has been designated for said

execution, and you will be at my office not later than 10:00
P.M. It is requested that you treat this communication as
confidential and inform me immediately whether or not you
will be present.

Under no circumstances is this invitation transferable.
Please bring this letter with you.

Very truly yours,
Richard J. Wallace
Superintendent

RJW:dp

Richard Wallace glanced at the letter John Pike had handed
to him. "So?" he asked, looking up at the deputy, who was
standing in front of his desk.

"Read the note on top," Pike said.

The superintendent looked back at the letter. In the top left
corner was typed a short message that he had not noticed. It
apparently was from the recipient of the invitation. It read:

Why I received this disgusting thing I do not know. How you
could think I would want to attend such a vile exhibition is
quite beyond me. Why don't you take this poor soul to
Yankee Stadium or put your despicable show on television?

T. L. Lewis

After reading the note Wallace looked up again. "What
happened?"

The deputy shrugged his shoulders as he sat down. "The
invitation went to the wrong Thomas Lewis. There are two of
them in the same town. There was a mix-up."

"Well, you didn't have any trouble getting another witness,
did you?"

"Hell, no. They're standing in line for the thing. But this
guy Lewis contacted the media. Apparently he thought we
sent them out at random. Anyway, a reporter called me about
it, so I thought I should mention it."

"Let's hope that's the only thing that goes wrong." Wallace flipped the invitation back to his assistant and leaned forward, resting his elbows on the desk, his face in his hands. The pressure of the execution had been mounting all week from every quarter. It was beginning to tell. He had been uncharacteristically abrupt with his staff and had smoked three packs of cigarettes that day. He lifted his head from his hands and glanced at his watch. It was almost midnight. Less than twenty-four hours, he thought. He rubbed his eyes and glanced up at Pike. "I've got to get out of here and get some sleep. How are things outside?"

"The demonstrations?" The deputy rolled his eyes. "Under control. So far, anyway. Some of them got past the barricade this afternoon and did a job on the corner of the north wall with some spray paint. That's about it. Tomorrow will be rough, though. Should be a lot of people out there. We're supposed to get another contingent of troopers in the morning. Say, what's this about expanding the press coverage? We've only got four benches in the execution chamber."

"We got a directive from Albany this afternoon. The Governor's getting heavy pressure from the media. If you squeeze them in, you should be able to get six people in each row."

"But we already have nineteen authorized people who have to come. The law is very explicit on who attends."

"That doesn't provide for the media." Wallace lighted another cigarette. "Look, John, let's face it. No matter how many they authorize, we have to squeeze them in. We've got no choice. Bring in more seats. You have over ten feet between the chair and the first row."

"But we can't put them right on top of the chair. They'd be too close. The inmate's sputum would spray all over them."

"You gotta get 'em in some way." Wallace took a deep drag on his cigarette and expelled a puff of smoke. "How's Powell holding up?"

"He was fine until a couple of hours ago. They say he's become very distraught. Wants to see his lawyer. That's the way it happens. They suddenly realize there's no way out; that it's really going to happen."

"Any other problems—in operations, that is?"

"No. Just the demonstrations in the mess hall. Everything seems okay. The place is really charged up, though."

"It'll be worse tomorrow. How about the dry run?"

"We're all set," the duputy replied. "Everyone will be assembled in the execution chamber at three P.M. Franklin, the executioner, got here this afternoon and checked out the equipment."

"Earl Franklin? I haven't seen him in over fifteen years. I hope to hell he still knows what he's doing. He must be getting a little old, isn't he?"

"According to the commissioner's office he's well qualified."

"Oh, he's qualified, all right," said the superintendent. "I only hope he isn't out of practice. Believe me, things can go wrong, even with him. I was with him at Sing Sing in the late fifties when he executed a man and a woman, both the same night. It was terrible!" He leaned forward and extinguished his cigarette in the ashtray. "The woman was hysterical. Had to be carried in. That wasn't bad enough. She'd gotten so thin the electrode fell off her leg—started sparking like a Roman candle. We had to stop the thing right in the middle and start over. The witnesses fairly ran out of the place when it was over."

John Pike squirmed in his chair. "He handled the execution down in Jacksonville a few months ago. Apparently everything went properly."

"A lot depends on Powell. If he comes unglued, it's tougher on everyone. You say he's beginning to fall apart? I'm surprised. He struck me as someone who could handle it."

"I don't know that he's falling apart. They just said he suddenly became very upset. Insisted he had to talk to his lawyer."

"Well, he can talk to him, but nothing will save him now. C'mon, let's get out of here. Tomorrow's going to be rough on everyone."

◇　◇　◇

PART
X

The Dancehall
July 1983

CHAPTER 40

"I'd eat it if I was you," Jackson said. "Food settles you down, man. Ask Doc Paget. He's seen lots of 'em go. He says the ones that eat do best."

Dave took the cardboard container of breakfast—four ounces of grapefruit juice, oatmeal, two slices of toast, one pat of margarine, and six ounces of black coffee that the guard handed into the cell. Earlier he had told the guard to give his food to the other inmates, but Jackson insisted he take it. The smell of the coffee nauseated him. He put the container on the edge of the bunk and ignored it. After pacing back and forth a few times he sat down, exhausted. He had been awake all night.

"Still no word from Olsen?" he asked.

Jackson, who was now stationed in a chair directly in front of Dave's cell, shook his head. "It's only seven, man. Hell, ain't no one out there in the world up yet."

"They should have contacted him last night," Dave said. "In case you've forgotten, I'm leaving soon."

"I keep telling you, Powell. Ain't no way he gets in here 'fore ten. Besides, you say he's down in Washington. Even if they reached him last night, it's gonna take him time to get back."

Dave moved back on the bunk so that he was resting against the wall. Within seconds he moved forward, sitting on the edge. "My God," he murmured.

"What's that?" the guard asked.

Dave shook his head but said nothing. Leaning forward, he buried his face in his palms. After a few seconds he straightened. "What if they can't find him?" He asked the question more of himself than of the guard. He knew Jeb was trying to contact members of the Supreme Court in a last desperate attempt to obtain a stay of execution.

"How 'bout we play a few hands of gin?" Jackson said. "Take your mind off things."

"No, no thanks."

"How 'bout some checkers?"

Dave did not answer. He sat staring vacantly at the guard, his mind once again on the photograph.

"You hear me, Powell? How 'bout some checkers?"

Dave focused on Jackson as though he had just noticed him. "What's that?"

"Checkers, man. Let's play checkers. Kolder says you gotta do things today."

Dave regarded him quietly, then said, "Look, it's my last day, right? You want to do me a favor?"

"You name it, man. Anything but the keys."

"How about moving that ass of yours down the tank a ways. Today is going to be tough enough without that ugly face staring at me."

"Yaw-haw!" Howell guffawed from his cell. "You tell 'em, Dave. You're bulletproof now, baby!"

"Why you gotta talk like that?" Jackson said, offended. "You know I gotta sit here. Kolder comes in and I'm not here, I'm in trouble, man."

"I know, I know," said Dave with a sigh. "Just don't bug me, will you?" He stood abruptly and started pacing once again between his bunk and the commode.

From the passageway came the noise of the keys and the

metallic clanging of the gate, followed by the sound of several feet. The moment he heard it, Dave knew they were coming for him. It was the first step in the long, agonizing trip to the execution chamber. But they were early. Kolder had said they would not come until seven-thirty—until after breakfast. He was being cheated of twenty minutes. A vague feeling of anger came over him. It left quickly. There was room for only one emotion. *Fear*. It crowded all other thoughts from his mind. He wished he could have gone directly from the CC's to the chair. Thoughts of the final hours in the Dancehall were terrifying.

His eyes were trained on the passageway when Kolder and two guards whom he had not seen before strode into view. The guards were large men in gray and black uniforms that included caps. The sight of the strange official-looking group accentuated his fear.

Jackson, with uncharacteristic alacrity, hurried to the gate to admit them. Kolder walked in toward Dave's cell while the two guards waited at the gate.

"It's time to go upstairs," Kolder said impassively.

"Any word from my lawyer?" Dave asked as Jackson unlocked the cell.

Kolder shook his head. "Nothing yet. The superintendent's office will let us know when they hear."

"May I take this with me?" Dave reached for the album.

"Leave it there," Kolder said. "We'll bring it up later."

"Let me take this picture, will you?" Dave retrieved the newspaper clipping of Sue from the front of the album. "It's my wife."

Kolder hesitated. He took the photograph and inspected it briefly. "We'll bring it up with the album."

"But . . . You won't lose it?" Dave implored. "It's very important. I have to give it to my lawyer."

"Don't worry." Kolder guided him by the arm toward the door.

As they filed out, eyes from the other cells followed Dave

closely, conveying a compassion known only to those who have shared a wait for death. It had not occurred to him that he would regret leaving those in the tank, but now he felt very much alone.

At the gate to the passageway he paused and looked back. "So long," he said, simply.

There was an immediate chorus of response as if the men in the cells were relieved to have the silence broken. "So long!" "Bye, Dave." As he moved with the death squad down the passageway, Howell called after him, his words echoing despairingly from the tank. "See you there, man!"

The guards took him from the passageway through another manlock to a windowless stairwell that twisted through dark brick walls to the roof. It was a dreary last mile. There was an almost medieval character about the area, unrelieved by the solitary bulb that cast a shadowy glow halfway up the stairs. Their footsteps reverberated off the walls as they mounted the stone steps. A closed steel door confronted them at the crest of the stairwell. Kolder produced a large brass key and inserted it in the lock. Opening the door, he motioned the others to enter.

Inside was a bright, empty corridor that contrasted with the somber stairwell. It was fifty feet long by fifteen feet wide, with a high ceiling. Bare, sand-colored walls and a highly polished terrazzo floor gave it a clinical look. On the right, running the length of the corridor, were several long windows extending from midway up the wall almost to the ceiling. Through the windows, the sky was visible.

The clean, almost antiseptic, appearance of the area was accentuated by a lingering odor of fresh paint. Apparently things had been spruced up for the event, Dave thought. As he stepped through the door, his nostrils detected something else—a faint, acrid smell of burning rubber.

Inside the door was the visitors' cubicle, similar to the one in the CC's, in which the condemned inmate received his last callers. As they walked, their feet echoed loudly down the corridor. Dave thought about the electric chair. It had to be close by. He could almost feel its presence.

"Where is it?" he asked suddenly.

"Where's what?" said the guard on his right.

Dave did not answer.

Near the end of the corridor they drew abreast of a closed door in the left wall. Kolder, walking a few feet ahead, motioned with his head. "It's in there. Just beyond the door."

Dave nodded. "I thought so. I can smell it." His voice was hoarse. He cleared his throat nervously.

They traveled a few more feet, made a sharp left turn around a corner, and came to an abrupt halt. Before them was a small, barren room with bars across the front, facing a blank wall. It was the last cell—the Dancehall.

Perhaps it was the closeness of the electric chair, or the faint odor of burning rubber lingering in his nostrils, but with the sight of the small cell a wave of nausea came over Dave. Taking a few deep breaths, he was able to fight off the feeling. He waited in front of the bars, looking into the cell as Kolder opened the gate.

It was a small enclosure similar to the CC's, with one difference. The Dancehall had two doors, one in the right front corner and one on the left. The extra door afforded another access for the death squad should they encounter resistance.

Kolder opened the door on the right. "Strip," he said matter-of-factly. Dave removed his clothes, and Kolder perfomed a body search.

"Okay, put those on." He pointed to some clothes folded on a metal bunk in the cell.

Dave entered and began dressing in the execution garments. He noticed the basted slits in the shirt and trousers that provided access for the electrode and stethoscope. He tried to relax his muscles to avoid shivering.

One of the guards, a powerfully built, light-haired man, took a position in a chair against the wall in front of the cell.

As Kolder locked the door, he motioned with his head toward the guard. "Barrows, here, will be with you from now on. Let him know if you want to see the chaplain." Kolder turned to leave. "Soon as we hear anything about your lawyer we'll let you know."

"You won't forget the photograph, will you?" said Dave.

"We'll get it to you, don't worry," Kolder said, walking away.

As sounds of the footsteps died in the corridor, Dave sat down on the metal cot. From where he sat he was able to see a circular institutional clock on the wall beyond the corner. The time was seven-twenty. From here he also was able to see through the top portion of the last few windows in the corridor. An expanse of bright blue sky was visible. He stared at it for several seconds, marveling at its beauty, and then leaned back against the wall.

His thoughts turned again to the newspaper clipping that had occupied his mind almost continuously since the previous night. Perhaps it had been his imagination. An illusion. Another product of K Gallery, where one's mind could conceive weird images.

"They won't forget the picture, will they?" he asked the guard.

"No, don't worry. Let me know if you want anything. Any hobby material—anything like that?"

"Just the picture. The picture is all I want."

The rest of the morning Dave spent alternately sitting on the bunk staring at the sky, or pacing in the cell. Occasionally he exchanged words with the guard, who appeared ready to talk, to listen, or to do whatever he could to help alleviate Dave's anguish. It was almost noontime when the sound of heels in the corridor brought him to his feet. Within a few seconds Kolder rounded the corner, carrying a lunch tray. Dave was relieved to see the album under his arm.

"Did you bring the photograph that—"

"It's inside the book." Kolder handed the tray and the

album through the bars. "Your lawyer will be here later. He's catching a plane out of Washington early this afternoon." As he turned to leave, he spoke to the guard. "See if you can get him to eat that lunch."

The news heightened Dave's anxiety. It would be late afternoon before Jeb would get to the prison. He placed the lunch tray on the bunk and sat down, balancing the album on his knees. Opening it, he found the clipping and again scrutinized the tiny object on Sue's neck. It was smaller than it had seemed before. Less obvious. Had he jumped to a false conclusion? But an enlargement would show for sure. He had to talk to Jeb. Shifting on his bunk, he looked at the clock. Almost twelve. He watched the long sweeping second hand make a complete revolution. One minute less.

"Powell, why don't you try some of that lunch?"

Dave sat staring at the photograph, oblivious to the comment.

"Powell," the guard repeated. "Here's your spoon. Try to eat something. It'll help."

Dave returned the clipping to the album and took the spoon the guard handed through the bars. Lunch was from the regular prison menu: ravioli, four carrot sticks, one piece of gingerbread with icing, and five ounces of milk. He started to eat the ravioli with the spoon, forcing the food down.

"You're left-handed?" Barrows asked, resuming his chair. "You were writing with your right hand."

"Yes, I know," said Dave quietly. "Sometimes I just eat with my left hand."

He took a few more spoonfuls of the ravioli and set the tray aside. Picking up a stubby pencil supplied to him with writing paper earlier, he returned to a letter that he was writing to Ida. It had been his intention to write four last letters. One each to Ida, Jeb Olsen, Dana, and the final one to Sue. He found it difficult to concentrate. Although he had started the letter to Ida over an hour before, he had written less than a page. With renewed effort he was able to finish the letter and to start the one to Jeb. As the afternoon wore on his anxiety increased, and he finally abandoned the chore. He would write to Dana and Sue later, after dinner. It would keep his mind occupied the last few hours.

He was sitting, his face in his hands, when Barrows spoke to him. "You sure you don't want the chaplain? It might help."

"No. I'm this close," Dave said wryly, "I might as well wait and talk directly to God."

It was almost four o'clock when Jeb Olsen arrived. He was waiting in the visitors' compartment at the end of the corridor when Dave entered. His drawn face reflected failure: the Supreme Court had denied his request for a writ of certiorari, a legal document that would have enjoined the state from carrying out the sentence pending a review of the lower court's handling of the case.

"Our only hope is the Governor," Jeb said. "I'm going to call Albany as soon as I leave. Cousins is up there trying to arrange an interview. If we can—"

"Forget the Governor," said Dave, cutting him short. "He's been telling the media for the past two weeks that he won't intercede. Listen, I discovered something last night that—"

"There's always a chance. We have to try. Maybe he's—"

"Jeb, for God's sake, *listen* to me, will you? We don't have much time. I have something to show you. I found it in the album Ida sent down. Look at this." He raised the clipping and flattened it against the glass partition.

Jeb put on glasses. "What about it?" he asked, studying the picture.

"Look at the date."

"I see it, July 1, 1962,"

"Now look at Sue—carefully. What do you see? Around her neck?"

"I don't see anything." Jeb adjusted his glasses while scrutinizing the clipping.

"Look closely. Don't you see it? On her neck—on the chain. *It's my medallion!*"

"Medallion?" Jeb continued to study the picture. "I see something around her neck. Whatever it is, it's partly covered by the dress."

"It's my medallion!" Dave repeated, his voice rising. "You can see the top of it."

Jeb looked at the photograph for several more seconds and then removed his glasses, an uncomfortable expression on his face. "Dave, I know what you must be going through—"

"You don't believe it's the medallion, do you?"

The lawyer shifted uneasily on the stool. Replacing his glasses he gazed once again at the clipping. "It could be anything. You can't see what it is. It's only the top of a little speck."

"You've got to believe me. I'm certain it's my medallion. You've got to get the picture enlarged right away." His voice was low, desperate. "Then we'll know for sure. If it *is* the medallion, then Sue had it with her in Newport. Don't you see? It couldn't be the one found in Ann Conway's hand."

"But it could be *anything*—a locket, a brooch of some kind. You've been under a severe strain. Why don't you—"

"I've got to see her!"

"What?"

"Sue! You've got to bring her here. I have to talk to her."

Jeb looked at him, bewildered. "But you've both agreed—"

"I know. I don't care. I've changed my mind. I have to see her. You have to get her to come *right away*."

Jeb bowed his head. Finally, he looked up. "There's nothing I can do. She'll never come. I'd rather tell you straight out than have you spending your last few hours waiting for her."

"You can try. You could go to see her. It's only thirty miles." He paused. "Please, Jeb. It's the last thing I'll ask."

They sat in silence for a moment. Finally Jeb said, "Of course. If that's what you want."

"And Jeb, promise before you do anything you'll have that picture enlarged. I know what you think, but it won't take long and then we'll know for sure."

"All right. Whatever you say. Give the clipping to the guard." He looked at his watch. "Traffic's tied up with all the demonstrators. I'd better get going. I'll try to be back before seven." He rose to go, hesitated, and turned back to Dave, his eyes filled with compassion. "She won't come. You know that."

Dave didn't answer. After the lawyer left, he stayed for a moment, head down, eyes closed. Was he going mad? Was it the strain, as Jeb had suggested, that caused his eyes to deceive him, his mind to play tricks? He looked again at the photograph before handing it over to the guard. It *was* the medallion. The shape, the pointed edges. Well, you couldn't really see the shape or the edges. When it was enlarged, it would all come out, though. He was certain. But how did Sue get it? He had to see her. He had to know before he died.

◊ ◊ ◊

CHAPTER 41

Richard Wallace paused outside the door to the Green Haven execution chamber. "What's that stretcher doing there?" He pointed to a folded green ambulance cot propped against the wall in the hallway.

"I had them bring it up from the hospital," John Pike said. "Kolder claims that during one of his last executions at Sing Sing a witness fainted."

"Well, get it out of sight," said the superintendent. "Everyone has to come in this way. They'll think we're using it to carry out the inmate."

He rapped sharply on the door. Almost instantly it was opened a crack by a guard who scrutinized them from inside.

"Yes, sir." The man opened the door wide so they could enter.

As he stepped across the threshold, Wallace experienced the uneasiness he always felt when he came to the execution chamber. His were not unusual feelings. The place could evoke queasiness in the strongest stomach. The room was an exact replica of the one used for six decades at Sing Sing prison to execute 576 people. Almost everything in the chamber had been moved there from Sing Sing—not only the electric chair but the benches for witnesses, the electric panel, and virtually everything else moveable.

The chamber was thirty feet long and twenty feet wide, with a ten-foot ceiling. The walls were the same beige as those next door in the Dancehall but seemed white because of six long illuminating panels affixed to the ceiling. The panels lit the room to an extraordinary brightness; one could fairly feel the heat radiating from overhead.

Immediately to the left of the entrance were four church pews, each ten feet long. Made of mahogany, they had a dark, baroque look. Next to the pews were an additional two rows of folding chairs that had been hastily assembled. To the right of the door, attached to the wall, was a small metal enclosure that looked like a breadbox. Inside was a telephone providing direct communication with the Governor's office.

In the left wall was a one-way glass window, behind which was the control room where the executioner performed his duties. On the opposite wall, a few feet from the far corner, was a closed door. Through there the condemned prisoner would be brought from the Dancehall. Above this door in large block letters appeared one word: SILENCE. There was nothing else in the chamber except, of course, the object that dominated all else—the electric chair.

It was a menacing apparatus located in the front center of the room, only twelve feet from the first row of church pews. Here, it was fastened securely to the hard terrazzo floor with heavy angle pieces, lag screws, and expansion shields. Larger than one would have expected, its high sloping back rose almost five feet from the floor. Squarely built, with broad arms and legs, it seemed to have grown from the stone floor and to have a durability that would keep it there long after the wood and plaster around it had turned to dust. Made in 1914 from kiln-dried red oak, the wood had taken on a black luster that added to the overall grisliness of the chair.

Its back consisted of four broad horizontal slats. A headrest, made of black corrugated rubber matting, was attached to the top three slats. The seat was planklike and had the same black rubber matting. Three legs supported the chair, but whereas the two in the rear were sturdy and conventional, the one in front consisted of a wide base that twisted down into a frame where the condemned prisoner's legs were strapped. A six-foot-square rubber matting covered the floor at the base of the chair.

From the chair dangled eight two-inch-wide leather straps. At the right rear of the chair two cables protruded from the floor. One went to a head electrode consisting of a copper mesh wire edged with leather and a fine sponge. These were attached to a leather helmet by a terminal post extending on the outside and fastened on top by a large wing nut. The helmet extended to within two inches of the base of the skull and was fastened to the head by a strap around the chin. A leather mask with holes for the nose and mouth completed the headdress.

The other cable went to a leg electrode made of copper mesh wire three inches wide by six inches long, edged with leather and sponge and attached to a terminal post. It covered the back of the right leg between the ankle joint and the calf and was fastened by the leg strap. Directly overhead, built into the ceiling like an exhaust for a large barbecue, was a ventilating system.

There were about a dozen men in the room when Richard Wallace entered. "Hello, Earl," he said, singling out an older man standing near the electric chair.

Earl Franklin took the outstretched hand and offered a restrained greeting that befitted the occasion. He was a thin man of average height, somewhere in his early sixties, with stringy gray hair that hung down on his forehead. Dark brown eyes were set deep in his skull, and his face was heavily lined. He was wearing a gray suit that looked as though it had had considerable wear. His manner was exceedingly sober. Even if he hadn't known, Wallace would have immediately picked him out as the executioner.

"Is everything in order, Earl?" Wallace asked.

"I was about to make a final check of the current to the chair with these bulbs." He motioned toward a large board that lay across the arms of the electric chair. The board contained twenty one-hundred-watt bulbs.

Wallace nodded. "Go ahead."

"Make sure everyone stands clear of the chair." The executioner strode to the door. "I'll tap on the window before I throw the switch."

The executioner's control room was the only significant difference between the Green Haven execution chamber and the one at Sing Sing. At Sing Sing the executioner remained in the same room behind a partition. Green Haven's control room was a small area, not much larger than a closet, containing a high, narrow electrical panel that resembled the dashboard of a vintage airplane. At eye level were a voltage meter and an amperage meter. Beneath each was a small knob used to regulate the number of volts and amps transmitted to the chair. Two-thirds of the way down the panel, in the center, was a stout black lever, eighteen inches long. This was the main switch that delivered the current to the condemned inmate. The panel was situated so that the executioner could stand before it and, by merely shifting his eyes to the right, view the electric chair through the one-way glass. In a corner, accentuating the combustibility of the control room, was a large fire extinguisher.

A few moments after Franklin had left the execution chamber a tap was heard at the window. Then a burst of brilliant light filled the room. Wallace watched, transfixed by the knowledge that the next time the switch was thrown, he would be watching David Powell die.

With the completion of the two-minute cycle, the superintendent turned to John Pike, who stood in front of the chair. "When Earl comes back, run through the procedures."

Within a few minutes, the executioner returned. Pike unfolded a single typewritten page and delivered a final review of the execution procedures. "Gentlemen, each witness will be thoroughly frisked before entering the execution chamber. A matron has been assigned to frisk the four women who will be in attendance. You will be particularly alert for concealed miniature cameras and recording devices. All witnesses must be seated no later than ten-forty. When the witnesses are in place, the superintendent will instruct them regarding their conduct. Should any of them become sick or hysterical, they will be removed immediately by the officers at the door. At two minutes before eleven, the superintendent and captain will proceed to the Dancehall and escort the inmate to the execution chamber. In the event there is physical resistance, the officers assigned to the death house will provide support. Should this become necessary, every effort will be made to avoid injuring the inmate."

"What's the condition of the inmate now?" Earl Franklin asked.

"Nervous," John answered. "But they don't think we'll have any problems with him."

The deputy paused for further questions. There being none, he continued. "The two sergeants will receive the inmate and strap him in the chair immediately. Each will strap in an arm and leg. Captain Morse will handle the two body straps and apply the headpiece. The superintendent will then give the signal to Mr. Franklin, who will proceed with the execution. Is that understood?"

"Just one point," Earl Franklin said. "Richard, it may be better if you give the signal to one of the physicians. If the doctor watches the inmate's chest and gives me the sign when the prisoner is exhaling, it will avoid that gurgling sound as the air is driven from his lungs. It makes quite a noise, and it's a little hard on the witnesses."

Wallace nodded his approval.

"Now, then," Pike continued, "after the current has been applied, the inmate will be examined by Dr. Paget, who will either pronounce him dead or order another application of current. Then the witnesses will be escorted from the execution chamber. When they're all out the body will be removed from the chair and placed on the autopsy table. The inmate has donated his eyes to the eye bank, so there will be a representative from that agency present at the autopsy. After the autopsy, the body will be placed in the facility morgue."

The duputy looked about the room as he folded his paper. "I believe that concludes things, gentlemen. Are there any questions?"

There were none. Sounds of shuffling feet on the stone floor filled the room as the group disbanded. As Wallace was leaving he paused and gave a final look back at the chair. He thought again of the things that could go wrong. There was a lot more to the process than they realized up in Albany. It wasn't simply a matter of bringing an inmate in, sitting him down, and pulling a switch. The entire prison was on edge. Emotions under such condit'ons were unpredictable—for both guards and inmates. Not only that, they were relying on old equipment. If the slightest thing went wrong, the results could be devastating.

◊   ◊   ◊

PART
XI

Tarrytown, New York
July 1983

CHAPTER 42

"Just what are you trying to prove, Mr. Olsen?" Emily Hunter's voice was strident. She flipped a photograph across the desk to where Jeb was sitting, "She's wearing a necklace. So what?"

They were in the handsome Edwardian library of the Powell estate, where Jeb had rushed with enlargements of the newspaper clipping. The pictures—large, glossy photographs—showed the medallion on Sue's neck in detail. It was identical to the one offered in evidence at the trial.

"What's the purpose of all this, anyway?" Emily asked. She had positioned herself at the desk with Jeb so that he had to speak over her shoulder to talk to Sue, who was sitting in front of three large windows on the far side of the room. It was apparent that whatever Sue Powell had to say, Emily Hunter intended to say for her.

Sue, unlike Emily, had said nothing when she saw the photographs, but from her manner Jeb sensed that they had made an impact. For a moment he thought he detected a frightened look in her cool, dark eyes.

"Sue, we have very little time," he said. "I'm sure you understand the significance of this."

"What significance?" Emily interjected. "I don't see any significance."

Jeb glanced at Emily briefly, then returned his attention to Sue. "Dave was convicted largely on the basis of that medallion. This clipping shows you wearing it two days before it ended up in that girl's hand. It raises all kinds of questions."

"Nonsense," Emily said. "I might have expected something like this. There could be dozens of medals like it. She could be wearing—"

"I beg your pardon, Mrs. Hunter," said Jeb, his voice rising, "but there aren't dozens of medals like it. The prosecution clearly established that." Lowering his voice, he spoke again to Sue. "It *is* the same medallion, isn't it?"

"You're trying to make something out of nothing," Emily snapped. "All this will do is give the press something else to write about. But maybe that's what you want. Your penchant for publicity is well known in legal circles."

The comment was too much for Jeb's frayed nerves. "For God's sake, have you no sense of morality? Unless I can show that there's a substantive flaw in the evidence, David Powell will die in less than three hours!"

Standing abruptly, he walked around the desk to where Sue was sitting, determined to talk to her without Emily's inhibiting influence. He drew a small straight-backed chair in front of the settee on which Sue was sitting. "Sue," he said softly, "listen to me, please."

As he spoke, he took her hand. Gently, but decisively, she withdrew it. After an awkward hesitation, he continued. "I've arranged a meeting with one of the Governor's aides. I'm going to show him these photographs and try to convince him the Governor should grant a reprieve until this is properly evaluated. They're going to be wary of any last-minute attempt to delay the execution. They won't do a thing unless we have the most compelling reasons for them to intervene. When this clipping comes to the attention of the authorities, they're going to be asking you lots of questions. They won't stop until they have the answers. Whatever you know, tell me while there's still time to save Dave."

"Will you stop badgering her?" Emily demanded. "I think you should leave, Mr. Olsen!"

"It's all right, Emily." There was resignation in Sue's voice. She rose from the settee and quietly looked out the window. Finally she said, "Emily, perhaps Mr. Olsen and I should talk for a moment."

"What?" said Emily, surprised. "Don't talk to him. Wait until tomorrow. I'll have my lawyers—"

"Please, Emily. I want to talk to him. Alone," Sue added firmly.

Emily paused, her hard eyes shifting from Sue to Jeb and then back to Sue. "Very well." She rose from the desk and walked stiffly toward the door, where she stopped. "I don't like this one damn bit, Sue. I don't know what you intend to say to him, but you're making a mistake. He's desperate. He'll use you any way he can."

Sue returned her attention to the window until Emily had departed. Then with a sigh, as though relieved that her friend had left, she came back to the settee, sitting down in a way that suggested exhaustion. "It's been very difficult, Jeb. These past months . . ." There was an uncharacteristic quaver to her voice, and for a moment the lawyer thought she might break down. In spite of the trauma of previous months, it was the first time he had observed any crack in her equanimity.

"I almost called you this morning," Sue said, regaining her composure. "I had a call yesterday. A detective from the New York City Police Department."

"What did he want?"

"He wanted to come to see me. I told him that he should talk to you. Did he call you?"

"He may have. They call me now and then. Mostly about depositions from Dave regarding the bodies in the well.

They've kept those cases open in the event his conviction for the Lake Placid matter were ever set aside. That way they can always try him for the other murders." Jeb shifted in his chair. "I wonder why he'd contact you about them?"

"He may suspect that I killed them." The words came out matter-of-factly, almost as though she were speaking of some item of casual interest.

"What!"

"He may have found out that Delaney was trying to blackmail me."

"What are you saying?"

"Delaney found out about my affair with Emily and was trying to extort money from me. But it doesn't make any difference now. Not with this." She nodded toward the pictures of the medallion in Jeb's lap. "The police will focus on me now."

Jeb, thunderstruck, half rose from his chair. "Sue, what are you telling me?"

"I'm responsible," she said almost lightly. "The deaths . . . all of them. I'm responsible."

The statement seemed nearly indifferent, a soft medley of words that, in spite of their horror, had an almost euphonic quality. Bell-like, her pronouncement lingered in the stillness of the great room, unmuted by the tapestries or the elegant Oriental rugs.

"It seemed like the logical thing to do at the time," continued Sue. "I never really had much choice."

Jeb was speechless. Was this some sort of final attempt to save her husband? His doubts faded as she supplied details about the bodies in the well.

"Delaney and Tom Lucas . . ." She paused, shaking her head as though reflecting on some mildly regrettable occurrence. "Delaney learned of my affair with Emily. He was trying to blackmail me. I knew it would never end. There was nothing else to do. The same with Tom Lucas. He was suspicious. He had Delaney's notebook. I had no choice."

Jeb reeled with the shock, trying to organize thoughts that whirled through his mind. He should call the New York City detective. But there was little time. How much would they believe in the Governor's office? They would be wary of a spouse's confession at this late date. Even the clipping would be suspect, viewed as a final ace in the hole, held until there was no time to establish its authenticity.

"Ever since that detective called yesterday I've been thinking of Dana." Sue stood and again looked out the window. The sun was setting, its fading rays reflecting on the leaded windows and diffusing around the brightly colored intaglios. "We've had wonderful times down there."

Jeb followed her gaze across the drive, past where the elm had been, to the small fence that enclosed the cutting garden. Through the entrance could be seen the rows of flowers, their colors, brilliant by day, now muted in the approaching darkness.

"There was nothing I could do for Dave. I had to put him out of my mind. Dana needs me." Her voice faltered, but she regained control. "But everything will come out now. They'll arrest me. That leaves only Dave to care for Dana. We've got to save him. The business will survive . . . with Emily gone."

"Emily gone?" Jeb said. "I don't understand."

"Oh, I'll see to that." Sue gave a toss of her head as she turned from the window, a serene, confident look replacing the troubled expression of moments before. Her dark eyes darted about the room as though considering options. "Don't you see? Emily had every reason to want Delaney and Lucas out of the way. Yes, the more I think about it, she'll be involved in it all. Very much so."

She paused and turned back to the window. "Actually, I was never as worried about the body in Lake Placid as I was about Delaney. I couldn't be sure he told me the truth when he said he was the only one who knew that I was the person having the affair with Emily. Dave was convinced that it was Elizabeth Raderman. In a way he may have been right. I've always wondered about them."

Turning from the window, she took a cigarette from a nearby humidor and lit it with steady hands. "Emily hates Dave," she said through a stream of smoke. "When I married him she was beside herself with jealousy. I'm sure that's why she married Henry Hunter; out of spite. When Dave started competing with Emily in Stamford it was more than she could take. She was out to destroy him. I've been caught in the middle. The affair with Emily. Her knowledge of Ann Conway. She was with me the night Ann Conway was killed. We'd driven up to Lake Placid from Newport that afternoon. My father had just bought me a new sports car. Emily agreed to help me drive it up to Camp Louise—on certain conditions. Even then she had strings attached to everything. But we were young . . . in love, I suppose . . ."

WARNING

CURVE AHEAD

30 MPH

The car flashed past the sign, tires squealing, taking the curve at fifty. Straightening, it picked up speed and soon the speedometer was registering close to seventy.

Sue Dickerson glanced at the tachometer on the dash that measured the engine rpm and then at the striking young blonde who was driving. "Emily, that sign said thirty."

"Don't worry about it," Emily replied, coolly. "That's for ordinary cars. This thing could handle it at eighty."

Indeed, the car held the road well. It was an English Jaguar with the steering on the right side. Its bright blue chassis and brilliant chrome fixtures glistened in the evening sunlight as it raced along the Lake Shore Drive toward Lake Placid.

The driver, her hair pulled back into an abbreviated ponytail, sunglasses adorning her thin, straight nose, seemed unconcerned. While one hand steadied the wheel, the other

314

dangled languidly over a side vent attached to the windshield. Her tanned, smooth face wore a look of boredom.

"What's the plan?" she asked. "Do you want to go straight to the camp?"

"Let's stop at the Dancehall first," Sue replied. "Dave may be there. We can ride out with him."

"Oh, no." Emily frowned. It was apparent that she did not like the Dancehall. Or maybe Dave Powell. Sue suspected it was both.

"You remember the Dancehall," Sue said, "The place we went to last fall."

"I remember," Emily said without enthusiasm. "What if this guy isn't there? How do we get out to the camp?"

"We'll borrow one of the Flemings' boats. They're neighbors. They won't mind. They're rarely there."

"You see an awful lot of this Dave fellow." Emily's smooth brow contracted. "Sometimes I wonder if it's all as innocent as you claim."

"I have to have an escort."

"I've heard that before. Next you'll be saying you have to have a husband, that all your friends are getting married. I know the pattern. And that silly medal he gave you." She shot a derisive glance at the medallion Sue was wearing on her neck.

"He didn't give it to me. I told you, he left it in his room when he came to visit me last week. He doesn't even know I have it."

"You're not thinking of marrying him, are you?" Emily asked. When Sue did not respond she looked at her quickly, "Are you?"

"I could do worse. He's very considerate. My dad likes him a lot, and my parents will expect me to get married. Besides, Dave doesn't press himself on me . . . like some others I know."

"What's that supposed to mean?" the older girl said sharply.

"I meant Bob. You're so sensitive."

"Sensitive! Listen to who's—"

"Emily! You drove right by the harbor road."

"Damn it! You've got me all screwed up." She braked sharply and brought the car around in a screeching U-turn. "Go ahead and get married," she said after righting the vehicle. "Who cares?"

"Relax, will you? I'm not getting married. At least not right now."

They turned onto the harbor road and drove in silence. Emily was the first to speak. "Don't forget your promise tonight."

"What promise?" Sue knew precisely what her companion meant but chose to appear vague.

"You know what promise."

"I didn't promise anything," Sue said. Then, defensively, "I said I'd consider it."

"You're too much," grumbled Emily as she pulled into the parking area across the road from the Dancehall.

"Oh, quit worrying." Sue leaned over and kissed her lightly on the cheek.

The Dancehall was already jammed. Sue led the way to the bar, where they ordered drinks. "I don't see Dave." She looked around at the crowd and then turned to one of the bartenders. "Do you know Dave Powell? Has he been in tonight?"

The bartender shook his head, not looking up. "I haven't seen him. He's probably playing ball. They usually don't come in until later."

They stood drinking, gazing around the room. A tall, attractive young man approached Emily. "Hi. You from around here?"

She barely acknowledged his presence. "No."

"How about a drink?"

"I've got a drink. And I'm busy."

The man hesitated, glanced at Sue, then shrugged and moved away. Within seconds they attracted yet another admirer, a shorter, jovial-looking fellow. "Hello there," he beamed. "A little crowded tonight."

"Yes, particularly right here." Emily said flatly. She turned to Sue. "Let's get out of here. I can't take this."

Sue paused, looking at the crowd. "I'd like to tell Dave that we're going to be at the camp. Let's stay a little longer. Maybe he'll—"

"You stay," Emily said peevishly. "I'll wait in the car."

"Oh, all right." Sue knew it wasn't worth it to upset her friend. She would nurse a grudge the entire weekend. "Come on, we'll go out to the camp."

Leaving the Dancehall, they walked down to the wharf and borrowed a small motorboat from the Dickersons' neighbor. It was dusk when they arrived at Camp Louise. Sue brought the boat into one of the unused slips at the end of the waterfront, farthest from the main house.

"You're sure nobody's here?" Emily asked, climbing out to secure the bow.

"No one's here. The caretaker lives in town."

"What about Dave?"

"He doesn't come out till late."

"How can you be sure?"

"What would he do out here all by himself? He only sleeps here."

"Maybe he's sleeping with someone."

"Not Dave." Sue climbed from the boat. "He's not the type."

As Sue stepped onto the landing, Emily slipped her arm around her waist, helping her up. "I'm glad I came," the older girl said, her voice softening. "It will be fun won't it?" As she spoke she drew Sue to her and brushed her lips with a kiss. "Do you love me?"

"Yes," Sue replied, indifferently.

"You never tell your shrink about us, do you?"

"Of course not. Anyway, I rarely see him any more."

"You haven't killed any pets recently?"

"Emily! I never killed any pet."

"Well, you pushed that puppy off the back of your boat. At least that's why your father sent you to the shrink. I told you, my mother heard all about it from your—"

"Emily, will you please stop! That happened a long time ago."

"I've always wondered about you," Emily continued teasingly, obviously enjoying her friend's uneasiness.

Sue started to walk away, but Emily held her by the arm. "Oh, c'mon, can't you take a joke?" She pulled her close and kissed her gently. "I love you, you know that." She kissed her again, more forcefully. "You *are* going to go through with this, aren't you, darling?" she whispered, nuzzling Sue's ear. "Tell me you are . . . please."

Sue, uncomfortable and tired from the trip, moved away. "It's so warm. Why don't we take a swim?"

"How can you think of swimming?"

"Come on. It will freshen us up."

"We can't go in like this. Let's undress and—"

"There are some swimsuits up in the house."

"Oh, take your clothes off." Emily began unbuttoning her own blouse. "What a prude."

Sue hesitated and then began to disrobe under Emily's watchful eyes. Soon they were standing naked on the dock. Although it was almost dark, Sue could still see the other girl clearly. Few had better figures, and Emily was keenly aware of it. She raised her arms over her head, as if fixing the back of hair. It was a calculated gesture. Sue had seen it before—a pose to raise her breasts and enhance her shape.

"Let's just sit and put our feet in," Emily said, moving close and embracing her. "Who wants to get all wet?"

Sue knew the signs. The thought of her bare back on the hard dock was too much. "Why don't we go to the apartment over the boathouse? We'll swim down."

"Will you do it with me?"

"Oh, Emily, you're like a broken record. 'Will you do it with me? Will you do it with me?'" she mimicked. "Who wants to listen to that all night?"

"You promised."

"All right, so I promised," Sue said, exasperated. "You ruin it all by talking about it. Let's just see what happens."

"That's what you've been saying since last summer."

"Come on. Let's go." Sue poised to dive in the water.

"What about our clothes? What if someone—"

Just then, a laugh drifted from the forest. Loud. Shuddering.

"Good lord, what's that?" Emily looked toward the woods, her eyes filled with alarm.

"It's just a loon. There must be a storm brewing. C'mon, let's go." Sue dived in, surfacing in a spray of foam a few feet from the dock. "Ooooh, it's marvelous." She turned and started swimming along the waterfront. A splash signaled that Emily was at her heels.

They arrived at the boathouse, out of breath, and mounted the steps to the apartment. "I hope there's something to dry off with," Sue said, walking toward the entrance that opened onto the far end of the balcony.

"It's stuffy," said Emily as they entered the room. "Open the windows."

The apartment was little more than a living area with a stone fireplace. An assortment of wicker furniture was scattered about, and an upholstered daybed rested against a far wall.

Sue opened a window on each side of the room, then picked up a large beach towel draped over the back of a chair and handed it to Emily. "Wasn't the water great? I feel ever so much better."

Emily dried herself quickly without comment and then began to dry Sue, wiping her shoulders with the towel. "Here, take off this silly medal." She started to remove the necklace.

"No, don't." Sue moved back. "I'll lose it."

"All right, relax. Don't be so jumpy." She drew Sue close and kissed her.

Suddenly, lights flashed on below.

"What's that?" asked Emily, startled.

"Just the dock lights. They come on automatically."

"Good God," said Emily. "Let's go over in the corner." She took Sue's hand and led her to the daybed, where they lay down. Soon Emily was kissing her intimately.

As she lay passively on the bed, Sue sensed the first stages of the ringing in her ears. She shifted uncomfortably.

"What's the matter, darling?" Emily asked. "You all right?"

"Yes. Yes, I'm fine."

"Do you like this?"

"Yes." Sue's voice was a whisper.

"You're going to do it for *me*, aren't you?"

Sue did not answer.

"Here, like this." Emily shifted her position. "You promised, remember?"

Sue had started to comply when she heard the unexpected drone of a boat. As the sound came closer, she sat up.

"Please," gasped Emily. "Don't stop."

"I think someone may be coming." Sue rose and walked to the window overlooking the waterfront. "I knew it. It's coming here!"

Emily joined her at the window in time to see Sam Wykoff's skiff glide in under the dock lights.

"It's the caretaker," Sue said.

"Let's get our clothes," said Emily, anxiously.

"Wait. He keeps his boat down on the other side. He'll never even see our clothes. See, he's going down to the other end." They watched as the skiff passed out of sight toward the far side of the waterfront. Soon they saw the beam from a flashlight as Sam mounted the path to the main house.

"Let's go while we have a chance," Emily said.

Sue remained calm. "Relax, will you? He'll probably leave right away. There's no reason for him to be out here now. He probably forgot something. If we go out, we're likely to run into him. Do you think I want him to catch us like this?"

"We could tell him we'd been swimming."

"No, it would look funny—up here in the boathouse . . . with no clothes."

Within a few minutes the flashlight reappeared and Sam headed back toward his skiff.

"See, I told you," Sue said. "He's leaving."

They watched in silence as the flashlight disappeared. Again came the wail of a loon.

"There's that crazy bird again," said Emily. "That's enough to scare the hell out of you."

Suddenly there was the sound of another boat on the lake. They watched as the lights of the Dickerson launch hove into view.

"Oh, lord," said Sue. "You won't believe this. It's Dave."

"Jesus! This place is like a marina."

"Shhh! Be quiet."

"He'll see our clothes," Emily said.

"No, no. The launch is kept down near Sam's boat. We'll go down the other end and get dressed while he's tying up the boat. He won't see us."

"What happened to the caretaker?" Emily asked.

They looked toward the spot where Sam had been, but there was no sign of him or the flashlight. Then they watched the launch as it came under the dock lights into the main landing next to the boathouse.

"He's going to dock it right here," said Emily anxiously.

The boat came to a stop and Dave emerged from the cabin. Then they saw the girl.

"Your boyfriend seems to have a girlfriend." Emily said.

"Shut up, will you!" The force of her response surprised even Sue.

After securing the launch, Dave started toward the main house, leaving the girl alone in the stern. Sue's eyes focused on her. Although it was difficult to see her clearly, she seemed attractive. Who was she, she wondered. Dave had never mentioned anyone else. She frowned and fingered the medallion uneasily.

From out on the lake she heard the distant noise of a motor. It sounded like Sam's boat. For some reason he must have paddled out to avoid Dave.

Dave reappeared shortly and joined the girl.

When it became obvious that the two were going to sit and drink, Emily grew impatient. "Now what do we do?"

Sue gave a toss of her head. "There's nothing we can do. We can't go out like this."

"Isn't there some way we can sneak past them up to the house? Maybe we could circle around back and get our clothes."

"No, with those dock lamps they'd see us. Maybe they'll leave."

Emily turned and walked back to the bed and lay down. "Let me know if anything happens. Remember, if they come up here, *I've* got the towel."

Sue continued to watch the couple closely, trying to catch snatches of their conversation, her feeling of resentment building. When they removed their clothes and went swimming, the feeling intensified. The ringing in her ears was louder now—a shrill whining.

Again came the sound of a loon, this time quieter—a faint lingering laugh. But it was heard by Emily. "What a ghoulish sound," she said. "You sure that's a bird?"

"Keep your voice down," snapped Sue. "They'll hear you."

The splash Dave made in diving into the lake brought Emily back to the window. "Oh, no. They're going swimming. We'll be here all night."

They watched in silence as the couple finished their swim

and began talking on the dock. When Dave cut his foot and they started toward the apartment, Emily became frantic. "We've had it—we'd better let them know we're here."

"Not yet." Sue's voice was flat, unemotional. "The way his foot is, he may go up to the house."

"No, listen. I think they're coming up."

Sue walked to the other side of the room to the window that offered a view of the balcony. Here, from behind a drapery, she watched as the couple appeared from the stairs. Her eyes locked on the girl. When Dave embraced her and removed her brassiere, Sue's resentment surged into anger.

"Did I hear you say Dave wasn't the type?" Emily whispered, peering over her shoulder.

Sue ignored the comment. The ringing in her ears was now a skull-splitting whine. Soon the headache would start. And then, deep within her brain, the dripping sound. She didn't tell Emily. She never told anyone. Only the psychiatrist understood. She should have filled the prescription; she was out of Thorazine.

"They're leaving," Emily said. "Let's get out of here."

"Wait, Dave's going up to the house. She may go with him."

The couple disappeared down the stairs, and Sue stepped back from the window. The headache had started now. It was severe. The agony registered in her face as she gritted her teeth against the pain. The dark eyes narrowed, the clamped jaw stretched her lips into the appearance of a smile.

Soon the girl reappeared carrying her bag. She paused to retrieve the clothes she had draped over the banister, then started down the narrow balcony toward the apartment.

"Here she comes," Emily hissed, wrapping herself in the towel. "What should we do?"

"As soon as she opens the door we'll walk out."

"What? But look at us. Look at *you*."

"What else can we do? Do you want to wait around and

introduce yourself? Come on, just follow me." Sue's voice was low and deliberate. "She'll be so surprised, she won't even see us. Our clothes are next to the boat. We can just leave." She crossed the room and stood next to the door. She felt no anger now—only the ringing and the excruciating pain.

The door opened and Ann Conway was silhouetted briefly in the entranceway. Sue moved forward quickly, knocking the form backward. The girl gasped—a scream choking in her throat—and stumbled back, her arm smashing a window pane. She clutched wildly at Sue as she toppled backward over the banister into the darkness. There was a short wailing sound—the start of a shriek that never came—and then the dull, thudding impact of the body slamming onto the dock some fifteen feet below.

"My God!" Emily cried. "What *happened*?"

"Be quiet." Sue stood on the balcony, listening.

"She's gone," Emily said, incredulously. She rushed to the banister and looked over. "Oh, my God! You pushed her over!"

"Shut up!" Sue continued to listen. Had Dave heard? No, there was no movement at the house. She went quickly to the stairs and descended to the dock, Emily close behind. The girl was lying in a pool of blood, eyes open and glazed, her tongue protruding. Blood oozed from a gaping wound in her arm.

"She's dead!" Emily exclaimed. "Oh, Jesus, she's dead."

Sue regarded the body for a moment. It evoked little emotion. Her only concern was how to get rid of it. At that moment, from nearby in the forest, she heard a low tremulous giggle. Of course! *Sally Wood*. They'd never found *her*. Her dark eyes traveled over the dock, finally coming to rest on the guideboat. It was so logical. Perfect, in fact.

"We'll tie her in that boat and sink it," she said calmly. "Over by Pulpit Rock. It's very deep. No one will ever find it."

"You're crazy!" Emily's voice was hoarse with emotion. "I always knew it. You're insane! I . . . I'm getting Dave . . . calling the police."

Sue turned on her, quickly. "Are you?" Her voice was steady. "What will you tell the police? That we were up in the apartment making love? They'll find out everything. All about your old girlfriends. They'll know every damn thing about you before they're through. Look at her. No clothes. You think they're going to believe she fell over that banister accidentally? We'll *both* be suspect, Emily." She paused significantly. "Just think of the publicity. Your parents. Your Newport friends."

Emily wavered. Her frightened blue eyes shifted to the body and then back to Sue. "I know you," she said in a cracked whisper. "You'd tell them I did it."

"Wait here," Sue commanded. "I'll get a canoe from the boathouse. We'll tie her in that guideboat. Don't worry, I'll do it. Get her bag and clothes from the balcony. You can follow me over to Pulpit Rock in the canoe." She paused for a moment and then added quietly, "Then we can make love. Any way you like."

As she walked toward the boathouse, Sue firmed up her plan. It would be best to leave Emily at Pulpit Rock, too. But it would be difficult. No, one body a night was enough to handle. She would have to take her chances with her friend. It would be a problem, though. Emily would have her in bondage; she'd never let her forget.

Once again the sound of the loon, but this time faint, distant; only the haunting whisper of a laugh.

The headache was almost unbearable now. She clamped her teeth together. At the corners of her mouth appeared the semblance of a smile.

◇ ◇ ◇

CHAPTER 43

"The execution will commence in eighteen minutes." Richard Wallace was standing in Green Haven's brightly lighted execution chamber directly in front of the electric chair, addressing the witnesses. His manner was austere. "There will be no talking. No one will be permitted to leave the room until the execution has been completed. Under no circumstances may you stand or leave your seat. Should you become nauseated or feel faint, take several deep breaths and put your head between your legs. Immediately after the execution you will be escorted from the room. I repeat, there will be absolute silence."

At the end of his remarks, the superintendent moved to one side of the room and stationed himself next to the closed door leading to the Dancehall. From here he was able to observe the entire room. To his left were the twenty-nine men and women who comprised the state's witnesses. Many of them represented international journalism and network and local broadcasting, coöperating with countless national and international press services. Beyond the witnesses near the entrance to the execution chamber, which was now sealed, was John Pike.

Directly across from Wallace were the two sergeants who would strap the inmate into the chair. To their left, in the control room behind the one-way glass, was the executioner. The prison physician stood near the window. Next to him, waiting to apply the electrodes, was Captain Morse.

In the corner, to the superintendent's right, in a position that would spare the inmate the sight of it when the door from the Dancehall opened, was the autopsy table on which his corpse would be removed.

But center stage, of course, was the object on which all eyes focused, the chair itself. For Wallace, the apparatus seemed to have taken on an even more grotesque appearance now that the execution was at hand. There in the white light it appeared darker, shinier, more lethal. He wondered if the cleaning detail, in its zeal to have things immaculate for the premiere event, had administered a coat of wax.

As the minutes passed he focused on the clock on the far wall. The slender black second hand swept silently and relentlessly around the white disk. At ten minutes before eleven he beckoned to John Pike, who came forward quickly. His eyes, like most of those in the room, were bright.

"How is everything back there?" the superintendent whispered, nodding toward the Dancehall.

"All right as far as I know. At least it was a few minutes ago."

"Is he going to make it?"

"I think so. They said he's just sitting on the edge of the bunk with his eyes closed."

"Is the chaplain with him?"

"Nope. He's waiting downstairs. Powell says he doesn't want him; that he's made it this far and he's going it alone. I don't think we'll have any problems."

"You never know," Wallace murmured. "Anything new from the Governor's office?"

"Nothing. Apparently they're getting the usual last-minute stuff. Powell's lawyer called them an hour ago, claiming he has new evidence. They expect such things. Our instructions are to proceed with the execution."

As the deputy returned to his corner, Wallace focused again on the clock. At five minutes before eleven, the captain moved forward and began soaking the sponges on the electrodes with a brine solution in a bucket near the base of the chair. The only sound in the room was the trickle of water.

Suddenly, a muffled cough from the congregation of witnesses shattered the stillness. It was a short, compulsive, gagging noise, and for an instant Wallace thought one of the witnesses had become ill. He looked quickly over the group, but nothing appeared amiss.

He shifted his eyes to the clock. Three minutes. As the second hand approached the two-minute mark, he braced himself and gave one final glance about the room. Then with a curt nod to the captain he turned and opened the door to the Dancehall.

◇ ◇ ◇

CHAPTER 44

It was approaching eleven. The night sky pressed down over Green Haven, a black lid on the prison walls, sealing off views of the outside world. Inside, death was present.

Nowhere was it more evident than in the Dancehall. Here Dave could feel it in every part of his being. It was in the shadows, waiting. Shortly, it would leave, taking with it whatever of his incorporeal remnants survived that blazing instant of electrical current.

He had despaired of a reprieve, of even hearing from Jeb. His execution was inevitable. He tried to avoid thinking of what was happening in the adjoining room, but the thoughts engulfed his mind. He knew they were all there. Executioner, guards, journalists—waiting for the clock to wind down so they could watch him die. But they would see only the finale—the last spectacular blast. Most of the dying had already been done in the Dancehall.

He thought again of the chaplain. Several times they had asked if he wanted him. Each time he had declined. Had he lived a religious life, it would be different. But now, at the moment of his death, to try to invoke the assistance of spirits in whom he had shown little interest during his lifetime seemed inappropriate. Besides, whatever ethereal experience awaited him after death—if, indeed, anything did—could be no worse than what he was now experiencing.

Earlier, he had finished writing his letters and had sat on the bunk watching the sky. With sunset it had become streaked with orange. It had reminded him of the evenings he had spent as a boy in a tall pine in the woods near his house. He had fashioned a tiny platform in a crotch of the tree where he had spent hours watching the sunset and the birds preparing for nightfall. There, high in the air, he had often imagined himself one of them—soaring endlessly in the evening sky on great horizontal wings.

But now the sky was a black patch in the beige wall. Thoughts of Sue crowded his mind as they had throughout the day. He had known she would not come. The matter of the medallion, like so many other questions, would go with him to the grave unanswered. With death moments away, it no longer mattered. He thought of Dana. By now she was up in bed, Lindsay close by, tucked under a blanket. He envisioned his daughter lying asleep on her side, mouth a little open, one leg drawn up, hair tousled. At the moment she had no problems, no unhappiness. Shortly it might be the same for him. His last thoughts would be of Dana. It would help him through it. If there were a life hereafter, she would be joining him there soon.

He wondered again if he should say anything—any last words. He thought not. Yet he wanted Dana to know that he would be waiting . . .

The sound of a door opening jarred him. He looked up quickly and saw the bright light from the execution chamber reflecting off the far wall in the corridor. He stiffened at the sound of approaching footsteps. They were coming. He felt weak.

As though on signal, the guard stood quickly and swung open the door. Within seconds, Richard Wallace and Captain Morse rounded the corner and stood before the cell.

"It's time, Dave." The superintendent's voice was quiet but firm.

Dave nodded, took a deep breath, and got to his feet. His eyes were shiny, and his skin had taken on a peculiar yellowish cast. Standing, he felt an urgent need to use the commode.

"Could I—" He cleared his throat. "Could I use the john first?"

As he started toward the commode, the guard moved quickly to the other door of the Dancehall. At the same time the superintendent took Dave by the arm, restraining him. "Easy, now. There's no time. Hold it in for a minute. It won't make any difference."

"But . . ." Dave hesitated, a helplessness in his sunken eyes. "I'd like to at least go with a little dignity."

"Come along." The superintendent tightened his grip and guided him toward the door. "Believe me, Dave, it won't make any difference."

"Please, I'm all right," Dave said, noting the guard enter the cell from the other door. He withdrew his arm from the superintendent's grasp. Clearing his throat once again he said, "Please, let me walk by myself."

"Sure, sure, I understand." The superintendent placed his hand on Dave's shoulder, guiding him from the cell.

"Will I have a chance to say anything?" Dave asked.

"If you really want to." Wallace arched his brows. "It will have to be brief, though."

With Dave in the center, the trio turned the corner into the corridor. Dave could feel the panic welling within him. In seconds he would be burned alive. He hoped it would be as quick as they had said. But he mustn't think. He had to control himself. He would walk in quickly, sit down and have it done with. No bravado. Just a last brief comment to Dana.

Walking resolutely, his head erect, he approached the door to the execution chamber. It was the last thing he would do. The bloody ghouls waiting there to watch him die mustn't see his terror.

As he turned from the corridor into the execution chamber, the glare of the lights blinded him. Then he saw it, and what strength he had, drained from his body. It was worse than he had imagined: larger, darker, deadlier. He saw it all at first glance, and nothing else in the room mattered. The mass of wires and electrodes; the death cap; the black matting on the high sloping back and on the floor surrounding the ugly, twisted, three-legged base; the straps hanging loosely. It waited for him in the brilliant white light, its tentacular parts dangling obscenely, its wide arms extended to embrace him in death.

Dave hesitated, but suddenly hands were on his arms moving him quickly toward the chair. Vaguely he saw the witnesses. Clusters of them. Scores of staring white eyes, awed by life's final moments. Then he was in the chair, arms and legs being strapped tightly—very tightly. Something was pressed on his head. It was cold and wet and he felt water trickling down the back of his neck. And then he could not budge, strapped so tightly that it was almost as though he and the chair were one unit. It was a terrifying sensation, the strap on his chest drawn so tautly that he could scarcely breathe. He closed his eyes. It would come now. In seconds it would strike him.

What was that? A voice. Did he want to say something? Yes. Yes, indeed! He did have something to say. It was very important. But would they loosen the strap on his chest? He couldn't breathe—couldn't speak. And then, the wide black death mask. Wait! Not yet! He wanted to talk. They were not giving him a chance. They'd promised. Please!

The room was utterly still then. Not a breath was taken; not an eye winked; not a muscle moved. And in that instant—when time itself had virtually stopped—a loud, sustained ring shattered the stillness. The ring continued, pounding against temples, threatening eardrums, reverberating off the hard, barren walls.

◊ ◊ ◊

PART XII

Tarrytown
Spring 1984

CHAPTER 45

It was dawn on Meadow Lane, hushed except for the sounds of awakening birds. The orange rim of the sun edged over the wall, reflecting off the dew in the tall meadow grass. A light haze hung on the meadow, but the sky was clear, promising a fine day. Even the reproachful expressions on the corbeled heads seemed to have mellowed with the fresh signs of spring.

A wren, no larger, it seemed, than a fifty-cent piece, hovered above the wall for a moment, beating its tiny wings against the air before disappearing into the ivy. It reappeared, an insect in its bill, and darted up past the gatehouse toward the estate. Seconds later it came to rest on a branch of a recently planted elm tree overlooking the cutting garden. Its arrival was not unnoticed.

"Look, Lindsay." Dana Powell pointed toward the bird from her chair in the garden. "There's a wren." She raised a pair of binoculars from her lap and focused on the bird. "He has something in his beak. Maybe he's going to build a nest in our new tree. Wouldn't it be nice to have some baby wrens up there, Lindsay?"

Lindsay was propped against a nearby chair, her blue eyes fixed on some far-off point. Lying on the ground next to the doll, impervious to everything but a large bee that buzzed beyond its nose, was Puff.

"Of course wrens like their nests closer to the ground," continued Dana. "But there will be other nests up there, just like before."

She turned her attention to Puff just in time to see the dog snap the bee cleanly from the air with its huge jaws.

"Oh, Puff! How awful!" said Dana, covering her eyes in disgust. Smacking loudly on the morsel, Puff climbed to her feet and lumbered across the garden.

"Now where are you going, Puff?" Dana called. "Oh, no! She's going to sit right on the tulips. Puff! No!" She watched helplessly as the dog lowered its frame in the middle of the flower bed. "Bad dog, Puff! Brandon's going to be very angry. Oh, well, what's the difference?" She gave a deep sigh. "The garden will never be right without Mommy."

Dave Powell overheard her comments as he approached the garden. Moments before, he had gone to the house for a sweater for his daughter. They were going for a bird walk, and the morning air was cooler than they'd expected.

Dana turned to him as he neared the entrance. "Daddy, look at the wren."

"Oh, yes, I see him."

"He's so tiny."

"Yes," said Dave, watching the bird admiringly. "But his song is bigger than the whole tree."

"Well, we'd better get started." Dana dropped the binoculars on her lap and reached for her father's hand. "I'll walk as far as I can, Daddy. Then I'll ride on your shoulders like I did last time, OK?"

"Remember what the doctor said. We mustn't overdo it." Dave helped her to her feet, and they started toward the gate. Suddenly he glanced back. "We almost forgot Lindsay."

Turning, he walked back and retrieved the doll. As he picked it up, he noted its deteriorating condition. A few months before he had patched one leg with adhesive tape, but

338

it was coming undone. One arm needed similar repair, and there were bare patches in the flaxen hair. He had noticed with a tinge of sadness that Dana accorded the doll less attention.

"Lindsay's hair looks a little like mine did last year," he said. "I think I'd better put some more tape on that leg, too."

"Oh, don't bother, Daddy. She's all worn out."

"No, no. She's fine. I can fix her." As he gave the doll to his daughter, Lindsay's vacant eyes stared up at him impassively, evoking memories. "I'm glad we didn't forget her. She would have been lonesome."

"Don't be silly, Daddy. She's only a doll. Dolls can't feel anything."

At the gate, Dave looked back at the dog. "Let's go, Puff. You're coming too."

The dog sat up on its haunches and gazed after them with the bewildered expression characteristic of St. Bernards.

"Look where she's sitting, Daddy," said Dana, disapprovingly. "Right in the tulips."

Dave regarded the dog affectionately for a moment, then began to sing:

> Here look in the gar-den bed.
> Some-thing beau-ti-ful is grow-ing . . .

"Oh, Daddy," Dana squealed. "You're so funny. She does look as if she's growing there." She joined in singing, her little voice striving for the right key:

> Bright, shaped like a cup-all-red,
> Tu-lip opens to the sun.

Laughing, they proceeded down the narrow path that tunneled into the woods, passing through strands of sunlight that filtered through the trees. The air was alive with the cheerful morning sounds of the forest.

◊   ◊   ◊

EPILOGUE

Green Haven Prison

Stormville, New York

September 1984

Not far beyond the somber buildings of Green Haven Prison lies a large forest. It stretches across the rolling hillside of Dutchess County, providing glorious scenery in sharp contrast to the grim prison wall. Here, one may view New York's spectacular changes of season.

Though close at hand, most of the beauty goes unnoticed by those within the prison. The wall intervenes. Yet seasonal changes are evident to inmates in other ways, particularly those of a nocturnal nature. For at night one tends to listen more in prison, and sounds from the nearby forest drift with the wind over the wall. In summer, for example, the forest is rife with the creaking cadences of life. It differs markedly from the profound silence of a winter's night when the wolf moon glitters off the hard prison snow.

And no wall, no matter how high, can deprive one of the celestial changes of season. The small pale disk that sails above the forest in the black winter sky, only to reappear in the fall as a magnificent harvest moon, is available for *all* to see. Nowhere is the sky viewed more intently than from the Dancehall. Through some chance design, perhaps providential, the last cell offers a striking final view of the heavens.

September 27, 1984, was a night of a moon. It was large and yellow, hanging in a navy blue autumn sky. In addition, there was an abundance of bright stars. At this particular time an occupant of the Dancehall sat smoking a cigarette, looking at the sky, contemplating life's final moments.

Earlier in the evening, there had been the usual preliminary activities associated with the death ritual: the execution garments; the last meal; visitors; the shaving of the crown of the head. At nine o'clock two shiny black hearses had been drawn up to the rear of the prison hospital. Shortly after ten, the witnesses had arrived.

Now, at eleven o'clock, death was but moments away. The condemned inmate, smoking and toying with a small bouquet of daisies and miniature pink roses, appeared relaxed, even serene. The scene was in marked contrast to that of only minutes before, when another prisoner had been hurried to the chair proclaiming innocence and retribution.

Around the corner of the corridor, the door to the execution chamber was closed, and beyond the door an execution was already in progress. Outside, it was quiet—quiet as only the Dancehall could be. The slightest sound—a cough, a footstep, even a sigh—echoed up and down the bare corridor. Suddenly, the silence was broken by a muffled, low, humming noise. It was a singular, distant, vibrating sound that was barely audible, but it was heard in the Dancehall. It was apparent from the way the prisoner stiffened and quickly inhaled the cigarette.

The sound continued for two minutes and then stopped. The waiting prisoner rose slowly and extinguished the cigarette in an ashtray affixed to the outside of one of the bars on the cell. Suddenly the sound came again. It lasted for another two minutes and then the corridor was quiet as a crypt. Soon the door to the execution chamber, unseen from the Dancehall, was flung open, and bright light spilled into the corridor. Two uniformed officers appeared, rolling an autopsy table between them. On the table, covered by a gray hospital sheet, was a slender form. The table trundled down the corridor and out the door. From inside the execution chamber came the loud whirring of the exhaust fan removing the odor of death.

In a moment, a tall black man emerged, a distraught look on his face. He was followed by a uniformed officer who dabbed with his handkerchief at a deep scratch beneath his eye. The two turned the corner and stopped before the door to the Dancehall. The inmate rose and nodded at the two figures as the matron stationed outside opened the door. The prisoner withdrew a small rosebud from the bouquet and, holding it by the stem, moved from the cell. Outside, the inmate paused momentarily to hand the flower to the matron and then, with a little smile, walked calmly into the execution chamber.

At night the forest beyond the prison wall assumes a different character. With darkness, it becomes a bundle of dark shapes and blends with the prison. It is then that one is reminded of its grimmer side. It overlooks the prison cemetery. Here, unclaimed bodies of dead inmates—of which there are many—are buried, including the charred remains of those who die in the prison electric chair. Pursuant to Section 620 of the New York State Correction Law, the body, after being covered with sufficient lime to ensure its decomposition, is buried in an unmarked grave. It is as though the law had been designed to eradicate all vestiges of the prisoner and his crime—and perhaps mistakes of the state as well.

But in spite of its forlorn setting, the cemetery does provide a quiet final resting place. Quiet, that is, except at night when there is a breeze. It is then that the tall pines beside the graves whisper their concerns, and a soft melancholic sound drifts over the prison wall. It is a low, moaning rhythm, disturbing to the ear—the requiem of the Dancehall.

◇ ◇ ◇